UNTOUCHABLE ZANE

DEBBIE CROMACK

Nicole,
Make your dreams
your reality.
Hugs!

This book is a work of fiction. All names, characters, places, dialogue, and incidents are the product of the author's imagination or are used fictitiously and are not to be represented as real. Any resemblance to actual events, locales, or persons, living or dead, is coincidental. References to people, establishments, or locations are intended only to provide a sense of authenticity and are used fictitiously. This story is fiction that the author has created for entertainment purposes only.

All trademarked brands and brand names mentioned in this fictional book are protected by their trademark and are referenced without infringement, dilution, tarnishment, or defamation.

Printed in the United States of America
Book cover by Lance Buckley (www.LanceBuckley.com)
Developmental Editor: Angela James (https://angelajames.co/)
Copy Editor: Lynda Ryba (http://fwsmedia.net/)
Proofreader: Annie Bugeja.
Interior Formatting: Qamber Designs & Media

ISBN 978-0-578-65420-1 (pbk.)
ISBN 978-1-7923-4928-7 (eBook)

This book is dedicated to Z.
You don't know me, but you've impacted me
more than you will ever know.
You were the most magnificent muse for this romance novel.
You fueled my imagination, you inspired me, you motivated me.
With all my heart, I thank you.

Acknowledgements

I truly believe that no one is a self-made anything. There are always people who help us along the way. I believe we get to where we want to be in life by helping one another. So, it is with heartfelt gratitude that I thank these wonderful people.

Monkey, thank you for giving me the space to explore and do what I love. I appreciate you, your support, and your love.

My high school friend, Carol B., thanks for asking me, many moons ago, "Debbie, did you write any of this down?!" Yes, I finally did!

Kim Argetsinger (IG: @kimargetsinger), how do I find the words? "Thank you" doesn't express the massive gratitude in my heart for your love, your support, your encouragement. Thank you for assuring me that ANYTHING is possible and that I'm not going crazy. And thank you for believing in me when I lost faith in myself. I love you!

My sweet Haylee LaRose (IG: @seekbalancedesign), none of this would've been possible without YOU by my side. You've been my anchor, my sounding board, and, above all, my friend. When we link arms, we can make anything happen. Thank you for standing with me.

Lisa Eaton Ling (IG: @lisaeatonling), Nicole Cheri Oden (IG: @nicolecheriodenlaw), Jena Rodriguez (IG: @jenarodriguez), and Heidi Garis (FB: @TapintoAbundanceNow)…I DID IT!!! I'm sending you hugs from across the miles. Your support and encouragement helped me get through each day. On rough days, you lifted me up. On wildly amazing days, you celebrated with me. Thank you for your love and friendship.

Dr. Danielle Gray, thank you for your support and encouragement through the years. And thanks for always being a shoulder to cry on when I needed it. I'm so grateful for you.

My amazing developmental editor, Angela James (IG: @ angelajameseditor), thank you for your tough yet gentle guidance. Thank you for encouraging me to keep going. Thank you for being in my corner on this wild ride.

My copy editor, Lynda Ryba. Thank you for your feedback and suggestions.

Annie, my proofreader (and so much more!). Girl, you GET me! I'm so grateful to have you in my life!!!

Christy Erasmus (IG: @mrs_eraz_author)...my confidant in Ellipsis Anonymous (See what I did there??). You've helped me grow as an author and my gratitude for you is endless. You helped me enrich this story and I appreciate you so much!

My wonderful beta readers, I am massively grateful for your candid feedback and your generosity of time. I appreciate you so much!! Thank you!

My outstanding ARC and Street Teams!!! I couldn't have done this without you!

And YOU, my new reader. I'm so happy you took a chance on my book. I hope you love it!!!

Visual Recommendation

I'm a very visual person. So, for each of my books, I create a Pinterest board that houses Pins of my hero, heroine, places they'll go, experiences they'll have, things from their past, and so on. To get a glimpse into the story of Zane and Desiree in Untouchable Zane, I invite you to visit their Pinterest board here: www.pinterest.com/debbiecromackauthor/untouchable-zane

Playlist

Music is powerful. Music can set my mood, help me change my mood, and intensify my mood. Along with being a visual person, I surround myself with music. When I write, I see my stories as though they're movies. And every movie has a soundtrack. I create a soundtrack for each of my books. Below is a list of songs you may want to check out as you read certain scenes and chapters in Untouchable Zane. They'll bring you even deeper into the story. You can find most of them on my playlist on Spotify: open.spotify.com/playlist/26OBuRfiXoIycy5OiCDR3C. I hope you enjoy them!

Chapters 7-10 - *Stardust* by Nat King Cole, *A Sunday Kind of Love* by Etta James, *The Way You Look Tonight* by Frank Sinatra, *All The Way* by Steve Tyrell, *Embraceable You* by Big Band Standards, *(I Love You) For Sentimental Reasons* by Laura Fygi, and *I've Got A Crush On You* by Steve Tyrell.

Chapter 18 - *Dreamsome* by Shelby Lynne

Chapter 21 - *A Little More Of You* by Ashley Chambliss

Chapter 22 - *Someone You Loved* by Lewis Capaldi

Chapter 23 - *Living Inside My Heart* by Bob Seger

Chapter 24 - *Why Does My Heart Feel So Bad?* By Moby

Chapter 27 - *I Gave You All My Life* by Brian Melo

You may be under the misconception that being hot, famous, and rich, makes it easy for a guy like me to find love. Sure, being all that makes it easy for me to get laid, but I don't want to get laid. I want to fall in love. I'm here to tell you that being all that makes finding *true* love incredibly complicated...almost impossible. At least that's been my painful reality over and over again.

There's only one woman I want to love and she's the only woman in the world who can break me.

~ 1 ~

Zane

Her face is beautiful, natural. Fair-skinned, emerald-green eyes, and caramel-red hair pulled up with pieces dangling around her cheeks and neck. A glow surrounds her and she smiles at me. As the image fades, a new image appears. The same beautiful face, but her hair is styled differently, her clothes are different, and the environment is different. That image fades and another appears.

The siren of my alarm blasts, jarring me awake.

I reach over to my phone on the nightstand, turn off the alarm, and lay in bed for a moment as the lingering images seep into my consciousness. Some of the dreams are different visions of her face. Some of them are us walking side-by-side, holding hands, and strolling through various places. And some of them are sexual; those are the most intense…and the most frustrating. It's like I'm watching a movie of us, so I can't feel her skin and I can't taste her lips. I can only imagine how silky her skin would feel under my fingers and how delicious her lips would taste pressed into mine. Annnnd something down below tells me it's time to get out of bed. *Dude, cut it out.*

The first streaks of dawn filter light into my room through the vast, floor-to-ceiling windows. Sluggish from my usual restless night, I sit up in my king-size bed, push aside my sheets, and sling my legs over the side of the bed.

Raking my fingers through my hair in frustration, I whisper,

"Who *are* you?"

Dragging myself out of bed, I make my way through my Hollywood Hills home. Being only thirty-one years old, I must say I'm pretty damn proud of what I've accomplished so far in my life. I was lucky enough to be a sought-after talent in Hollywood at the age of fourteen, I've starred in numerous block-buster movies, worked with industry icons, and started my own production company. Okay, so I don't have an Oscar yet, but I'm working on it.

As I head to the kitchen, the cold beneath my feet mirrors the coldness of my environment. I poured tons of money into having my house professionally decorated and, while I admire and appreciate the Zen-like ambiance of what I wanted at the time, it feels empty, barren. It doesn't feel like home. It lacks love. The love of a woman's touch…and presence.

I microwave some glass-bottled spring water and pour in a packet of Four Sigmatic coffee. I've worked hard on my physique my entire life and that includes my diet. No regular coffee is going in this temple. As I drink my coffee, I whip up a protein shake to drink on the way to my grandparents' house. Grandma passed a few years back and all us grandkids do our best to rotate spending time with Grandpa to keep him busy and active.

Grandpa and I are going fishing today. After my first stint in rehab, I vowed to make more time for my family and time with Grandpa always makes me feel good. He's my hero and I love listening to him share his wisdom through his life's stories. Being his first-born grandson, I have a special bond with him. It feels like he started taking me fishing as soon as I started walking. Now, I get to take him fishing and I cherish our time together even more.

It's a typical, sunny California day, so I drive my gray convertible '64 Mustang that Grandpa gave me last year. Even before I had it restored, it was my favorite in my collection of cars because it was Grandpa's. He's the one who got me hooked on cars and fueled my love of them. When I was a kid and a car show was in town, Grandpa always took me. We'd spend hours walking up and down the rows and rows of cars and he always bought me a hot dog and soda.

He favored the antique cars, looked at them like they were fine art hanging in a museum. One time I asked him why he liked the old ones so much. Briefly taking his eyes off the *1927 Ford Model A* his eyes were savoring, he knelt down on one knee and told me, "They hold memories." Then he smiled at me with a sentimental gleam in his eyes. When we went to the shows, he always drove us in his '64 Mustang and one time on the way home, he told me the story about the first time he kissed Grandma; it was in the Mustang. As I got older and more successful in my career, special times like this with Grandpa became few and far between.

As I pull into their driveway, Grandpa's tinkering with his rickety old fishing pole.

"Hey, Grandpa," I cheerfully greet him. "Why won't you let me get you a new rod?"

"Hey, Zaney," he responds, keeping his eyes on the weathered old pole like it's a timeless, priceless treasure. "Nah, this pole's like a trusted friend now. Works just fine. Catches fish. No need for those fancy new ones." Holding onto the pole, he picks up his beaten-up tackle box. "Ready to go?"

"Yup, let's do it."

We load our gear and a cooler full of water and snacks into the back seat. I drive out to our favorite fishing spot; the lake is calm and there aren't any other people there. Taking our time, we unload our gear and walk down to the lake where we patiently prepare our fishing rods with lures. With years of practice, we have our routine down to an easy ritual.

Fishing bibs on and poles ready, we wade into the water and stand in our usual spots in the lake, close enough to talk and hear each other and far enough to not cross our fishing lines. A slight breeze rustles the leaves in the trees surrounding us. The calm of the lake relaxes me and the babbling water is a gentle symphony in my ears. We fish in silence, letting the peacefulness soak in.

"The redhead was in my dreams again last night." I stare blankly out over the water as I cast, seeing her, not the lake.

"Oh?"

"Yup. The same images over and over." I glance over at him.

Grandpa wears an impassive expression as he casts back into the water, flicking his wrist in a way only expert fishermen can do after years of fishing. "And you're sure you never met her before? Or maybe seen her somewhere?"

I look back over the lake as the water ripples out in concentric circles from where his lure sunk. "I'm sure. But something…feels like I know her. But I know I don't."

"It's been a lot of years she's been visiting you in your dreams."

"Tell me about it." I smile at him, grateful for the years he's listened to me talk about her without judgment.

"Do you think she's the reason you keep yourself from falling in love?" He doesn't look at me, but keeps his eyes on the water.

Damn, Grandpa. He's not one to beat around the bush. He and Grandma met when they were kids. He loved that woman every day, in every way, with every part of his being. They shared a love I think we all desire, but is hard to come by these days.

"Y'know, I don't know, Grandpa." Sadly, this is true. I have no idea.

Okay, so my love-life has been less than stellar. I had one long-term relationship when I was in my early twenties followed by a series of six-to-eight-month relationships. The women I fall for usually end up in one of two categories: One: physical attraction only or Two: they have a hidden agenda and just want to be associated with me because I'm a celebrity. So, the relationship lasts a while and then fizzles. And don't think because I'm a muscle-head, I'm famous, and I'm rich that it doesn't hurt…because it does.

While I confide in Grandpa about a lot of things, I'd never admit to him that I'm worried I'll never find love. At least not the kind of love he and Grandma had. My lifestyle doesn't lend itself to any kind of normal relationship, that's for damn sure.

The years are going by and I want to settle down with someone and build a future together. I want a wife to come home to. Someone who genuinely wants to know about my day. Someone to make my sterile house a home. Someone who loves me for *me*.

I don't think she exists.

Turning my attention back to fishing, I reel in my line and cast back out. As my lure plunks into the dark water, I accede to the realization: my longest relationship is with a mystery woman who's been haunting my dreams for fifteen years.

~ 2 ~

Zane

After fishing with Grandpa, I head to Virtue Fitness to film a YouTube episode for my show, *Hit the Gym*, and get in my workout for the day. The gym is my sanctuary. It's the one place I can go to relieve stress and stay fit for my next role. I get to put on my hip-hop music, shut out everything around me, and escape into my own world; a world with no paparazzi and no expectations, just me and the weights.

With filming complete, I head out to my car to grab my gym bag with a change of clothes for my workout. As I'm getting my bag out of the back of my car, I hear a soft voice from behind me.

"Excuse me. My friend and I are looking for a gym. Do you know if they have a day pass or a week pass here?"

I look up at her from my bag and the invisible force of what feels like a sonic boom knocks me off balance, causing me to adjust my footing and face her. Flashes of the images of the woman from my dreams for the past fifteen years race through my mind, landing on the one with her black Nike hat. And now, she's standing right in front of me, wearing a black Nike hat, looking at me with her striking green eyes that have become so familiar to me.

Holy shit!

"It's you." Adrenaline shoots through every inch of my body as I examine her face and try to compose myself. *Damn, she's freaking beautiful. Even more beautiful than my dreams, she's breathtaking.* I stifle the full-on freak-out raging inside me.

"I'm sorry?" She tilts her head and a crinkle appears between her brows.

I think I'm in shock. I can't seem to move or speak. I can't wrap my head around the fact that she's standing here. Barely able to form a coherent sentence through my muddled words, I stammer, "I'm — I'm sorry, what did you say?" *How's this possible? How is she here?*

"My friend and I are looking for a gym. We're only here for a few weeks and we can't seem to find one that offers a day pass or a week pass. Clearly, we didn't do enough research on Google." She smiles and I think I'm going to fall over. "Do you know if they have passes here?"

Her friend glares at her. It doesn't seem like she knows who I am which is both odd and refreshing.

"Um, I think they might. Let's check." I turn my head down toward my bag and shake it, trying to clear away the images. Grabbing my bag, I turn toward the gym, completely awestruck. "Come with me."

"Okay, great," the redhead, the incredibly gorgeous siren from my dreams, responds as they follow me into the gym.

My heart beats wildly in my chest.

"I happen to know the owner." I motion for them to sit on the L-shaped bench in the lobby area. "Sit here and I'll check for you."

"Okay, thanks so much." The redhead sits on the bench while her bleach-blonde friend peers around the corner as if to get a better look at the gym.

As I head to Johnny's office to tell him the ladies are looking for a gym for a few weeks, all I can think is that things like this don't happen. Her being here isn't possible. It's just not possible. Yet, she's sitting at the end of the hall.

Virtue is an exclusive, private training facility reserved for celebrities, the Hollywood elite, and high-profile athletes. It's *not* the kind of place that has day passes. Since Johnny and I are friends, he agrees to let them work out here for a week.

As Johnny hands me waivers for the ladies to fill out, we hear them talking through the speakers in Johnny's office and realize a microphone is still on in the lobby area where they're sitting from the *Hit the Gym* episode I just finished filming. We can't help but listen to their conversation.

Desiree

From the moment he looked up from his bag and his deep blue eyes locked onto mine, he captivated me. Like one of those steamy, electric moments in a movie. Strange, I'm not typically attracted to a man in such a lustful way...and he's so young. Well, we *are* in L.A. and L.A. is overflowing with hot men. But there's something about this guy.

"Don't you know who that *is*?" Bella's tone is scolding.

I shake my head slightly. "Should I?"

She lunges her body forward, gripping the edge of the bench. "Oh my God. That's *Zane Elkton*."

Heat flushes through my face. "Oh my gosh, I feel so foolish."

"You're an idiot. Maybe he'll give me an autograph. I think he's single," she gushes.

"Look, I don't follow all that celebrity stuff like you do. Of course I know who he *is*, I just didn't recognize him — immediately. I'm sure he would like his privacy respected and not to be ogled over by another seemingly love-struck fan. Besides he's an Untouchable." I have a theory about hot celebrities, one that keeps me immune to ever becoming their prey.

"What's an Untouchable?" The skin between Bella's eyes creases.

"You know, a celebrity under the watchful eye of the world. Every movement either praised or scrutinized by the public. Every misstep catastrophized. Every glance at a woman misinterpreted as his newest love interest, which is probably true, but who knows. Millions of women across the world fantasizing about him, but untouchable by anyone not in that world." My mouth goes dry and my palms start sweating. "Let's go." I put my gym bag strap on my shoulder and stand.

Bella grabs my arm. "Wait. We can't just walk out. He's trying to help us. Damn, he's smokin' hot." She waggles her head and shimmies her body. "Mmm…mmm what I wouldn't give to see in real life that fine body people like us only get to see on the big screen."

As she talks, I recall a quick clip I saw of him on *Ellen* once, comparing his ripped abs to the sculpted abs of a wax figure of himself. Never having seen a man with such a shredded body in real life, I feel heat crawl up my neck to my cheeks as I visualize what it would be like up close. *Cut it out.*

I plant my hands on my hips. "I'm sure he has better things to do. Let's tell them we have to go and get out of here." An intense urge makes me want to slip out and vanish, yet there's a tugging in my gut that makes me want to stay.

"Let's just see what he finds out."

With hesitation, I sit back down.

"You have to admit he's gorgeous. I bet *he* could give you an orgasm." Being condescending is like an art form to Bella.

My entire body stiffens and I snap my head toward her. "*Really?*" I whisper-yell. "You're bringing that up right *now*?"

Bella has no filters and no damn boundaries. Although, she's probably not wrong. Being a gorgeous celebrity, he probably doles out orgasms like nurses hand out lollipops at the pediatrician's office.

"Come on, forty-three years old? I've never heard of someone your age not having an orgasm from sex."

I don't know why I *ever* let that intimate piece of information slip out of me, especially to Bella. It's not like we're close friends. She's one of the few people who has time to get together with me for a quick lunch every now and then and she's usually pretty tolerable. I'm already starting to realize that spending almost a week with her and her friends is *not* going to be tolerable. The minute she invited herself and her friends on my trip when I told her I was coming out here, I should've politely uninvited them.

Tension pinches the base of my neck and I lean in toward her. "Shhh," I scowl. "Would you please keep your voice down? I'm sure he'll be back any second."

So, I've never had an orgasm from sex. Okay, I've never had an orgasm from a man in any way. There. I said it. It's not a big deal and I'm sure I'm not the only woman in the world who hasn't. I've simply never been with a man where there's that raw, lust-filled, passionate attraction like I imagine there would be with someone like Zane Elkton. On second thought, I should *not* imagine that.

"Come on, admit you think he's hot."

I know her well enough to know she isn't going to let this go so I appease her. "Oh, my gosh. This is ridiculous. Yes, he's devastatingly handsome and his eyes are…hypnotic, okay? And he's probably been with hundreds of women." The thought sours my stomach. This is exactly why I have never nor will I ever date anyone as hot as him. With so many women throwing themselves at him, his type just can't keep it in their pants. Plus, I'm no hottie and men that gorgeous aren't attracted to plain-Jane's like me. "I think we just need to leave the guy alone."

Bella grins broadly. "Yup, I knew it." She snaps her fingers and her grin shifts into a cocky smile as she leans back against the bench. "Kinda makes you tingle, huh?"

"Cut it out. Here he comes." I don't see him, but want to cease Bella's relentless babbling.

Zane

Trepidation fills my body as I listen to the redhead describe an Untouchable. I've never heard a celebrity described that way before. I've never heard *myself* described that way before. Sadly, she's pretty much right. It's what I've become used to. It's become a normal way of life. Damn, it sounds pretty awful the way she talks about it.

I head toward them with pens and the waivers on clipboards. "Here you go," I hand everything to the redhead. "Just fill these out and you're all set. I could only get you in for one week though."

"That'll be just fine. Thanks a lot." She takes the clipboards and pens from me and hands a set to her friend. "Oh, I'm Desiree and this is my friend, Bella." She gestures to the bleach-blonde.

Desiree, meaning "desire." Of course, because that's what I'm feeling right now as I soak her in, unable to believe she's sitting here.

"It's nice to meet you both. I'm Zane," I say and sit down next to her as they fill out their waivers.

Bella bounces up and takes a few steps toward me then bends down, giving me a clear shot of her large breasts, and extends her hand to shake mine. "Oh, we know." She winks at me and sits back down on the bench.

Desiree fills in her name, address, and phone number. Then she stops and stares at the form: Emergency Contact ______________. She glances at Bella.

Bella eyes the form where Desiree's hand is frozen. "Just put me," her words rush out in a whisper.

I catch Bella's eyes and the corners of her mouth turn up slightly as she shifts her head back to her waiver.

I return my attention to Desiree. "Is everything okay?"

She swivels her head toward me and the corners of her mouth turn up slightly, similar to the smile Bella gave me, but the smile doesn't reflect in her eyes. "Yes, everything's fine."

I feel like I'm missing something here.

They sign their waivers and hand them back to me.

"How much is it for the week?" Desiree asks.

"Oh, there's no charge. Not for a pass like this."

"Really? Wow, that's great. I'm surprised. This place looks really upscale. Please thank the owner for us. And thank you for your help."

"His name's Johnny. I will. The locker rooms are to the right. You ladies have a good workout." I flash them a smile.

"Yeah. You too." Bella beams back at me.

"Thanks." Desiree politely smiles and turns, heading toward the locker rooms.

On my way back to Johnny's office, I take a picture of Desiree's information with my phone. There's no way I'm letting this chance pass me by. No way.

The mysterious woman from my dreams has a name: Desiree Capstone.

As they work out, I barely catch a glimpse of Desiree. It almost seems like she's avoiding me. I do see a lot of Bella who seems to make sure she's in my line of sight.

Before I leave, I scan the gym and find Desiree in the free weight area, working out her shoulders. As I head toward her, her toned body catches my attention. Her frame is small with a tiny waist and long legs. I can't take my eyes off her; a savage desire pulses through me. *Woah, down, boy.* I slow my stride. *Grandma's underwear, Grandma's underwear.* It takes two more repetitions before I can walk normally.

"Will I see you here tomorrow then?" I'm both hoping and planning to see her.

"Um, I'm not sure what time we're coming tomorrow actually. But thanks again for your help. We really appreciate it."

"Well, that's too bad. Yeah, you bet. Hopefully I'll catch you again during the week." *I'll make sure I see you again.*

"Yeah, maybe."

"Take it easy," I say as I turn and walk away. The fact that she's here still feels surreal.

"You too," she calls out.

I turn halfway around, give her a quick salute with a smile, turn back around, and go find Johnny.

"Dude, I don't have time to explain right now, but I need you do to me a favor."

"Sure. What's going on?" Johnny asks.

"If you learn anything about them before they leave, I want you to call me, text me, whatever and let me know. Okay?"

"You got it."

"Thanks, man."

Desiree

Bella and I finish our workouts and I want to make sure we thank Johnny before we leave. I saw his picture hanging on a wall so I know what he looks like.

"Hi. You're Johnny, right?" I ask.

"Yup, that's me." He smiles brightly at us.

"I'm Desiree and this is Bella." I motion to her. "We just wanted to thank you for the pass for the week. You have an amazing facility here."

"You're welcome. Zane's a good friend so I'm happy to accommodate his request for you. What brings you ladies to L.A.?"

Bella jumps in before I can speak. "We're on vacation. Well, Desiree's here for over a month house-hunting. The rest of us are on vacation for a week." She grins at him.

Bella has always been one to blurt out unnecessary information. She's really getting on my nerves. I don't know how I'm going to survive the week with her.

I halt her from continuing. "Can you tell us if this is usually the time Zane comes to work out? We'd like to respect his privacy and avoid bumping into him during the week."

"I'm sorry. As much as I'd like to help you out, privacy is of the utmost importance with my clientele and I wouldn't be able to share that even if I knew. Honestly, it depends on what he has going on so it varies."

"Yes, of course. That makes complete sense. I'm sorry to have asked. Okay. Well, we're heading out. Thanks again. We'll see you tomorrow."

"I'll be here." He smiles at us.

We turn and head toward the exit.

"Let's shoot for around two tomorrow. You and the girls can hit the beach in the morning and then we'll come here afterwards," I suggest.

"Okay, sounds good."

There's a strange twinge in my stomach. Though I want to avoid running into him, I also find myself hoping to see him tomorrow.

~ 3 ~

Desiree

We head back to the Airbnb and Zane is swirling around in my head. He really is pretty darn gorgeous. And that was nice of him to help us out, he certainly didn't have to do that. *Ugh. Get out of my head, cute young boy.*

It's only our first full day in Los Angeles and I'm regretting my decision to let Bella and her friends come along on the trip. They're all much younger than me, they're ridiculously catty, and they're annoyingly into celebrity-hunting. I definitely should've come alone. Too late now.

Thankfully, they want to go the beach and then go shopping and looking for famous people. I don't want to do any of that so I stay at the house and my introverted self is delighted to be alone.

I'm always hungry after working out so I order some food because we haven't yet gone to the grocery store. I'll go after I eat. I need to stock up since I'll be here a while.

I grab a quick shower while I wait for my food to arrive. As I eat, I Google to find the nearest Whole Foods and head out once I'm done. Not being in a hurry, I take my time figuring out where things are in the store and load up my cart with fresh fruits and vegetables, fish, chicken, some healthy snacks, and a few other things.

I roll my cart into the checkout line and there he is…Zane, on the cover of a tabloid. My entire body tingles like that feeling you get when your foot wakes up after falling asleep. *What is wrong with me?*

I ignore the feeling, check out, and head back to the Airbnb to get some work done and look for Realtors. Zane keeps popping into my thoughts. The next thing I know, I'm on Google typing in: "Zane Elkton."

There are over thirty-six million results. He's on display for the world. I find all sorts of images from when he was a little boy to more recent ones. There are loads of images of him with no shirt and, *good heavens*, I have to admit that his Zeus-like physique is definitely nice to look at. In some images, his eyes are crystal-blue with long, dark, luscious lashes any woman would pay to have.

His hair styles and hair color varied throughout the years, some of them make me laugh out loud. *Ooo, the crimping, no, no, no.* I linger on a few of the present-day images — thick, dark hair, a little longer on top and tousled with sideburns, hypnotic eyes, strong jawline, and an adorable crooked smile. Here comes that tingle again.

I also watch a few interviews and read some articles. While you obviously can't believe everything you find on the internet, he actually seems respectful, kind, and down-to-earth. Other actors and industry professionals he's worked with speak about his dedication to his craft, his confidence in his abilities, and his passion and professionalism in his work. The more I read and watch, the more enamored of him I become — I didn't expect that.

The next morning, I spend a few hours researching houses and looking for a Realtor, without much success. Bella and her friends head to the beach for the day and Bella's meeting me back here just before two o'clock so we can go to the gym together.

I put on my workout clothes, grab my hat, and head to the bathroom. As I pull my hair through the hole in the back of my hat, I stare at my reflection and my nerves surface. *I wonder if he'll be there. Why's he in my head?*

Just then, Bella pops her head in, startling me out of my thoughts. I didn't hear her come in the house.

"I'm here," she gasps on an exhale of heavy breathing.

"Okay. We're not in a hurry. I'm ready to go when you are."

"Okay, let me get changed."

She changes into bright blue shorts that barely cover the bottom of her butt cheeks and a white sports bra that doesn't do much to harness her voluptuous breasts. Her long, silky, platinum hair is in a ponytail. As soon as she's ready, I drive us to the gym with butterflies darting around in my stomach.

When I pull into the parking lot, I don't see Zane's car. Whew, he's not here. *This is a good thing. Why am I disappointed?*

About fifteen minutes into my thirty-minute run on the treadmill, he crosses in front of me looking oh, so good. He stops, doubles back, and stands in front of my treadmill, giving me a wave. Pangs of conflict wrestle inside me and I want to disappear. Seeing as I can't disappear, I give him a quick wave back.

Focus on your run. RUN.

Bella practically bounces her vivacious self over to him.

Zane

"Hi, there," Bella chirps in an overly excited tone.

"Hey, Bella," I greet her and look back at Desiree. "She keeps a good pace," I say as I cross my arms.

"Wait until the end."

"What happens at the end?"

"Where most people trail off at the end of a run, she kicks it into high gear."

"Yeah?" I glance at Bella and she shifts her body toward me, her breasts lightly grazing my arm. While I love a nice set of breasts, I've gotten tired of seeing women leave almost nothing to the imagination. I'm much more interested in the perky breasts of the woman from my dreams who happens to be running on the treadmill in front of me.

She shakes her head. "You've never seen her run."

That sounds like a challenge. I'm up for it. I get on the treadmill next to Desiree's and start running.

Desiree

Why's he running next to me? Go away, you gorgeous boy. He points to his ears and raises his brows as though trying to tell me he wants to say something. So I take my headphones out of my ears.

"Let's see what you've got." His playfulness is devilishly charming.

He winks at me with a cunning smile. That radiant, crooked smile is distracting and my legs come close to buckling beneath me.

"Are you sure you're ready?" *Stop flirting and breathe.*

"Bring it." He jets his chin up.

"The last five minutes." I catch a breath. "We increase speed by .5 each minute."

He nods in acknowledgement.

I put my headphones back in my ears and look straight ahead. *Concentrate.*

As the treadmill timer hits 24:55, I look at him, motion five fingers, and put my thumb up. We both increase our speed by .5. At 25:55, I motion again and again we increase. Right on cue, my favorite running song, "Sandstorm," blasts into my ears. By the end of the fourth increase, he hits the "Cool Down" button. I look at him and smile as I put up my index finger and swirl it in an upward motion. Shifting my head forward again, I increase my final .5 for the last minute. "Sandstorm" hits its climax and it's as if my legs have separated from my body, sprinting. Just to taunt him a little more now that he's bailed, I bump the speed up to 9.0 for my last thirty seconds. My legs are strong and powerful as I push out my final strides and sweat drips down my face and chest.

Hitting my "Cool Down" button, I pluck my headphones out of my ears and turn my face toward him. His skin glistens with sweat and he's breathing heavily. Either sweat is pouring into my mouth or my mouth is watering at the sight of him.

"What happened to you?" I chuckle, trying to catch my breath.

"What *was* that?" He laughs. "I'm fast. You're crazy." He points a finger at me, shaking it.

"What can I say? My legs were made to run."

"Well, now you have to let me redeem myself somehow."

Redeem himself? "No redemption necessary." I park my hands on my hips as I walk and focus on steadying my breathing.

"Oh it's on now. I can't go down like this."

"I told ya." Bella winks and smiles at him then goes back to her workout. I have no idea what she said to him and, frankly, I don't care.

We continue walking in silence until we're both cooled down. I had only just started my workout when he came in and now I want to leave. He's a distraction. *Why am I so drawn to him?*

"What are you doing for dinner?" he asks.

Dinner? What does he care what my dinner plans are? "I think the girls are going out to eat and then probably to a night club."

"And are you going with them?"

"Nah, not my scene. Besides, I need to find a Realtor. After they leave, I have five weeks to hopefully find somewhere to live out here." *He doesn't need to know this.*

"Well, you need to eat. Come join me for dinner at my parents' house."

"You want *me* to join *you* at your parent's house for dinner?" *Excuse me, what?*

"Yes," he says, deadpan.

"Why?" I shake my head. *Zane Elkton is inviting me to his parent's house for dinner?*

"Why not?" His sultry eyes lock onto mine, weakening me.

Let's see, my options are: One: go to an uncomfortable dinner with three girls I don't actually like and put up with them trying to bully me into going out drinking and dancing; Two: stay at the Airbnb by myself; or Three: go to Zane Elkton's parent's house with him for dinner.

After researching him the night before and now this little running race, I'm definitely curious about him. And let's face it, how often does an old woman like me get asked to dinner by a young, hot, charming guy?

"Um, okay?" My stomach flips as I answer in what sounds more like a question.

"Great. Where are you staying?" He grabs his phone. "I'll pick you up at five."

I give him the address of the Airbnb. "Pull a few houses down when you get there. Bella's friends will eat you alive if you come into the house."

"Okay, noted." He smiles. "I'll see you tonight," he says as he turns, gets off the treadmill, and walks toward the weights.

His walk is like a cowboy who's just gotten off his horse, slightly bow-legged, and, *my goodness,* what a cute butt.

What did I just do?

When we get back to the house, Sarah and Jane are there, laying on the sofa, watching TV and eating snacks.

"Someone was getting chummy with Zane Elkton today." Bella's teasing annoys me.

Jane jumps right in. "Oh, *really*? Celebrity sighting!" A broad smile stretches across her beautifully tanned face.

"Celebrity *interacting*." Bella exaggerates.

"Anyway." I cut off any further chatter down that road. "I connected with one of my friends who lives out here and we're meeting up for dinner so I won't be joining you tonight," I lie.

"Okay." Sarah sounds like she's relieved. "You don't know what you're missing though," she says as she gets off the sofa and walks down the hall to her bedroom.

Since I'm staying for a while, I get the largest bedroom with my own bathroom. I shower, do my usual minimal makeup, and put on distressed skinny ankle jeans, my flowy floral tank top, and taupe strappy heels. Simple diamond stud earrings finish my outfit.

Grabbing my purse, I go to the living room where I wait for Zane and listen to loud club music coming out of Sarah's room. One by one, the girls pop out of their rooms, each wearing some version of Saran-wrap-tight mini dresses with plunging necklines, showcasing all their assets. They're in bright colors, shimmery fabrics, and lariat necklaces dangling between their breasts. They've got their makeup loaded on, stiletto heels, and body parts are barely covered.

"You girls look ready for a fun night." I affirm as I grab my phone to check the time. "Have a great time." I walk out the door and down the street a bit for my secret meet-up...with Zane Elkton.

Are my underarms wet? Why am I nervous?

~ 4 ~

Zane

Being dubbed a "Hollywood Heartthrob" at a young age and "The Sexiest Man in the World" as an adult, I'm extremely confident around women. But, when she walks out the door, *damn*, an involuntary shudder runs down my spine and I feel like a nervous twelve-year-old kid.

One of the images from my dreams, matching her appearance, flashes quickly through my head. I can't pry my eyes from her and rash excitement rushes through me.

"Hi." I pull up to the curb where she's walking.

She scurries over to the car, quickly gets in, and scooches down. "Hurry, hurry, go, go." She giggles.

I hit the gas pedal and put the windows up so her ponytail doesn't become a tangled mess. I've learned women hate that.

"I think we're clear," I say with a sigh.

She sits up and puts on her seatbelt.

"Sneaking out, huh?"

"Yeah, well, it's better this way, trust me. If you came in, the girls would've been tripping over each other to talk to you. They're the star-struck type."

I'm used to that. Most women fall all over themselves in my presence, but not Desiree. She seems indifferent to my celebrity status which I kind of like.

"Not you though?"

She smiles. "No, not really. I mean, at some point, you were all everyday people like us. Certainly, what you've accomplished in your life is impressive and something to be admired and respected. I just think that some people's reactions to your very existence can be rather extreme and unnecessary and kind of silly actually."

"You get used to it."

"I don't think I could ever get used to that."

"So, now that I have you captive, tell me more about needing a Realtor." I want to learn everything I can about her.

"Well, I'm hoping to move out here."

"Where from?"

"Pennsylvania." She pulls on the seatbelt strap, adjusting it around her small frame.

"Is that home for you then?"

"Yeah, for a long time now."

"What brings you out this way?'

"Um..." She hesitates, clasping her hands in her lap. "A change."

I sense a similar tension in her as when she got stuck filling out her waiver at the gym.

"And sunshine." A natural smile spreads across her delicate face.

"You'll get plenty of that out here. So, I think I can help you." I'll do anything I can to connect myself to her.

"You can? How?" She shifts a little in her seat to face me more.

"I have connections." I grin.

"Ah, of course you do." She chuckles. "That would be really great actually. Right now, I'm just blindly searching online and it's hard to know who to trust, who's good, who will actually look out for you, you know?"

"I'll hook you up with my guy."

"Are you sure I'm not too small-time for him? I don't want to waste his time. I might even start out with an apartment if I can't find a house. I mean, I'm not going to be a big commission for him."

"No, no, he's a really good guy and he'll take care of you. Do you want to live around here or closer to the beach?"

"I'm not sure really. I just know I want something small and cute." She squishes up her cute nose as she shrugs. "I know, great criteria." She mocks herself.

"Hah. Okay. Square footage and number of bedrooms?" Let's probe a little here to see if there's a husband and kids who'll be joining her. My stomach knots.

"Doesn't really matter. One bedroom, maybe two, for an office or guest room."

"So, it's just you?" I clench my fingers around the steering wheeling, hoping she says yes.

"Just me."

Yes. A burst of hope rises in my chest. "Jerry will be able to help you find something. Do you know what kind of place you want?"

"Not really. I know whatever's out here is going to be very different from where I am now."

"Yeah? What's it like where you are now?"

"It's beautiful and surrounded by nature. I live in an old stone farmhouse, oozing of charm. It's my dream home really. I'm lucky to have been able to live in my dream home for so long. Creaky wooden floors and big window-sills." She animatedly creates an imaginary window sill with her hands. "It's cozy and homey. There's an old outhouse and even a smokehouse and a huge barn." She pauses and sighs. "And because Pennsylvania is one of the oldest states, there are so many antique places to shop. I have lots of unique vintage and antique pieces."

"Yeah? What is it about those old pieces that you like?"

"Well, I like to daydream about their history, their journey before I found them. It's like my house, within its walls it holds the past, stories, someone's memories. From hardships, to celebrations, to love stories. I don't know. I guess they make me think of simpler times. I'm going to miss it there, a lot."

Though everything in my house is new and modern, Grandpa's love of vintage and antique cars instilled in me an appreciation for them. I can't help but admire her similar fondness and cherishing the memories as Grandpa does. "It sounds incredible. What brings you out here then, work?"

"No." She pauses. "I need a change. I'm planning to attend the National Holistic Institute here in L.A. and get licensed in massage therapy while I build up my business here."

I whistle. "You'll be in high-demand for that out here." This is Tinseltown and there's a ton of people I know who are often looking for a good, trustworthy massage therapist who's not out to exploit them. Hmm, maybe I can help her here too.

"That's what I'm hoping for," she says as she raises her eyebrows.

"What is it you do now?"

"I'm a professional organizer."

That's not what I expected. "So, you organize people's kitchen cabinets and things?"

"Well, that, but I have a more holistic approach to it. Being organized is something so much deeper than just *being organized.* Our habits are deeply seated in our lifestyle and keenly connected to our emotions. Most people don't initially realize that and think it's just about me helping them put stuff into containers. I'm not about swirling in, tidying up, and moving on. I get to know the person; what they're about, what their lifestyle is like, what stresses them out, and what makes them feel good and at peace. My goal is to create a space for my clients to feel organized and tranquil with processes in place that serve them long after I'm gone while leaving a lasting impression."

"Very cool." I admire her approach to her work. It sounds much more professional and in-depth than what I thought an organizer would be. "Okay, we're here."

I pull into the driveway and go around to open her door, but she's already getting out. I hold the door open and she tilts her head and smiles, acknowledging my attempted gesture of chivalry. Closing the door, I lead her into the house. It's my childhood home and somewhere I can be completely myself and not paranoid about lurking paparazzi.

We walk into the living room where my family is gathered,

sitting and chatting. Mom's home cooking fills my nostrils.

"Hey, Grandpa. This is my friend, Desiree."

"Hello, dear," Grandpa's voice is cheery. He stands up and shakes her hand, clasping it in both of his.

I point around the room, introducing each relative by name. My uncle Tom; aunt Mary; cousin Janelle and her husband, Paul, and their two kids, Nicky and Tammy; cousin Grace; my brother Declan; and my dad Dan. They each smile and greet her and she politely smiles back.

"No Jasmine tonight?" I ask Declan.

"No, she and Sherry are off doing wedding things," he replies.

I shift to Desiree. "Sherry's my other cousin. She's getting married in a few weeks."

"Your mom's in the kitchen," says my dad, pointing toward the kitchen.

"Okay, thanks." I take Desiree's hand in mine and walk to the kitchen. I like the way her small hand feels in mine. I knew her skin would be soft.

"There's my boy." Mom stops cutting lettuce, wipes her hands on her apron, and puts her arms around me.

I let go of Desiree's hand, embrace Mom, and give her a kiss on the cheek, releasing her.

"Mom, this is my friend, Desiree. Desiree, this is my mom, Sabrina."

"How nice to meet you, Desiree." She puts her arms around Desiree and hugs her.

"Oh." The surprised look on her face is adorable. "It's so nice to meet you as well." She hugs Mom back.

"You're a wisp of a thing, aren't you?" Mom smiles and releases her. "Here, let me get you an apron. Do you mind helping me?"

"Not at all, I'd be happy to help."

"Okay, you." Mom motions to me, shooing me away. "Get out of my kitchen and let us finish up here so we can eat."

"Okay, okay." I laugh and go back to the living room.

I beeline for Grandpa and look him squarely in the eyes. "Grandpa, it's *her*," I whisper as my temperature rises what feels like ten degrees.

"Who *her*?" The wrinkles between his eyes deepen with confusion.

"From my dreams. Desiree is the woman from my dreams."

Grandpa's white bushy eyebrows raise as he slowly nods and the deep wrinkles shift to his forehead in surprise. "Ohhhhh."

Desiree

Sabrina gives me an apron and I slip it over my head. She grabs the ties behind me and ties a bow.

"You *are* a tiny thing." She says, putting her hands on my hips.

"Yeah." I chuckle, slightly self-conscious, tucking away an errant piece of hair that's escaped my ponytail.

"I'll have you prepare the salad, okay?"

"Oh thank goodness. A salad, I can do. I'm a dreadful cook." I laugh nervously.

"No. Really?" She arches her body a bit as though my confession surprises her.

"Oh, yes. I could destroy ramen noodles."

"Hah! Okay, we'll stop at the salad then." She smiles and hands me a cutting board, knife, the lettuce she was chopping, cucumbers, tomatoes, carrots, avocados, red onions, and croutons.

Not quite sure what to say to Zane Elkton's mother, I know one thing I need to do is to be gracious. "Thank you so much for having me here with your family. I hope I'm not intruding."

"Intruding? Not at all. It's been quite some time since Zane brought a girl home."

I feel her eyes on me and look up from my vegetable-chopping, shaking my head. "Oh I'm not a girl. I mean, I'm a girl, but I'm not — we've only just met and he's…" I shake my head and shrug, "…

he's just being a nice guy. He seems very kind." As I turn my head back to my chopping board, I catch Zane watching me and smile at him. I quickly look back at Sabrina, who also appears to catch the moment.

"He is. He has a big heart." Her smile is broad with pride.

"I can tell that about him. He's offered to connect me with his Realtor to help me find a place to live out here."

"So, you're not from around here then?"

"No, I'm currently over on the east coast."

"What brings you out this way? Family?" she asks as she dumps a boiling pot of potatoes into a strainer in the sink.

"No. It's just time for a change in my life."

"Do you know anyone out here?" She looks away from her potatoes and shoots me a concerned, motherly look.

I pause and put my attention back on my vegetable-cutting. "There are a few women I know online from my business, but I've never met them in person. I don't know anyone else."

"That's pretty brave to make such a big move all by yourself."

"It's…" I sense her gaze on me again and keep my eyes focused on my vegetables. "…something I need to do."

"Well," she says cheerfully, "now you know us."

I smile at her, feeling like she truly means it.

"Quick." She waves her hand at a chocolate cake. "Hide that cake before my Chocolate Bear comes back in here and sees it. It's for *after* dinner."

"Chocolate Bear?" I pick up the cake and tuck it around the corner.

"That boy loves his chocolate." The corners of her mouth curve up as she shakes her head with her hands on her hips. "Ever since he was little."

Together we finish cutting and chopping and prepping. Then she sends me out to the living room to visit with the family and get to know them. After about ten minutes, she enters the living room and announces that dinner is ready. She asks the girls to help bring the dinner bowls to the dining room table and we all fall in line behind her to the kitchen.

Once the meal is on the table, everyone sits down and starts passing around the bowls and filling their plates. Sabrina walks around with a bottle of red wine and a bottle of white wine, offering some to each person.

"Wine, Desiree?"

"None for me thanks." I smile.

She doesn't offer any wine to Zane. In researching him online, I learned that he was in rehab for alcohol addiction. It seems like he takes his recovery seriously. *That's good. Not that it makes a difference to me though.*

During dinner, childhood memories and family vacation and holiday stories are shared around the table.

"Do you guys remember the story Aunt Sabrina told us when Zane was like six years old and she went into his bedroom to check on him before going to bed and he was standing on his bed with his sheet pulled up under his chin?" Grace starts with glee.

A dopey smile forms on Zane's face and he hangs his head, shaking it.

"And when she asked him what he was doing, he told her he wanted to see what it was like to sleep standing up like a —"

His two cousins, Aunt Mary, and Sabrina say in unison, "Horse." Everyone erupts into laugher as he looks at me, shrugs, and starts laughing as well.

"How about the time we were at that park — what's the name of it? The park that had all the swings and monkey bars," Declan chimes in.

"What *was* the name of that park? Is it even there anymore?" asks Janelle.

"Anyway," Declan continues, "there was that Around-the-World monkey-bar globe thing and I had it spinning so fast. And Zane decides to fly through the air and try to grab hold of a bar."

"Oh, I know this one." Sabrina rolls her eyes as she breaks into a smile.

"He grabs a bar for about two seconds and then loses his grip and goes flying through the air again, crashing onto the ground and rolling into a huge puff of dirt."

Everyone bursts into laughter again.

"Hey, I still have a scar from that," Zane chides.

The storytelling continues through dinner and dessert. His cousins scour their phones for humiliating pictures to share with me and they find some doozies. I take a brief moment in the midst of it all and realize that I feel like part of the family. It's unlike anything I've ever felt within my own family. Dinners together aren't something my family does, nor did we even when my parents were still together. This is comforting to my soul.

"Get together." Grace motions to me and Zane with her phone ready to take our picture.

He puts his arm around me, gently caressing my shoulder. A bolt of heat rushes through me and my breath gets stuck in my throat at his slightest touch. I like the feel of his hand on my skin. His arm remains around my shoulder and I'm surprised by how natural it seems.

Grace snaps the picture. "Desiree, give me your number and I'll send it to you."

We exchange numbers and Grace texts the picture to me.

After we devour Sabrina's scrumptious homemade chocolate cake, it's time to clean up.

"Come on, Dec, we're up," Zane says to Declan as he gets up and starts gathering plates.

Sabrina waves her hand at them. "Zane, I'll get it later. You have a guest."

"Nope. That's our deal. You cooked, we clean. Besides, it'll go faster with all of us pitching in."

"Such good boys." A gleam dances in her eyes as she folds her hands together.

Everyone joins in, bringing the dishes to the kitchen and piling them up at the sink where Zane starts washing them.

"I'll dry," I announce. "Declan, how about you put everything away since I don't know where anything goes."

"You've got it." He complies.

Once the dishes are done and the kitchen is mostly tidied up, we head to the living room to join the rest of the family. As I walk into the room, Grandpa's lifting the stylus on an old record player and carefully touches it to a record. Nat King Cole's smooth voice, along with the crackle and hiss of the old vinyl, fills the air with the lyrics of "Stardust." Walking farther into the room, I head toward Zane, but Grandpa stops me, stepping toward me with his arms extended in invitation to join him. I willingly and happily oblige as he scoops me into his arms, a proper distance from himself, with his arm poised just so, gently clasping his fingers around mine in his hand. He moves and sways so gingerly as he hums along with the music and grins from ear to ear.

Paul wraps his arm around Janelle's waist and takes her in his arms, swaying to music. Declan walks over to Grace, bows, and holds out his hand.

"May I have this dance?" he asks, feigning his best attempt at a proper royal accent.

"Why, I'd be delighted." She plays along, exaggerating her acceptance of his hand.

They laugh as he tugs her in and they dance together.

Zane smiles at Sabrina who joins him, and they dance next to me and Grandpa.

The song ends and Grandpa bows while I curtsy. Then me, Grace, and Janelle join Sabrina on the sofa. She's brought out some old photo albums and they start sharing more memories and stories.

Nicky and Tammy busily run around the living room playing when Nicky runs over to me.

He gazes up at me with his big brown eyes. "You're pretty," he says and runs off.

"Aw, thank you." I chuckle and watch him run away.

Zane

Watching Desiree interact with my family warms me deep in my soul. I'm still in awe that she's even here.

A couple hours after dinner, everyone starts to head out.

"Will we see you tomorrow night at Zane's?" Grace asks Desiree.

"I don't know. I don't think so." She shakes her head, looks at me and then back at Grace.

"You *have* to come." Grace looks at me. "Make sure she comes, okay? Good night."

Grandpa takes Desiree's hands in his. "It was lovely meeting you, Desiree. Thank you for the dance. I hope we see you again soon."

She releases his hands and wraps her arms around his neck. "Thank *you*, Grandpa. It was a pleasure. Good night." She kisses him on his cheek and a big, wide smile forms on his wrinkled face as though he's a child who's just been given his favorite candy.

Mom is next in line. She squeezes Desiree in her arms. "Desiree, we loved having you here. Thank you for all your help. You have family here now. Come back anytime. And let us know if we can help with anything to get you settled in when you find a place to live."

Her beautiful smile lights up the room. "Thank you so much, Sabrina. I enjoyed being here and meeting all of you. I sure will."

She moves on to Dad. "Thank you for having me. Good night."

"It was our pleasure. Good night." Dad's a man of few words.

Mom hugs me and whispers in my ear, "I *like* this one." She takes my face in her hands and kisses me on the cheek.

I chuckle. "Good night, Mom. Thanks for dinner." Dad hugs me and gives me a manly pat on the back. "Thanks, Dad. Good night."

I take Desiree's hand and we leave, turning back to wave. This time, I get to her car door before she can open it. She gives me a big grin of appreciation as she gets in.

Backing out the driveway, I know I'm not ready to end our night. "Where to next? Do you want to come back to my place?" I still haven't spent any time alone with her and I'm eager to learn more about her.

"I should probably get back to the house."

"Okay." A heaviness sinks in my chest, but I respect her wishes and head toward her house.

"Do you all get together often?"

"My mom tries to get as much of the family together as she can about every other month. We're a pretty close family." I pause. "I drifted from them for a long time, but now I know how important they all are to me."

"What made you drift?" A question I don't feel ready to answer drops out of her mouth. I know it'll come up at some point so I may as well get into it.

After such a great night, I don't want to end it in a crappy way, so I answer somewhat vaguely. "My line of work can be pretty demanding and, for a while, I let it take over my world. I didn't see my family much and got pretty consumed in the darker side of stardom. But that's behind me now."

"I'm glad you found your way back to them. It's really nice how close you all are." She's quiet for a moment. "I learned a lot about you tonight."

"Yeah." I laugh. "My family is full of embarrassing stories."

"I haven't laughed like that in so long. I really had a good time. They're all quite endearing."

"Thank you for coming. I'm glad you had a good time." I pause. Nerves crawl up my throat and I push past them. "So…I'm having some friends over tomorrow night." I hesitate. Will another invitation so soon scare her away? I don't know, but I desperately want to see her again. "I'd like you to come. You already know my cousins will be there. You can bring your friends. You can't tell them where they're going, but you can bring them. I'll send a car to get you and my driver will take your phones. Can't have it splashed all over social media, you know?" I take a breath. "What do you think?"

She doesn't answer right away. *Shit, I freaked her out.*

"Well, they'll be in heaven for sure. Um, I guess we could come. I don't think they have anything planned for tomorrow night."

That hopefulness I felt before fills me again.

"Why do I get the feeling you don't like these women all that much?"

"It's not that I don't like them, it's just, we're very different. Bella's kind of my friend, but Sarah and Jane are Bella's friends, not mine. Bella's a good person. We just have different views of life and values and morals, that's all." She pauses. "Okay, I don't like them very much." She lets out a small chuckle.

"I see. And you didn't have anyone else to bring here with you?"

"No." Her response is matter-of-fact. "I don't have many close friends and the couple I do have are busy moms with jobs and families. Bella invited herself and, at the time, I didn't want to come alone."

"And you don't know anyone at all out here?"

"There are a couple women I met online, but we've never met in person. I'm hoping to connect with them while I'm here."

My heart sinks for how alone she seems. "I think Grandpa was smitten with you."

"Heh. He's adorable."

"I think my mom kind of liked you too. Heck, my whole family did. And little Nicky was right, you're very pretty."

She ignores my compliment. "They're all so warm and welcoming." She pauses. "I really had such a nice time. Thank you for inviting me."

"You're welcome."

I pull into an open parking spot in front of her house, turn off the engine, and shift my body to face her.

"So, will you come tomorrow night?" I rub the back of my neck.

She hesitates. "Okay, we'll come, Chocolate Bear." A shit-eating grin smears across her face.

A heatwave shoots through my chest. *She's coming.*

I laugh. "Ah, Mom's divulging family secrets, I see." I hold out my hand. "Here, give me your phone."

She gets her phone out of her purse and hands it to me. I key in my number and text myself even though I have her number from her waiver...she doesn't know that.

"Plan to come over around eight. When you and your friends are ready, text me here and I'll send Bill to get you. Remember, don't tell them where they're going, just tell them they're going to a party. And make sure everyone gives their phones to Bill before they get in the limo." I hand back her phone.

"Okay."

When I get out of the car, she stays put until I open her door. Together, we walk in silence to the front door and stand under the dim, yellowish overhead light on the porch. As we face each other, I clumsily shove my hands in my pockets to keep myself from grabbing her in my arms and tasting her lips. My throat is parched. I'm standing inches away from the woman I've been dreaming about for over fifteen years. All my breath rushes out of my lungs. I've never wanted to kiss a woman so badly in my life. Silence hangs in the air as we stare at each other, transfixed.

She looks up at me from under her lashes and breaks our trance. "I used to give my boyfriend a kiss after a nice dinner out."

Boyfriend? A tightness threads through my entire body. *I didn't see* that *coming.* Despondence engulfs me. I turn my face slightly and touch my finger to my cheek.

She delicately touches my shoulder and presses her soft lips to my cheek. "Good night, Zane." The sound of my name as it trickles out of her mouth makes the hairs on the back of my neck stand up. It takes all my willpower not to wrap my arms around her and devour her.

"Good night, Desiree."

She lets herself in and closes the door behind her.

Boyfriend? Shit.

Desiree

I lean back against the door. *Zane Elkton just put his phone number into my phone after having me at his family's house for dinner and inviting me to his house for a party. What is happening?*

~ 5 ~

Desiree

The bright California sun beams through the slit in the curtains of my room, waking me up earlier than I want. Between the girls startling me awake at two o'clock in the morning when they got home and then waking up dripping with sweat from my dream about Zane in the middle of the night, I did *not* sleep well. *I don't have sexual dreams about men. What* was *that?* I lay in bed and recall how hot and bothered I was when he kissed me in my dream. There's that foot-waking-up, full-body tingling again.

Why did he invite me for dinner at his parents' house? And why in the world is he inviting us to a party at his house? This is all very strange. My mind replays bits and pieces of the night before. I have no idea why he held my hand, but it felt so natural and I liked it. *Stop it. Stop thinking about him.* My scolding is in vain. I can't keep him from my thoughts. Watching him with his family and learning about him through their eyes brought such a realness to him. A realness I didn't expect.

The intensity of his cobalt-blue eyes encased me as we stood face-to-face the night before. Without my permission, my mind begins fantasizing; he reaches his fingers through my hair, circling them around the nape of my neck, and tenderly draws my face close to his. His strong, muscular arm encircles my waist, pulling my body to press against his. I wrap my hands around his sculpted arms. Inch by inch, his lips get closer to mine until I feel their warmth melting into me. They part mine as his tongue slides into my mouth.

Oh my gosh, girl! I cover my face with my hands and groan. *Get up and stop this.*

I toss off my covers, put my feet into my slippers, and grab my robe, putting it on over my camisole and satin shorts.

"Oh, shoot. He never gave me the name of his Realtor." *Ugh, I really don't want to text him for it.*

Instead, I eat breakfast and go for a walk to clear my head. As I step outside, the warm air wraps around me. The sun soothes me, instantly confirming that I've made the right decision to move here. I swear my hunched posture is a result of being cold all the time back home.

When I get back from my walk, the girls are up and I let them know a friend of mine is having a party tonight and we're invited. They, of course, are thrilled to have a party to go to. Bella and I decide to hit the gym before we all spend the day together, shopping and roaming around town.

As we pull into a parking spot, I see Zane's car. A surge of energy washes over me. I don't want to see him…and yet I *do* want to see him.

"Ooo, Zane's here." Bella coos and practically skips into the gym.

I head for the treadmills and Bella goes for the weight machines. She's scanning the place, clearly looking for Zane.

"Hey, you." His thick, sexy voice sends a warm flush to my cheeks.

I turn around and he somehow looks even more gorgeous. "Hey, there."

"Okay, this time, I'm ready for you," he coaxes as he broadens his shoulders and puffs out his chest a little.

"Ready for what?"

"Redemption." He playfully shakes both fists in the air, causing the muscles in his arms to tense. *Oh, those tight muscles.*

At this point, I know he's not going to let this redemption-thing go. "Okay." I wave my hand, motioning from him to me. "Out with it. What is it?"

"Chin ups. Well, I'm doing pull ups and you'll do chin ups."

"What? That's completely unfair. You're like, three times the size of me." I spread my arms up and out.

"Maybe four." He winks at me and smiles. That crooked smile is like kryptonite. "Come on."

I follow him to the bar where he jumps on, his back toward me, and starts pulling himself up and dropping slowly down and up and down and up and down; the muscles in his arms are tight and rippling. *Don't drool.* Bella is, of course, immediately by my side, nearly panting like a dog in 100-degree heat with its tongue hanging out. Even through his black T-shirt, his physique is unreal. When he reaches twenty, he drops off the bar.

"Hey, Bella." He's not even out of breath.

"Hey, yourself," she says flirtatiously. "That was impressive." With her hands on her hips, she sways from side to side.

He turns to me. "I'll stop there for now. Your turn."

"Is this a battle?" she asks him as I go over to the bar.

"No. It's my redemption from the run yesterday."

I look up at the bar and know this is such a bad idea. I'm going to humiliate myself. "I can't even reach it," I say, stretching my arms as high as possible.

"Here." He promptly lifts me up. *Oh God.* I like the way his hands feel on me.

I grab the bar and hang for a second, praying I can at least do *one*. Up I go and back down. *Whew!* The second attempt is shaky. I get about halfway up and my muscles quiver. His hands are around my waist, guiding me up and back down. *Please, stop touching me. You're distracting.* I release the bar and he holds me until my feet are on the ground. I'm slightly dizzy from having his strong hands wrapped around me.

"Ha-ha. Redemption!" he shouts, his tone oozing of triumphant testosterone and trite victory as he thrusts his arms in the air. "Yyyyeeeessss," he growls deeply as he shakes his hands with manly pride. He's seductively charming.

"Yeah, yeah." I concede, placating him. "That was a completely unfair competition."

"That *I* won." The playful immodesty in his tone tells me that he's pleased with himself. "I'm heading out. You ladies have a good workout."

"Bye, Zane." Bella's ditzy-voice is in full force and it makes my jaw clench.

"Take care." I wave and turn to Bella. "Okay, let's get to it."

We finish our workouts, go back to the house, and get ready for our day of shopping and touring the town. Bella, Sarah, and Jane spend loads of money on clothes and shoes and jewelry and belts and hats and tons of other junk. The only things I spend money on are lunch and dinner. I'm more frugal than they are and don't need more *stuff*. We head back to the house after dinner to relax and get ready for the party.

As I figure out what to wear, I'm caught off guard by my excitement to see Zane. I have no idea what to wear to a party at a celebrity's house and I certainly didn't pack for such an occasion. I pick out a different pair of skinny jeans from the night before and a casual light tan floral blouse with three-quarter length sleeves and a wide, delicate-ruffle elastic neckline that can be worn off-the-shoulder, but I wear it up on my shoulders. I put on my strapless bra in case the wide neckline shifts, I don't like to have my bra straps showing.

Around seven-forty, I check to see if the girls are ready. Similar to the night before, each pops out in some version of tight, plunging, sheer, revealing clothing; dolled up and ready to party. When I go to text Zane, I can't find his number in my contacts. I know he texted himself so I check there...and find him: "Chocolate Bear." Warmth spreads through my chest and I text to let him know we're ready.

About fifteen minutes later, there's a knock on the door and I open it.

"Are you Miss Desiree?" asks a tall, broad man who looks to be in his early sixties. He's sharply dressed in a black suit, white dress shirt, black tie, and shiny patent leather shoes.

"Yes, I'm Desiree."

"I'm Bill." He nods, smiles warmly at me, and clasps his hands together. "I'll be taking you ladies to the party."

"Okay, great. Thanks so much."

The girls are huddled behind me and, as we step onto the porch, Bella squeals, "A *limo*?"

"Ooooo, fancy," Jane chimes in.

"*Who* is your friend?" Sarah asks.

Bill interrupts them. "Excuse me, ladies, I'm going to need your phones."

"Our phones?" Jane asks.

"Yes, ma'am. In order to attend this party, you'll need to give me your phones for the evening. You'll get them back when I bring you home later."

Sarah turns to me as she hands her phone to Bill. "What's going on? What kind of party is this?"

"Oh my God," Bella yips. "Is it *Zane's*? Is that where we're going? Eeeeeee!"

"You'll know where we are when we get there," I reply, keeping my expression and tone neutral.

Bill's husky voice interrupts us again as he holds open the door to the limousine. "Ladies, please go ahead and get in." He holds out his hand for the rest of our phones.

We hand them over and climb into the limousine. About fifteen minutes later, we arrive at Zane's house. Bill gets out and opens the door, offering his hand to help the girls out, but they ignore him and pile out excitedly. He then offers his hand to me and I accept it.

Even in my heels, I have to stretch up to whisper, "Am I supposed to tip you?"

He laughs heartily. "No, ma'am, that's not necessary."

I grin. "Okay."

"Just down those stairs and enter in the door on your right,"

Bill instructs us.

The girls giddily head down the stairs and into the door. As I enter, pushing open the thick mahogany door, Zane is letting them hug him one by one and each of them gush and tell him what big fans they are which is probably only partially true. They're fans of *any* celebrity.

"Thank you so much. I appreciate that. If you brought purses, I can put them in my bedroom." They raise their wrists, dangle their new wristlets at him, and burst into giggles. "Okay, great. Alcohol and food are in the kitchen. Make yourselves at home. Everyone here's very friendly. Have a good time," he calls out as they make their way, heels clicking on the hickory-wood floor, into the group of people standing in the kitchen.

The low, rhythmic thump of club music fills the air along with the buzz of chatter from small clusters of people. While this is definitely an environment the girls thrive in, the introvert in me considers turning around and leaving when, unexpectedly, Zane lifts me off my feet into his massive arms like I'm a feather.

He spins me around and returns me to the ground, still holding me in his arms. I'm lightheaded and it's not from the spin. My hands are on his arms, the warm skin on his arms that wraps around his muscles. I've never had my hands on someone so luscious.

I'm quick to remove my hands from his arms, but he doesn't let go of me.

"It's good to see you. I'm glad you're here." The sincerity in his voice is unshakable.

I'm a little startled and wonder if *I'm* lingering in his arms or if *he's* frozen in the moment. Finally, he releases me and takes my hand in his. Again, I find this hand-holding strange, but I also like it.

"Come on." He walks toward a small group of people in the spacious living room.

"This is my assistant, Eric. He's also one of my oldest friends," he says as he introduces me.

"Hi. It's a pleasure to meet you." I hold out my hand.

"Nice to meet you, Desiree." He smiles politely and shakes my hand.

Grace springs out and embraces me. "You came!" The girl exudes joy and it makes me feel at ease.

"Yeah." I'm happy to see Grace and Janelle again.

Grace turns to a girl who shares her facial features and long, dark hair. "This is my other sister, Sherry, who wasn't there last night."

"It's so nice to meet you, Sherry."

"Likewise. I heard I missed a fun night of roasting Zane." She looks at him and winks.

He smiles and puts his hand on my back. Goose bumps run up my spine. "Give me your purse and I'll put it in my room."

I hand him the small purse I brought. "Thanks."

"I'll be right back," he says and disappears.

Feeling out of place, I stand quietly, listening to his cousins and friends have conversations. About an hour passes and he hasn't returned.

I touch Grace's arm and lean close to her ear. "Where's the bathroom?"

"Just down that hall on the left. You'll see it."

"Thanks, I'll be right back."

I walk slowly, taking in the ambiance. I've never been in such a massive house. While perfectly appointed, it's starkly different from my cozy farmhouse. I'm guessing he hired a professional decorator. The kitchen cabinets and island are a dark teak wood topped with thick marble that's swirled with a light teal, tan, and cream. Wide windows above the double-sink look out over the twinkling city. The view is amazing.

As I walk down the hallway, I pass a water fountain; the lull of the water adds a tranquility to the space. When I get to the bathroom, it's just as grand as what I'd already seen and minimalistic in décor. The counters are a smooth mahogany and a glass bowl serves as the sink. One contemporary blue and green painting hangs on the wall and a round black-rimmed mirror hangs above the sink.

While it's not at all my style, it's peaceful.

When I return from the bathroom, I don't see Grace or anyone else from the group I was standing with earlier. I wander through the kitchen and living room, out through the opening where glass doors have been pushed open, to the balcony. Standing at the railing that stretches the length of the house, I take in the view. It's spectacular; shimmering lights of the city as far as I can see in panoramic view over to the ocean. I look down to the level below and see a lighted pool with several groups of people talking. There are probably thirty to thirty-five people there altogether.

The thump of the music and idle chatter morph into a low hum in my ears. A warm, soft breeze glides over my skin, gently swirling my hair. I rest my hands on the cool, steel railing and close my eyes, immersed in the moment.

Warm fingers whisper down my neck and move my hair, causing my shoulder to involuntarily lift in response and my blood to race. The movement shifts the collar of my blouse just off my shoulder as the fingers trace from my neck to my exposed shoulder. I shudder. A body barely meets mine. I know it's him…Zane. A shallow breath sticks in my throat and heat bolts through me as I open my eyes and turn slowly around.

He seduces me with his eyes. "Hi."

"Hi." My breath escapes.

"I'm sorry it took me so long to get back to you."

I adjust my blouse back onto my shoulder. "Oh no, it's fine. You're the host. I totally get it."

"Maybe we can sneak into a quiet corner…"

"Zane, dude, I think you're out of beer," one of his friends shouts from behind us.

He closes his eyes, squeezes his lips together, then opens his eyes and smiles.

Before he leaves, he sets down a beer bottle on the small glass table next to me and my eyes linger on it, probably longer than seems normal for someone to look at a bottle of beer. "I'm sorry, do you want one?"

"No." Sharpness cuts my voice.

His head jerks back and his eyebrows shoot up. "Okay. Don't go anywhere. I'll be right back."

"It's okay. Go."

He turns and goes; leaving me intoxicatingly off balance by his touch and my response to it. I'm also a bit shaken to see him drinking. *Well, that's disappointing. Not that it matters.*

I spot Grace, Janelle, and Sherry in a group down by the pool and join them. A little over an hour passes. I look up at the balcony and see Zane and Bella talking. She's touching him, groping his chest and his arms. A twinge of jealousy pinches me, though it shouldn't.

Zane

I pick up my beer and take a swig as Bella clumsily uncrosses and re-crosses her legs.

"So, I didn't get twirrrrrled around with my hug," Bella slurs. "You know, you don't want to get involved with her," she says snidely. "She's messed up."

"What do you mean, 'messed up?' How?" I ask, taking another swig of beer.

"She's been a hot mess ever since her cheating, alcoholic boyfriend, Brad, flipped his Lamborghini upside down and died six months ago."

Holy shit. I'm stunned. I put down my beer, my eyes drop toward the pool, and I see Desiree watching us. My heart aches for her. I can't even begin to imagine what she's been through.

Bella runs her index finger across my chest that tightens immediately. "I'm available though. With nooooo baggage." A sloppy smile drips across her face.

"Excuse me a minute," I say as I turn to go down to Desiree.

Desiree

Though I'm standing with a group, I'm not listening to anything being said. I can't stop staring at Zane and Bella.

"Your friends are very…different than you," Grace says as she nudges me out of my trance and looks up at Zane and Bella on the balcony.

I turn my body to her and refocus my attention. "Yeah." I acknowledge. "We're not really close. I wouldn't even say we're friends." *What am doing here? I need to leave, now.* "I…I think I'm going to go. It's getting late."

"She's not his type." Grace looks back up at them. "*At all.*"

My gaze follows. "It's really none of my business." I'm sick in my stomach.

"No?" She cocks her head to the side with curiosity in her eyes.

"No." I shake my head and hug her and then Janelle and Sherry. "Good night everyone." I wave at the group. "It was so nice meeting you all."

Grace grabs my hand. "I'll call you tomorrow."

"Okay," I say quietly and force a polite smile.

I turn to go find the girls and let them know I'm leaving when I see Zane coming down the stairs toward me. *Just be gracious and get out of here.*

"Thank you again for inviting us. This was fun." I barely slow my stride.

"Wait, you're leaving?" A tinge of alarm sits in his voice as he gently grabs my arm.

Go, just go.

I stop and face him. Releasing my arm from his grip, I rub the area he was just touching. "Um, yeah, it's…it's getting late and I, uh, I'm getting tired," I lie, unsure of what to say.

"I'll drive you back."

"No, you can't do that. You're the host. You need to stay here with your guests." I inch backwards from him.

He steps toward me. "They're my friends, they don't need me here."

"Really, it's fine. I'm just, uh, going to find my friends and let them know I'm leaving. Do you think it's okay for Bill to take a second trip to bring them back later?" I look away from him, pretending to look for the girls, but desperately trying to avoid making eye contact with him.

"Yes, it's fine." He reaches over and takes my hand in his, summoning my eyes to his. "I wish you would stay."

My gaze returns reluctantly to him. "I can't. I really need to go." Pangs of uneasiness dart frantically in my chest. I let go of his hand. "Looks like Bella's really into you." I look away briefly and immediately want to take back my childish remark. There's a sinking feeling in my stomach.

"*I'm* not into Bella." His blue eyes glow with a stark seriousness.

"I…I really need to go. Good night Zane." I walk away and find Sarah and Jane, tell them I'm leaving, and then go upstairs to find Bella. And there she is…passed out on the sofa. Zane isn't far behind me.

"Here, I'll get her." He picks up her dead weight like he's picking up a pillow.

I follow him as he carries her down the hall into a bedroom where he lays her down on the bed. Taking off her shoes, I put her wristlet on the nightstand and fold down the sheets and blanket. He helps me roll her under the covers.

"Thank you." I sigh. "Is it okay if I stay here with her? I wouldn't feel right leaving her here alone."

"Yes, of course."

"Okay, thanks. I'm going to let Sarah and Jane know. I'm so sorry about this."

"Hey, it's not your fault."

The guests have thinned out and only about fifteen people are left. I find Sarah and Jane and tell them what happened and that I'll be staying here with Bella. They decide to leave and Bill takes them back to the house.

When I go back into the bedroom, there's a neatly stacked pile of a black T-shirt, gray sweatpants, a pair of socks, and my purse. I undress and put them on; grateful for the comfortable clothes.

What the hell am I doing here?

It's late and I'm tired. And I know I'm not going to sleep well. As I lay in bed under the covers, images of Bella touching Zane sneak into my thoughts.

Cut it out. This is all so surreal. Tomorrow you leave and focus on what you came here to do...find a house and create a new life. Now, try to sleep.

My brain won't quiet down and my body is restless. Involuntarily, my thoughts jump to the dark side and he's kissing Bella and touching her back. *Argh!* I'm so confused. One minute he's inviting me to his parent's house for dinner and holding my hand and the next he's flirting with freaking Bella. Or was he? *She* was touching him, but did he like it? I didn't see him touching her back. *Oh good Lord! What does it matter?* There's *nothing* going on between us. He's just being a nice guy, that's *all.*

I throw the covers off and sit up on the edge of the bed. Every muscle in my body is tight and my mouth is dry. I get out of the bed, tiptoe to the door, and open it a crack, listening for people talking. It's quiet.

Lights from the kitchen help me see where I'm going when I step out into the hall. I pad down the hall as quietly as possible, making sure to peek around the corner first in case anyone's still there. The living room's empty and it looks like Zane cleaned up a little. I grab a bottle of water out of the refrigerator and go out to the balcony to breathe in the view once more, hoping it will relax me. The sky is clear and filled with stars and the moon sits suspended. The slight chill in the air causes me to shiver.

"Couldn't sleep?" His velvety voice evokes a gasp.

"You keep sneaking up on me." I turn and glance at his handsome face, laughing quietly.

"Do I?" His smile is broad and knowing. "Heh, I figured they'd be big on you." He examines his clothes on me.

I chuckle as I look down and wiggle my toes in his floppy socks. Raising my head, I hook a stray strand of hair behind my ear. "Thank you for these."

"Let's sit by the fire."

I follow him to the fire pit and sit cross-legged in his baggy sweatpants on the overstuffed cushion of a light rattan chair teeming with pillows the color of autumn leaves. Putting my water on the matching side table, I grab a puffy burnt-orange pillow and hug it to my chest.

"Got cool out." He turns on the fire.

"It did. Thanks." I rub my hands in the warmth of the heat.

"I'm going to grab some water. I'll be right back."

He leaves and comes back with a bottle of water and a blanket that he drapes over my shoulders.

"Thank you."

"It's a nice night." Sitting down next to me, he tucks the blanket around me.

"I think it's morning."

"Yeh." He chuckles. "What has you up?"

"I don't sleep well when I'm not in my own bed. How about you?"

"Insomnia. I slept great as a kid, but I can't seem to get more than two-to-three hours a night these days." *Hmm, insomnia...one indicator of substance abuse. Stop it. It doesn't matter.*

"That's awful. How do you function? I'd be a zombie."

"I've gotten used to it." He leans back into the puffy cushion.

We sit quietly, gazing into the flames. Golden flecks from the fire flicker in his eyes.

"Can I ask you a question?" His gaze shifts from the fire to me.

Please don't ask me something I don't want to answer, I beg, my stomach queasy. "Sure."

"Why'd you want to leave tonight? Weren't you having a good time?" he asks, sounding disappointed. "I'm sorry I couldn't be with you much." His voice is deep and rugged yet gentle.

I don't *want to answer this.* "No, I *was* having a good time. I really like your cousins and your friends are all very nice. I just...I don't belong at parties. I don't fit in. I think I was the oldest person here, except maybe Bill who was outside in the limo." I laugh. "I don't belong *here*."

"Well, I'm glad you're here. I feel bad about *why* you're here, but I'm glad you're here." His eyes hold mine so intently.

We're silent.

I break his comforting gaze and look at the fire.

"Hey, I forgot to give you Jerry's information last night. Let's make sure you get that before you leave."

"Yeah, that would be great."

"Stay right here," he says as he gets up and goes into the house.

The air fills with the silky sound of Nat King Cole. He approaches me and holds out his hand expectantly.

My mind plays emotional tug-of-war. *Don't do it. But I want to. Nothing can happen. He is who he is and you are who you are. It's just a dance.* I unwrap from the blanket, rise from the chair, and float into him. He holds me the same sweet, old-fashioned way his grandpa did. Without my heels on, my eyes are at the level of his delicious lips. *I wonder what they feel like.*

"I think I was a little jealous of Grandpa." His words are quiet off his tongue.

"Oh, yeah?"

"Mmhmm." He pulls me closer. *Oh God.*

Nearly fused together, we sway to the languid beat of the music. I forget about his celebrity status, forget about the beer, release my battling thoughts, and seep into the moment. Locked in the security of his embrace, I rest my head on his chest.

Zane

For the first time since we met, her silken, caramel-red hair is down. I knew it would smell good. With her pressed against me, I inhale and the faint scent of something like a creamsicle fills my nostrils. I want to bury my face in it.

The song ends and we part our bodies slightly.

She steps back from me. "Zane, what am I doing here?"

"I want you here. Don't you want to be here?"

"You're..." She shakes her hands at me and takes another step back. "*Zane Elkton*. What am *I* doing here? Why did you invite me here? Is there something you want from me?"

"No, I don't want anything from you." That's not entirely true. "I..." I hesitate. I know I need to tell her about my dreams, but this does *not* feel like the right time. "I like you. I enjoy your company."

"You don't even know me."

"I want to." *More than you know. I want to know your mind, your body, and your heart.*

Creases form between her brows as she shakes her head. "Why? I'm nobody in your world."

"Maybe that's what I like about you. You're real and unpretentious and not caught up in my celebrity-ism, if that's even a word." I chuckle.

"But you *are* a celebrity, Zane." There's an edge to her voice. "That will *never* change. *That's* your world." Her words sting me with reality. She backs away from me. "This is all a little much for me. I need to try to get some sleep."

"Desiree, wait." I step toward her. "Come back and have dinner with me tomorrow night. No family. No friends. Just us."

She takes another step back, her gaze drops to the ground then back up to me, and she shakes her head. "I don't think that's a good idea."

"We can actually have a conversation without interruptions or drunk friends." I pause. "Please, Desiree."

Not meeting my eyes, she says, "I'll think about it." Then she grabs the blanket from the chair and walks back into the house, briefly looking back at me. "Good night." Her delicate voice makes the hairs on my neck stand on end again.

"Sweet dreams." *I have to tell her.*

~ 6 ~

Desiree

I climb back into the bed in Zane's spare bedroom, curl up under the covers, and pray for the night to drift away. I'm trying to ignore the irrational longing for him that's growing stronger inside me. My head wants to push him out, but my heart is nudging me to open up. The battle doesn't allow me to fall into a deep sleep. Instead, I lapse in and out of surface sleep and awake, bereft of rest, to the smell of coffee and bacon.

Bill still has my phone so I have no idea what time it is. Suffering from a disquieted night, I get up slowly. Bella's snoring away.

I climb out of the bed and go into the attached bathroom. *Ugh.* Staring at myself in the mirror, I shake my head. *How can I possibly have feelings for this boy? I'm 12 years older than him. I don't know him. He doesn't know me. He belongs to the world. His job basically requires him to be intimate with different women. I'm sure, personally, he's a total ladies' man and has been with dozens if not hundreds of women. And he drinks. None of this is good.* I wipe off the smudged eyeliner on the puffy pockets under my eyes. Looking at his clothes on me, the conflicting thoughts in my head unsettle my stomach.

I've got *to get out of here.*

"Mmm." Bella sniffs. "I smell coffee." Her voice is groggy.

"How are you feeling?" I ask, coming out of the bathroom, secretly hoping she feels like crap and irritated she put me in this situation.

"Where are we?" she asks with a groan as she kicks the sheets off her.

"We're in Zane's guest bedroom."

"Oh my God." She sits up, holds her head, and drops backwards onto the bed. "I feel like shit."

Good. "Well, you should. You had a *lot* to drink last night."

"Did you say we're still at Zane's house?"

"Yup. Sarah and Jane went back to the house last night and I stayed here with you." Not that she's going to bother thanking me for staying with her and making sure she was okay.

She sits up again. "Oh my God, I can't let him see me like this. Do you have any makeup?"

"Bella, I'm sure he won't care. And no, I don't. Let's get some food in you."

She stands up and nearly falls backwards. I grab onto her to hold her up.

"I'm good. I'm good." She steadies herself. "Wooow." She takes a deep breath. "Okay, let me just touch up my face."

I sit on the bed and wait. A few minutes later, she comes out, somehow looking gorgeous, puts on her heels and grabs her wristlet off the nightstand.

"Okay, I'm ready."

Still wearing Zane's clothes, I grab my clothes, shoes, and purse.

The click-clack of Bella's heels echoes as we walk down the hall and into the kitchen where Zane's cooking scrambled eggs and bacon. There's also a glass container full of berries on the counter along with gold-rimmed white plates, gold-tone silverware, and crisp white linen napkins.

"Mmm, someone knows how to cook." Even hungover, Bella manages to ooze flirtatiousness.

"Look who's up." He smiles at her. "How's that head feeling this morning?"

"Throbbing." She looks at me. "I'm *not* going to the gym today."

"I kind of didn't think you would."

"I wasn't sure what you ladies wanted so hopefully something here will satisfy you. I made some coffee too."

Bella grabs a plate and kisses him on the cheek. "You're the best." She fills her plate, pours coffee, sits at the glass-topped dining table, and starts eating.

I take a plate and scoop some eggs and berries onto it.

"Hmm." He surveys me. "You look kinda cute in the morning," he whispers then winks and looks affectionately into my eyes. "Coffee?" He holds up the pot.

Cute? I must look a mess after the night I had. I look away, trying to avoid his impenetrable eyes. "No thanks. Do you have any other flavors of the Four Sigmatic?"

His packet is still on the counter. "You like Four Sigmatic?" He raises his eyebrows.

"I do." I smile.

"Yeah, help yourself. It's in the pantry." He points in the direction of the pantry.

"Thank you. You didn't have to do all this."

"I love cooking. I'm pretty good at it too." He winks at me again. "So, what are today's adventures for you ladies?"

"I think I'm gonna hang in bed for a while and watch TV." Bella groans.

I come out of the pantry and prepare my Mushroom Elixir. "I think Sarah and Jane wanted to go to the beach for the day before we go to the casino tonight. So, I might head to the beach with my computer and check out some houses."

"Right." He slides me a piece of paper with Jerry's phone number and office address written on it. "Here's Jerry's number for you. I let him know you'd be reaching out."

"Thanks again. This'll be a big help."

Bella finishes eating and walks toward the large U-shaped black leather sofa, passing Zane as he starts cleaning up and loading the dishwasher. "Don't you have someone to do that stuff for you?"

She reaches the sofa and lays down.

"I do, but that doesn't mean I can't also clean up after myself or should leave a massive mess for her."

Hmm. Brownie points and respect earned on that one. I finish eating and grab my plate and mug and Bella's dishes and bring them to the sink. He's washing and rinsing the pans and I grab a towel and dry them, putting them on the counter.

Bella sits up and sneers. "Well aren't you two all cute and domestic."

"Bill's waiting outside whenever you're ready to go back to your house," he says to me, taking the dish towel from me and slinging it over his shoulder.

"He is? How long has he been waiting?" I ask, hoping he hasn't been waiting long.

"It's okay, there's no hurry," he assures me. "I pay him to be at my disposal."

Okay, I can't even grasp that concept. "Come on, Bella. Let's go."

Bella slowly gets to her feet and we all head to the door.

She flings her arms around his neck and kisses him on the cheek. Tension twists from my shoulder blades up to the base of my neck as I watch her. "Thanks for everything. I had *such* a great time." And with her clickety-clacking shoes, out the door she goes.

After a strange night of conflicting emotions, right now all I can think about is how I wish I had never agreed to attend Zane's party. Then Bella wouldn't have gotten drunk here, we wouldn't have stayed in his house, and I wouldn't be standing here alone in front of him, waiting for him to ask me the question I didn't answer last night. A question a part of me wants to say yes to, but I know I should say no to. Maybe he forgot.

"Thank you for making breakfast for us."

"Of course. I couldn't have you going home on an empty stomach. Thanks for your help with the dishes." He shoves his hands in his pockets and tilts his head down, looking up from under his lashes with a bashfulness that melts me. "So, will you come back for dinner?"

He didn't forget.

"I can't tonight." *Why is he so persistent?*

"I know, casino with the girls, which, something tells me you're not going to enjoy." He offers a sympathetic grin as he winces in mock pain.

"Probably not, but that's what they wanted to do so we planned it and I said I'd go. And I don't back out of my commitments unless there's an emergency."

"Tomorrow night then."

"Zane, I don't…" My throat clenches and my stomach twists into a knot.

"Please, just say yes."

He's wearing me down. And, if I'm being honest with myself, I want to see him again, even though I know I shouldn't. "Okay, I'll come." I'm unable to control the slight quaver in my voice as my throat constricts and the knot in my stomach winds tighter.

"Good, it's settled. I'll pick you up at your house at six o'clock tomorrow night. Anything I need to know food-wise for the menu?"

"I'm a bit difficult. No dairy. No gluten. Nothing spicy. No sauces, gravies, or spices. Plain chicken cooked in avocado oil is a pretty standard meal for me. Think plain, boring, and healthy." I grit my teeth and give him an I-know-I'm-a-pain-in-the-butt smile.

"Ah, a challenge. Okay." He takes his hands out of his pockets, steps toward me, and cups my face in his hands. *Don't faint.*

My heart rate quickens as his hypnotic eyes drill into mine.

He lowers his head and presses his warm lips to my forehead, his masculine scent entering my nostrils. "I'll see you tomorrow night," he whispers, sending a wave of goosebumps over my body.

Oh boy.

~ 7 ~

Zane

In one of my dreams, there are pink peonies so I take a chance she likes them and get a bunch for our dinner tonight. Playing it safe with my meal, I get chicken, asparagus, and avocado. I watched her pick through the salad bowl at my parent's house and I get only the things she put into her bowl.

I've been waiting for this night for days...well, almost half my life. I take my time getting ready and go with all black from head to toe; Armani dress shirt and dress pants, impeccably tailored, with my black leather Christian Louboutin belt and dress shoes. My TAG Heuer watch is the finishing touch. I take a look in the mirror. *Dressed to impress.* I'm eager to spend time alone with Desiree and get to know her. Excitement streams through me.

Hmm...I should've planned this better. I'm a closet romantic and I want to have the candles lit and music playing when she walks in. I grab my phone and text her.

Me: Small change of plans. I'm going to have Bill pick you up.

Desiree: Okay.

Desiree

Bill arrives at six o'clock on the dot.

"You look beautiful, Miss Desiree," he says as I approach him.

I'm wearing my pale-yellow floral dress that has ruching through the bust and short sleeves, an elastic scoop-neck, and is fitted through the torso. The bottom flows gracefully below my knees.

"Thank you, Bill. Please just call me Desiree. Miss Desiree seems so formal."

"Okay, Desiree." He holds open the back door of a smaller, sedan-type black limousine.

"Would it be okay if I sit up front with you?"

"Why, I'd be delighted." A big smile spreads across his chubby face.

He closes the door and walks around to the passenger side with me, opening the door to let me in. And we're off.

"How long have you worked for Zane?"

"Oh, I think it's been over ten years now I've been working for Mr. Elkton. He's a good man."

"Yes, he does seem to be." I pause. "We live in very different worlds."

"It's a unique kind of life, being a celebrity. Mr. Elkton has always handled it with grace and that's not always easy to do."

"I don't know how he does it. It seems so invasive to me. They can't even go to the grocery store or get gas or eat out without people taking their picture or asking for autographs."

"He works hard at not letting it get to him."

"It must be tough. I think I'd crack under all that pressure and spotlight." I gaze out the window. "I don't even know what I'm doing right now," I say quietly.

"I think you're going to have a nice dinner with a really good guy." He tilts his head as he smiles at me.

We finish the ride in silence. He pulls into Zane's driveway and opens my door, offering his hand to help me out.

"Enjoy the evening." His tone is gentle.

"Thank you, Bill." I go down the stairs to the large mahogany door.

Zane

I hear her knock and quickly survey the rooms. Candles are lit in the living room, on the dining table, and out on the balcony. Vases of pink peonies are scattered around. Our place settings look like a picture from a 5-star restaurant. A playlist of music with artists like Nat King Cole, Etta James, and Frank Sinatra is set to play for hours. I'm ready...and nervous.

I open the door and freeze, soaking her in, as this very image of her from my dreams flashes through my mind. She's angelically beautiful.

"Come in. Dinner's almost ready."

She hands me my clothes from the night before. "Thank you. I washed them. It smells good," she says, walking past me. "Oh, Zane. It's lovely in here." She stops. "Pink peonies." She turns toward me, her deep green eyes twinkle. "They're my favorite flower."

"Lucky guess." I smile as I lie and put the pile of clothes on the kitchen counter. "Do you want something to drink?"

"No, thanks. I'll wait for dinner."

"I, uh, turned on the fire pit if you want to sit out there while I finish up in here."

"Do you need any help?"

"Nope. It'll be ready in about ten minutes."

"Okay." The glass doors are open and she walks out onto the balcony and sits on the big, puffy-cushioned rattan chair.

Ten minutes later, I go out to the balcony, take her hand, and walk back into the house. I love holding her soft hand. Pulling out her chair, I push it under her as she sits. Then I get our plates from the kitchen and set hers in front of her. The dish is simple and professional-looking.

"It's not fancy."

"Good, I don't like fancy." She smiles.

"If there's anything you don't like, we can order out."

"It looks delicious," she says, draping the linen napkin across her lap.

"Do you want some wine?"

"No." There's that sharpness. Her glare nearly singes me.

I'm missing something again.

I take the wine glasses off the table and put them in the kitchen. *Damn, I want some wine to calm my nerves, but I'm getting the feeling I shouldn't have any.*

"I hope you like it." I sit down across from her. "How's the house-hunting going? You got in touch with Jerry, right?"

"I did." She softens. "We have a few appointments to see some places the day the girls leave. Once they're gone, I'm going to spend some time driving around and getting a feel for things. Figure out where banks and dry cleaners are and check out different neighborhoods. I also want to tour the National Holistic Institute's campus."

"I'm between projects right now. I could be your tour guide if you'd like."

"Oh, that's..." She shakes her head and looks down at her plate. "Not necessary. I'm sure you have plenty of things to do to keep you busy." She looks back up at me as she cuts into her chicken.

"Actually, I don't. Not right now anyway." I study her eyes for a spark of interest. "It's helpful to be with someone who knows their way around. Plus, it doesn't sound like you know many people out here."

"I'll think about it." She takes a bite. "Mmm, it's good."

"Good. I'm curious, what prompted the decision for massage therapy?"

She sighs and shifts in her chair. "Well, my entire life I've done what I was supposed to do: went to college, graduated *cum laude*, got my MBA, got a six-figure job at a Fortune 100 company, and now I'm the CEO of my own company."

"Impressive." I clench my teeth to keep my jaw from dropping open. I suddenly feel intimidated.

"Maybe, but none of it made me happy."

I offer an understanding nod.

She gazes at the candle on the table. "Sometimes it takes a jolt from life to force you to really look at things and take stock of your life." She moves her gaze from the flame and into my eyes. "So, here I am, trying to make a new start for myself. To…follow my heart for the first time in my life and live my desires if I can. I love getting massages and I've always been told I'm good at giving massages." Now I'm picturing her hands on my naked body. It's a good thing I'm sitting and have a napkin on my lap. "So, I figured I'd learn the proper techniques and bring in some money while I start up my business here."

"Big change." I admire her courage at making such a bold move all by herself.

She nods. "Big change. Scary."

"What made you leave the corporate world?"

She swallows a bite. "After twenty years, it occurred to me that I wasn't actually *doing* anything in this world. Something I always said when I was younger was that I wanted to make an impact; to touch people's lives, to help them. And I was *not* doing that in corporate America. I mean, I worked my tail off and I know my team appreciated me, but I wasn't actually helping another human being and *that* was what I wanted to do. So, I left. I started my own business where I call the shots and do work that's meaningful to me and is truly helpful to others." She sighs. "Now, here I am, about to start over, and I'm a little scared. I built up a good reputation and had repeat clients and referrals. Here, I'm starting from scratch."

"You seem like a woman who can do anything you put your mind to. I have no doubt you'll be up and running faster than you think."

Her eyes widen and tiny lines crinkle her forehead. "I wish I had your confidence."

"With everything you just told me, I know you can do it." I pause. "You're coming here for a pretty big change, so what do you want for your life then?"

Her lips press together and her shoulders rise toward her ears. "I'm a pretty simple person with pretty simple desires. I want to be lit up by the work I do, make a positive impact by helping people, and make a decent living doing it. And I want to experience more places and travel a little. I don't need a lot to be happy."

"That's the life part. What about love?" The question comes out of me without much thought and suddenly I wonder if it's too soon to just blurt it out. Too late now. I continue eating, trying to appear nonchalant.

"Well, wait. What about you? What do *you* want out of your life?" She sidesteps my question.

I stop eating and fold my hands above my plate. "Me? I want to build a legacy. I want to be known for being really damn good in all kinds of different roles and doing all my own stunts. I want to be a mentor to young actors. I want to continue using my money for good; to help those in need, those who don't have the privileges I have. I also want to enjoy the money I earn. I want to take care of my family and travel the world and buy nice things." I pause. "And I want to fall in love. Get married someday and maybe have kids."

She nods with a hint of a smile on her lips. "You're already building that legacy, you know." Her compliment fills me with pride.

"So, you avoided my question."

"What? Love?" She shakes her head. "Love is a fallacy," she says flatly as she moves the food around on her plate.

"You don't believe in love?" Sadness drapes my heart as I sit back in my chair.

"It sounds all dreamy and perfect in your line of work, but in real life…" She shakes her head again. "It's an empty promise. That pure, connected from soul-to-soul, I-would-die-for-you-and-die-without-you kind of love, it doesn't exist."

"I believe in love," I confess as I unfold my hands.

"Yeah? So, what's love for you?" There's a softness in her voice.

I shift forward. "At its core, I believe love is knowing a person on the surface and cherishing what lies beneath. Celebrating their brilliance and embracing their darkness with them. It's knowing what drives them and what terrifies them. Knowing what triggers them and working hard to avoid those triggers instead of using them as a weapon. It's being by their side through the good times and still being there when you're mad at each other. Sharing a piece of yourself that no one else knows. Accepting them for who they are and not wanting to change them. It's loving all facets of them, no matter how scarred or damaged. It's a connection you feel deep in your soul that you can't explain. It's enjoying conversations with each other and caring about what they care about. It's about communicating and respecting one another. And building a life together that's filled with what you both want. Love is blissful and scary and magical."

Her lips part and her eyes are glassy and staring at me.

"Desiree?"

She licks her luscious lips and closes them as she blinks. "That was...beautiful."

"It's what I believe love is. Or at least how I want it to be for me."

She clears her throat. "I'd imagine relationships are tough for you."

"Heh. They're certainly challenging. As hard as I work to keep my private life private, the press and paparazzi manage to catch something innocent and splash it all over social media and the tabloids." I wave my hand through the air.

"I can't even imagine." She pauses. "You must feel so much pressure when it comes to dating. I imagine there's a lot of expectations based on your image."

"How do you mean?"

"It's just...you know, you're depicted as one of the hottest men in the world and you do these steamy love scenes and what if, in reality, you're not even a good kisser? That's a lot of pressure." She blinks quickly and looks down into her plate, moving food around again.

"So, you think I'm not a good kisser?" I prod as I lean forward again with my elbows on the table and clasp my hands together.

She lifts her head and shakes it, looking like a deer caught in headlights. "No, that's not — I'm sorry. That's...not what I meant," she stammers as she looks around the room, down at her plate, and around the room again, completely avoiding eye contact with me. "I...I don't think that at all. I mean, how would I know? I'm sure you're just fine at...kissing and...other things. I...uh..." A crimson hue flushes her cheeks. She's the most enticing little thing I've ever laid eyes on.

"Just fine?" I laugh. I enjoy watching her squirm. Taking in a deep breath, I let it out as I lean back in my chair. "It's not so much their expectations. It's tough to trust people. Even when it's someone in the industry and they know what it's like to live in the public eye. Even behind closed doors, there's an agenda. And whenever I've tried dating someone who's not part of this industry, most of the time, it's the connection to fame they're interested in and not really me, as a person."

She shakes her head slightly as her chin tightens. Her eyes shift down then back up to mine. "I'm so sorry. I can't even begin to imagine what that must feel like for you."

"You do start to wonder if the real thing will ever come along." I pause. "I'm not giving up hope though." I pause again. "So, you don't believe in love. Were you ever in love?"

She's quiet.

Grabbing her glass, she takes a sip of water. "I thought I was. Then...I think I *loved* him, but wasn't *in* love with him."

"The boyfriend you mentioned?"

"Yes, Brad. We were together a long time, five years."

"Five years and you never got married?" I'm trying not to sound shocked.

"No, he had a rough marriage and then a rough divorce so..." Her voice trails off. "It was kind of like we were married because we lived together and he made sure I'd be taken care of if..." her eyes move back to the flame. "...something ever happened to him." A mistiness coats her eyes.

"So, you're not together anymore?" I want to see if she'll open up to me. I can't let on that I know what Bella blathered to me.

"No," she answers emotionless.

That answers that. We sit in silence. I don't want to push her for more.

"Were you ever married?" I ask.

"Nope. Never married. Never been asked."

"Really? You've never been asked? How can that be?"

Her eyes open wide as she cocks her head to the side. "Lots and *lots* of bad decisions when it came to men." She chuckles. "Then I would stay in the relationship too long. I usually ended up becoming more of a maid or a mother. And then they would cheat. I never understood that." She pauses and looks at the flickering flames. "I want a partner. Someone who wants to take on the world with me. Someone who wants to grow and expand and evolve as a person alongside me. Someone who respects me and sees me as their equal. Someone who wants to spend time with me and live life together and build a future together. Someone who makes me laugh, hugs me when I'm crying, and holds my hair back when I'm vomiting. I want someone who challenges me and enhances who I am." Her gaze returns to me. "I don't think that person exists for me. I'm just..." She looks back at the flames. "...done with relationships."

Done with relationships? Well, shit.

~ 8 ~

Zane

It's clear she's been hurt…badly, and love is a source of pain for her. That makes my heart ache.

Time to lighten things up a little.

"How was casino night with the girls?"

She contorts her face. "Just as dreadful as I thought it would be."

I can't help but laugh at how cute she is. "Why didn't you back out?"

"I told you, I don't back out of commitments unless there's an emergency."

"Is that a personal rule of yours?"

"As a matter of fact, it is." She shoots me a playful smile.

"And is there a story behind this rule? Because it feels like there is."

"Actually, yes." She picks up her glass and finishes her water. "When I was twelve years old and my family was leaving Kuala Lumpur for good, I made plans to sleep over my friend Kim's house a few days before we left. I was supposed to run down and meet up with her between our houses and then we'd walk back to her house together. As I was packing my sleepover bag, I got a call from my best friend, Daisie, and *she* wanted me to come sleep over. Since I was leaving forever, of course I wanted to see my best friend. I quickly called Kim to change plans, but she was already on her way to meet me. This was way before cell phones so I couldn't reach her another way. I ran as quickly as I could to meet Kim and let her know I wouldn't be sleeping over. When I got to her and told her that I basically chose Daisie over her, the pained expression on her face stabbed me in the gut. I can still see her face and it tears me up. So, I vowed, at that very moment, that I would never back out of commitment unless there was a true emergency."

"Wow. And you've stuck by that?"

"I have." Her delicate smile and deep integrity knock me back in my seat.

"Do you have any other personal rules?"

She looks into the candle flame and then back at me as she folds her hands in her lap. "Don't rely on anyone." Her expression turns stony.

"Does this one have a story?" She continues to fascinate me.

"Not specifically." She pauses. "If there's one thing life and relationships have taught me, it's to not rely on other people because you'll be let down every time. I understand a little about you not being able to trust people. It tends to backfire when you do."

"Kind of keeps people at a distance, doesn't it?" It sounds like we've both had our share of being let down by people.

"It does. But, for me, it's helped me be independent and not feel like I have to *need* anyone. I've gotten very good at figuring things out on my own and getting things done. I keep my expectations of myself high and my expectations of everyone else low. That way the only person who can disappoint me is me."

Jesus, she's a female version me. Though I've never sat down and thought about it or would ever put words to it, she's described me to myself. With the exception of knowing I can always trust and rely on my family and very few close friends, she's nailed me to a tee. I'm starting to understand why she's so guarded. I don't know what she's been through that caused her to build her protective walls so thick, but I'm getting the sense it's some pretty tough shit.

Her glass is empty. "More water?"

"Yes, please. Do you have any that are room temperature?"

"Sure do." I bring over a bottle and fill her glass.

"I noticed you don't like wine." Something in my gut tells me to tread cautiously.

"No, not really. I'm not a drinker. I maybe have eight drinks a year, if that."

"Is it the taste?"

"No. I don't like to not be in control of myself. Plus, too many alcoholics in my family; my father, my brother, my boyfriend." *Damn.* Bella's words pop into my head — her cheating, *alcoholic* boyfriend. "Nothing good ever came from drinking."

Shit. I choke down the knot in my throat as a wave of unpleasant heat surges in my chest and my own demons of alcohol addiction slither into my thoughts.

An ominous black cloud hovers at the edge of my thoughts. The gripping at the center of my chest squeezes tighter. My battle with the complex disease is egregious. *No wonder.* Now I understand her reactions to my beer the other night and my offer of wine tonight. *Shit, how am I going to handle* this*?*

"It's in my blood, I think. I really scared myself one time." She crosses her arms at her chest.

"Yeah? What happened?"

"It was back in college and I had gone to visit a friend of mine at Georgetown. She and her roommates were having a party and we were all drinking and talking. I finished a fifth of Southern Comfort and went down to the liquor store and bought another fifth. I know I was tipsy and I wasn't any bigger than I am right now, but I wasn't drunk."

"Holy crap." *How was she not dead?*

"I know. I remember her friends looking at me like, 'How is the girl standing?' That night really shook me. Now, I have one martini and I'm goofy." She laughs.

"I'm sure you're a lightweight. You're so tiny."

"I imagine your world runs rampant with alcohol and drugs."

My stomach sours. "Yeah, they definitely numb you from some of the stress." I shift back in my chair and drop my eyes to my plate. Scotch is my Lucifer. I'm not going to hide my struggle with addiction from her. Besides wanting to be fully transparent with her, I also know she can easily search the internet and learn about it if she hasn't already. And, right now, I'm scared as hell this is a deal-breaker for her.

"You had fame really young."

"Looked me up, did you?" I'm flattered.

"A little." Specks of amber twinkle in her eyes from the candlelight and the sweetest, almost shy, smile forms on her lips.

"Ah, you have an advantage now." I wink. "So, what did you learn about me?"

"Some things. But you can't trust what you read on the internet. I'd rather learn about you *from* you."

"You got it. Yeah." I acknowledge. "I did. It was kind of a weird way to grow up, but it was what I knew. You feel totally exposed and completely isolated all at the same time. Everywhere you go, there's some kind of press or paparazzi taking your picture. I spend a lot of time in my house and sometimes it makes me feel like I'm going crazy. When I was younger, there were girls and drugs and alcohol everywhere, being shoved into my hands. You've met my family, they're amazing. But my parents couldn't protect me from all of it."

"Mmm." She nods.

"When I was working, I was working. All-in. A hundred and ten percent. In between projects, I'd get antsy and that's when it got bad for me. I'd party a lot. It got to the point that when a project came along, I'd work my ass off and couldn't wait for the weekend so I could party. When the workdays became rough from the aftereffects, I knew I was in bad shape. I got…lost in it all. And I didn't even feel comfortable in my own skin anymore. One day I woke up on my bathroom floor, naked, hungover, and feeling so disgusted with myself, not even remembering the night before."

Her eyes fix on me as she listens intently.

"It was that day I decided I no longer wanted to numb myself and I wanted to find a better way to cope and *live*, really live. So,

I went to rehab. The media love to exploit that kind of thing, but I'm not ashamed of it. I don't think people should be made to feel bad when they seek help for self-destructive behavior. Unless you live in this environment, you don't understand what it's like. I love my life, but it's not all fame and wealth and happiness. There are definitely demons to battle."

She reaches her hand across the table and puts it on top of mine. Man, I love her touch. Looking into my eyes, she gently squeezes my hand. It's like I can see her ache for me. "Thank you for sharing that with me."

"So." I clear my throat and change the subject. "How was your dinner?"

"Absolutely perfect." A sweet smile forms on her face.

"I'll expect my kiss later." I wink. "I know you're a dessert girl, I saw you scarf down my mom's chocolate cake." I flash her a saucy smile.

Her smile grows more pronounced.

"How about we make some chocolate chip cookies?" I ask as I stand up, grabbing my plate.

"Ohhhh, you're tempting me," she says teasingly.

She grabs her plate and follows me to the sink. I wash and she dries; it's becoming a comfortable routine. I collect the dry ingredients from the pantry, along with Mom's recipe card, and bring them to the kitchen island.

"Oh, you mean business. I thought you meant the break-and-bake kind."

"Oh no, I don't mess around when it comes to chocolate chip cookies. Will you grab the butter and eggs from the fridge? I have some dairy-free butter in there."

She gets the butter and eggs while I turn on the oven. Step-by-step, we follow the recipe on an index card my mom wrote for me a long time ago. She tosses in the dairy-free chocolate chips and stirs until everything is mixed. I hand her a spoon and she scoops out a spoonful onto the cookie sheet.

"No, no, no," I say, shaking my head. "You have to scoop it

into your hands," I say while air-demonstrating with my hands, "and make a ball out of the dough. Otherwise you'll get weirdly shaped cookies."

"Okay, cookie connoisseur," she says playfully as she scoops dough into her hands and begins rolling it into a ball.

She rolls a few and places each in a row on the parchment paper on the cookie sheet.

"You know, there's something I've been wondering."

"What's that?" she asks, curiosity alight in her eyes.

"Well, I've been wondering if you're *ticklish*." I poke at her sides.

"Ah!" she screams and laughs. "Zane! Stop it." She laughs harder as she tries to squiggle away from me with cookie dough covering her hands.

She runs around the island and I chase after her. *I could do this for the rest of my life.*

"No, no, this isn't fair," she shouts playfully. "You're rotten," she roars. "I'm going to tell your mother."

"Now *that's* playing dirty," I jeer and stop chasing her. "Come on, let's get these in the oven. I want to eat them." I wiggle my eyebrows.

"Rotten," she whispers and smiles at me.

Getting back to rolling the cookie dough balls, she puts them on the cookie sheet. I slide the sheet into the oven while she washes her hands. Closing the oven door, I take her in my arms and dance to the music. I think I surprised her because she lets out a little gasp, but then settles into me. We're cheek-to-cheek and I get a deep whiff of her. *Man, she smells good.*

"I love this music." Her voice is like sweet nectar and her breath tickles my neck. *Grandma's underwear, damnit, Grandma's underwear.* "I'm a bit of an old soul."

"Me too." Nat King Cole's, "When I Fall in Love," fills the air and I sing the lyrics softly in her ear. I marvel at how perfectly she fits in my arms. This is far better than any of my dreams. She feels like home and I don't want to let her go. My heart is falling for her.

Instantly, time doesn't exist. I sing and we sway, melding into one another.

Bddddding, the timer goes off.

~ 9 ~

Desiree

I can't believe I'm in Zane Elkton's arms — his strong, muscular arms — and he's singing an old love song in my ear while we dance and wait for chocolate chip cookies to finish baking. This feels unbelievably amazing. *I'm in dangerous territory.*

He pulls himself back from me, still holding my body tightly to his; the space between us is scorching. He looks into my eyes and, for a brief second, my breath catches in my throat. *God, I want him to kiss me.* Did I mention *dangerous territory*?

"Hot, gooey cookies, comin' up." He releases me. "Can you grab a cooling rack out of that cabinet?" he asks, pointing. He turns off the oven, takes the cookies out, and grabs a spatula.

I find the cooling rack and bring it to him. He slides off all the cookies, grabs a plate, and puts six cookies on it. "Ooo, ooo, hot, hot," he chirps, shaking his fingers as he laughs. He's downright adorable. "Grab our waters."

I grab the waters and follow him out to the fire pit where we sit in the rattan chair; it's becoming our usual spot.

"Tell me more about home."

I pick out a cookie and take a bite, tapping the crumb I feel on my lower lip into my mouth with my finger. "I live on the outskirts of New Hope in Pennsylvania. It's a quaint little town with a bunch of bed and breakfasts and tons of little shops. There's a little over four acres that the goats love to run around and play on."

"Goats? You have goats?" His beautiful eyes widen as his

eyebrows shoot to his forehead and he leans forward.

I can't help but laugh at his stupefied response. "Yes, I have goats." I take another bite of cookie. "Mmm, so good. I have a friend watching them now and I'll probably give them to her when I move here."

"I can't believe you have goats. What are they like?"

"They're very entertaining and more lovable than I would've thought. Patches is my snuggler. All he wants is to be loved. And Tiny, well, he's like a bull in a China shop. He bullies little Patches, but Patches usually holds his own and sneaks his digs in when he can. When Patches was little, he doesn't do it much anymore, but when he was little, he used to sniff my face at night. It was the cutest thing. I'd come down after getting ready for bed and I think he liked the way my moisturizer smells. He'd put his nose, ever so delicately, almost touching my forehead and sniff his way around my face. You haven't lived until you've experienced hot goat sniffs across your face." I chuckle.

"*How* did he do it?"

I get up and sit hip-to-hip, facing him. *Danger, danger!* "Close your eyes," I say, my voice feather-thin, and he does. I'd lose all control if he didn't. I put my nose a whisper away from his skin and slowly move around his face, sniffing softly in and out, mimicking Patches.

"That tickles," he says as he opens his eyes and fixes them on me, like he knows their power over me.

His lips are so close. Oh God. Get up!

I clear my throat and escape. "But beware of goat sneezes."

"They sneeze?"

"They blast-sneeze. Hay mixed with snot *every*where." I grimace.

"Oh, gross." He laughs loudly, squishing together the features on his face.

"I think Tiny is learning the word, 'kisses.' I'll say, 'kisses' in a sing-song voice and he lifts his face up for me to kiss his nose.

Sometimes I end up with a mouth full of goat tongue which isn't so pleasant, but…"

"Oh, nasty. Nothing like being French-kissed by a goat." He cringes and puts a cookie in his mouth.

"Kind of like my first French kiss in twelfth grade, *horrible*." I stick out my tongue. *Stop talking about and thinking about kissing.*

"You didn't have your first French kiss until *twelfth* grade?"

"Hey, I was slow in that department," I defend my good-girl status.

"What happened? Why was it so awful?"

"Well, I had braces on my bottom teeth and wore a retainer for my top teeth. I remember it was after school and it was with a boy who was more popular than me that I kind of had a crush on, but he was also kind of a jerk; clearly that became my M.O. for most of my dating life. Anyway, I have no idea what we were talking about or why we kissed, but I remember thinking to myself, 'Ew, this is so gross.' And my retainer loosened a bit and I pulled away. I have no idea what we even said at that point. I just remember being mortified." I laugh, clapping my hand to my chest.

He laughs with me. "That sounds pretty bad. My first French kiss was on camera. Talk about pressure."

"No." I put my hands over my mouth and can't hold back a loud gasp.

"Ohhh, yes. Of course, I had *no* idea what I was doing. It's not like someone teaches you that stuff when you're an actor. And I was pretty young."

"Oh no. What did you do?"

"The only thing I *could* do. I'd seen movies so I stuck my tongue in her mouth. But I think it was more like when you stick your tongue *out* at someone rather than trying to kiss them."

I erupt into an uncontrollable belly-laugh and he joins me.

"That sounds terrible."

"Thankfully, I've improved since then." He winks at me. *Whoosh*, here comes that tingling feeling again.

Change the subject — quickly. "Oh, I got an offer on my house today."

"Hey, that's terrific."

"Yeah, I was pleased." I frown. "They're offering twenty thousand dollars over my asking price because they want it furnished, which, I mean it's great, but if I leave everything behind, then I have nothing for my house here. And I like a lot of my furniture and decorations, especially the vintage ones."

"I'm sure you can negotiate the deal to take only what you want to bring here and go back with a counter-offer."

"I guess so. It's weird, it's some kind of straw buyer with a cash offer. Very mysterious. I just hope it's legitimate and doesn't fall apart on the last day."

"Wow, interesting." He leans over and takes another cookie, popping the whole thing in his mouth. "Well, you'll be able to close quickly with that kind of deal."

"Yeah, my Realtor said things should be all done during the first week I'm back home. I'll miss that beautiful old house." I pause, reminiscing. "Okay," I lift my leg up onto the chair and tuck it underneath me, facing him. "What's the most rebellious thing you've ever done?"

"What? Those are forbidden secrets. I can't tell you that," he jokingly scoffs then smiles. "Hmm, give me a minute." He pauses. "Ah, so, Declan and I got grounded because we were playing football in the house."

"In the house?" I tilt my head and give him a side-eyed glare.

"It was raining out and we were throwing a Nerf football," he says, in a vain attempt to defend his poor choice.

I purse my lips in disapproval.

"We ended up breaking some dish and my mom grounded us for a week. But a friend of ours was having a party that Saturday night and we wanted to go. So, we snuck out, ran to our friend's house, and got drunk and had a blast. As we were sneaking back in through my bedroom window, my mom was sitting on my bed and she was *pissed.*" He laughs. "I think we were grounded for a month."

"You should've been." I laugh and poke him. "Mischievous boys."

"Okay, your turn."

"Hah. I took my father's car." I shake my head as I swallow a bite of cookie. "But I didn't just take it, I got it *stuck.* I was in high school, a junior, I think. My mother was in the psych hospital after her first attempted suicide and my father was traveling for two weeks for work so I was home alone. I went to school, did my homework, went to my job; I was a good girl. It was winter and it had snowed a lot. Every day, I drove the opposite way of school to pick up my friend, Beth. So, I drove us to school and then after school we went to the mall. By the time I dropped her off, it was getting dark.

"We lived far off the road, up a winding stone-covered, single-lane driveway that was probably a quarter-mile long. We were in one of three houses tucked back in the woods. I'm slipping and sliding my way up the driveway." I pretend to hold a steering wheel, imitating my movements of turning the wheel from side to side. "All of a sudden, I somehow manage to drift off the driveway and land smack in the middle, *lengthwise,* between two trees. There was probably only a foot of space in front of the car and behind the car." I spread my hands about twelve inches apart.

"My father was due home early the next morning. Well, I panicked. Of course, I spun and spun and spun the wheels, going nowhere. Then I ran up to the house and grabbed a shovel and some cardboard. First, I tried digging up some dirt to put under the wheels, but the ground was like ice. Then I tried to get the cardboard under a tire, total fail. I was at it for hours.

"Thankfully, I was at least off the path so others could get by and I went to bed. I knew a kid who worked at a gas station and hoped he could help me. I got up at like five o'clock in the morning, took my mother's car, and went to the gas station. I got so lucky he was there and willing to come help me. He came over and got the car out and it was covered with mud and snow. My father would've had a *fit*. So, there I was, in the dead of winter, washing this big old Ninety-Eight Oldsmobile boat and I remember I cut my knuckle and was bleeding all over the place. I did *not* want to get in trouble."

"Hah! You wild thing, you. Did you ever tell him?"

"Yup." A giggle erupts. "About three years ago."

He laughs. "You waited *that* long?"

"Uh-yup. I knew by that time, I couldn't get in trouble."

"Your mom tried to kill herself?" he asks cautiously. "That must've been pretty scary for you."

I did kind of breeze right past that. I don't usually talk about this stuff. Disdain bubbles to the surface as I recall how alone I felt through the bulk of my teen years. Though I had compassion for what my mother had been through, it made me angry that she chose to try to end her life and leave us rather than teach us how to take the bad things that happen in life and learn how to survive and move forward. Through that disappointment, the lesson for me was that I never wanted to be a person who just gave up. It's made me incredibly resilient so for that, I'm grateful.

I probably shouldn't be baring my soul to someone I barely know and will probably never see again once I leave, but something inside me feels safe in telling him. He doesn't even seem annoyed talking about some pretty deep stuff. Zane Elkton is definitely not the typical surface-level type of guy I'm used to, and certainly not what I expected of someone of his status. I'm actually kind of astonished right now.

I sigh. "Yeah, she had a tough life of broken dreams. My father moved us overseas when my brother, sister, and I were very young. She had no friends there, no family, and didn't know anyone. Just plopped into a foreign country and he expected her to be okay with it. And with his drinking and cheating and lying, she finally fell apart when we came back to the United States."

"Jeez, I'm sorry. That's awful." He shrinks back in his chair.

"It is what it is, I suppose. Everyone's family has its share of drama." This is feeling a little heavy.

"You've made me even more grateful that I have such an incredible family." He pauses. "So, overseas, huh? I wanted to come back to that. Earlier you mentioned Kuala Lumpur." His eyebrows raise.

"Mmhmm. When I was one year old, we moved to Kuala Lumpur. We were there for seven years."

"Wow, that's incredible."

"Yeah, I'm very fortunate to have experienced different cultures and lots of traveling in my life. There's a lot I don't remember though because I was so young, but I'm grateful." I grab another cookie. "Okay, how about a hidden talent, whatcha got?"

"I can move my tongue like a wave. Wanna see?"

Oh...dear...God. I look away from him. "That's okay, I trust you."

"Here, watch." He ignores my decline and leans toward me. I can't *not* look at him. He begins moving his tongue like a wave, watching my eyes watch his devious tongue. An intense tingle shoots between my thighs.

My rebellious body leans in, my mouth is extra wet. I can't take my eyes off his enticing, wiggling tongue. *Good Lord.*

He closes his mouth and my eyelids flitter.

"Good," I choke out as I draw my body back. "That's some skill right there." I grab my glass and take a gulp of water. I'm not the kind of woman who has dirty thoughts about a man, but *holy crap*. My mind is reeling about the things I'd like that magical, swirling tongue to do to me. I've also never been within inches of a ragingly hot man who's tormenting me with the sensual, wavelike movements of said tongue. *Breathe.*

"Now you."

"Well, I'm not sure I can top that." I linger. "I can snap my toes," I state proudly.

"What? No way. Let's see this."

I uncurl my leg, unbuckle and remove my shoe, and proceed to snap my big toe against my pointer toe.

He laughs and takes my foot in his hand. "That's crazy. Look at those toes move."

"Ah!" I recoil my leg and laugh. "That tickles."

"I've got one. What's something you've always wanted to do, but never done?"

I look up at the sky. "Hot air balloon ride."

"Really?"

"Yeah. You know how people ask, 'If you could be an animal, what would you be?'"

"Uh-huh."

"I'd love to be a bird. Fly around to anywhere you want to go in the world and see how beautiful it all is." I spread my arms like the wings of a bird. "Free." I pause. "I think a hot air balloon ride would feel something like that anyway. What about you?"

I imagine nothing is off limits or out of his reach…nothing.

~ 10 ~

Zane

She's smart and cultured and driven and funny. I can't believe this is happening right now. The glow of the fire kisses her skin and makes her eyes sparkle like emeralds.

"I'm very fortunate and can pretty much go anywhere I want and do anything I want. So, let me think about this." I pause in thought. "Oh, wait, okay, I've got one. I've never been to Africa. I think it would be pretty cool to go on a safari trip. I've heard the sunrises are amazing."

Her eyes fly open and shine like she has a secret. She jumps up without saying a word and hobbles into the house with her one shoe still on. Then she's back with a tattered piece of paper in her hand and she sticks it in front of my face, pointing at it.

I take it from her. "What's this?"

"It's my Life List. I made it *way* before the movie *The Bucket List* came out." She points at one of the bulleted items, *Watch the sun rise in Africa.* "I can't believe you just said that."

"Well *that's* ironic. What else is on here?" In looking at the condition of the paper, I can tell she's had it for long time.

She tries to grab the paper from me. "Oh, um, no. That's just — you don't..." She shakes her head. "You don't want to read that. It's silly stuff really."

I hold it in my lap. "I want to read it. Can I?" I ask permission.

She hesitates. "No one's ever seen that list." The look in her eyes and gravity of her voice tell me how precious the list is to her.

"I'd really like to read it, if that's okay with you," I match my tone to hers to let her know I respect the seriousness of our conversation and her list.

"Okay." She gives me approval and sits down slowly across from me, biting at her lower lip.

I hold the paper up so the light of the fire can illuminate her writing.

Life List

- Hot air balloon ride
- ~~House with fireplace, front porch, and garage~~
- Ice skating in Rockefeller Center
- Horse and buggy ride around Central Park
- Window shopping on Rodeo Drive
- Try on a wedding dress
- Horseback riding on the beach
- Gondola ride through Venice
- Spa vacation
- Learn to speak French
- Learn to play piano again
- Save someone's life
- Dance under the stars with someone I love
- Make love in the rain on a warm summer evening
- Watch the sun rise in Africa
- ~~Cirque du Soleil~~

"Ah, hot air balloon ride."

One side of her mouth curls up as she shrugs the same shoulder and tilts her head toward it.

I finish reading through the list. "I like it."

"Silly wishes of a young, naïve girl."

"The crossed off items?"

She straightens her spine and perks up. "Those are the ones I did." She smiles.

"Just these two?"

She hunches a little. "Well, yes." Her deflated voice tugs at my gut.

Idiot, she's clearly proud of the two she's done.

"How long have you had this list?"

"Gosh, I don't know. At least twenty-five years, I suppose."

"Did your boyfriend know about this list?"

"Brad? Yes, he knew I had a list, but I never showed it to him. Over the years I told him a few things that were on it."

"And you never did any of them?"

Her expression wilts and her eyes cast down. "No." A weak smile appears on her face and the green of her eyes dulls. "It's okay though. I told you, silly wishes." She reaches out her hand.

I revel at the glimpse into her life-wishes. Knowing she's never shared the list with anyone else makes me feel even more connected to her. She's tugging on my heart.

Knowing how personal this list is to her, I take care in folding it back up and hand it to her. "Thank you for letting me read it."

She scurries into the house and returns, sitting back down and tucking her one bare foot beneath her.

"Alright, I've got one," I say. "What's your biggest regret?"

She sighs. Her body curves in a little as she looks into the fire, the dangling of her delicate earrings glinting in the firelight. "Waiting so long to ask myself what I really want in life." Her lips clench. "Letting fear be the driver of my life and not figuring out what I truly want, what my heart desires. I guess I wasn't ready until now." She looks at me with an earnestness that hooks into my heart. "And you? Any regrets?"

"Definitely not going to college. My career was taking off around the time I would've gone to school and I chose to follow this path. I'm incredibly thankful for how my life's turned out, but I regret not going. I know I can always go back, but at my age and with my career..." I shrug. "The time never seems to be right."

"It really is never too late, you know? I didn't go back for my

MBA until ten years after I graduated from college. It was really hard to get back into a routine of notetaking and studying and writing papers, but I'm glad I did it."

"Where'd you go to school?"

"University of Pennsylvania for undergrad and Villanova for my MBA."

"Wow, both good schools."

"Yup. Most of my MBA was online, but I lived in the city on campus for undergrad. I learned quickly that I'm *not* a city-girl." Her eyes bug out.

The horrified expression on her face makes me laugh. "Oh, yeah? Why's that?"

"Gosh, let's see. Our apartments were broken into, my car was broken into, my computer was stolen, it was noisy all the time and dirty, I got mugged —"

"Wait, you got mugged?" A wrecking ball smashes into my chest as I lurch forward.

She blinks almost as though she's wincing at the memory. "Yeah. I got lucky it wasn't too bad though."

"Wasn't too bad? You were *mugged*. What happened?" *Jeez, Zane, maybe she doesn't want to talk about something traumatic like getting mugged. Again, I'm an idiot.* "I mean, you don't have to tell me if you don't want to," I say, leaning back against the chair, trying to temper myself.

"No, it's okay." She takes a breath. "I was walking home from my job at The Gap and it was the middle of summer so, even though it was late in the evening, it was still light out. I'm pretty street-smart so I was doing my best confident walk, heading straight home, and had my purse strapped across my body. I was about a minute from my apartment and I noticed two adolescent boys. One was approaching me and the other was to my left. The one in front of me walked right up to me and sucker-punched me on the left side of my face."

"Jesus." I'm becoming enraged that someone would hurt her.

"I think I was in shock and all I could think to say was, 'Get the fuck away from me.' Well, he didn't like that very much. He grabbed my shirt and started whaling me in the face with his fist, *hard.* There was a third boy who must've been behind me who smashed me in the back of the head with some kind of rock or brick or something."

My mouth drops open. "Desiree, *Jesus.*" I'm not a violent guy, but right now I'm so furious I want to find the guys and beat the shit out of them.

"The next thing I know, I'm on the ground in the fetal position."

"They knocked you out?" I instinctively dart forward again.

"Yeah, I don't remember falling down and I'm not sure how I got up, but I did. I started screaming and I remember seeing this little old man across the street just standing there."

"He didn't try to help you?" I grip my thighs.

"No, he looked confused. Then the boys ran away and I stood there clutching my purse. I only had sixty-three cents on me."

"Desiree, I'm so sorry that happened to you." I'm trying to stifle the rage throbbing in my veins. "What did you do?"

"Well, I went back to my apartment and my roommates weren't home, which was fine because we weren't really all that friendly with each other anyway. My mother was in another psych hospital after her second suicide attempt so I could only call her, which was also fine because she's certainly not a person I go to for consolation. But, I called her because I felt she should know. And when I called my father to let him know, he was wasted. So incoherently drunk and it sounded like he was on drugs or something because he couldn't comprehend anything I was saying."

The wrecking ball swings back, shattering my entire body. I have such an amazing support system in my family and my true friends. She doesn't seem to have anyone. Her mom tried to kill herself *twice*? What the hell? It's painfully obvious she doesn't have a good relationship with either of her parents. I wondered why she kept referring to them as Mother and Father instead of Mom and Dad; so formal, almost detached. My heart is breaking right now.

"Anyway." She continues, emotionless, like she's pushed the pain down deep. Not only the painful memory of the incident, but also the solitude of having no one to even go to for help or comfort. "I knew a bunch of guys at a fraternity and I called the hall number because I knew I needed to go to the hospital and was scared to go back out alone. One of them ran down to get me and took me over. I had some cuts and bruises, but no concussion, so I really got lucky. I do have a ringing in my ears to this day from the rock-smash to the back of my head. It's a daily reminder of what happened." She pauses. "It was one of the scariest things that's ever happened to me."

I'm a mixture of anger and compassion and heartache. I can't even find words to comfort her. I sit back in my chair, tuck a hand into my underarm, and cover my mouth with my other hand. It's like I'm feeling everything she's shutting out. She must see the anguish in my face.

"You don't need to pity me. It really could've been a lot worse."

"I'm so sorry that happened and you got hurt and didn't even have anyone to turn to." My words don't even come close to conveying the intensity of what I'm feeling.

"It's fine. It was a long time ago and I'm clearly okay." She pauses and clears her throat. "Is there anything that scares you?"

I'm riveted by her inquisitive nature and savoring the depth of our conversation. I can't recall ever talking to a woman this way and I love it.

"Yeah." I pause. "A lot actually. I'm afraid of not living up to my potential. It took me *years* to shed my Disney-kid image. To be honest, I'm still not sure I have. And it's not that I'm not grateful, because I am, I'm extremely grateful. It's just that I want roles that challenge me and push me to my limits. That's where I thrive. I want to prove that I can be so much more as an actor. I want to do work that has an impact on people and moves them and makes them think. I'm not so different from you in that way."

"Can I ask you a question?" She shifts her foot and rests her arm on the back of the chair.

"Of course. Anything."

"You don't have to answer it if you don't want to."

I'll answer anything you ask me. "Okay." She has my full attention.

"Do you want to win an Oscar?"

While I'm a little taken aback by her bluntness, I have to admit that this unexpectedly bold side of her is pretty damn alluring. "Of course I do. I mean, that's the biggest honor in my industry."

"So, why do you hold yourself back?"

"I…I don't." I've never had anyone be so brazen with me, except maybe Grandpa. And, she's freaking right. *Damn, she sees right through me.*

"Don't get me wrong, you're obviously well-known for your physique and that's highlighted extraordinarily well in many of the films you've made, but you *are* so much more than that. You have a gift. You have so much untapped, raw talent, but you don't seem to put it out there." She pauses. "It makes me wonder what you're afraid of." *Zing!*

With one brutal statement, delivered with so much tenderness, she shines a light on one of my biggest insecurities: I'm afraid I'm not good enough.

Even though she's not attacking me, my self-defense instinct kicks in. "I'm not afraid." I deflect, not willing to verbally admit to it, to her or to myself. "What makes you think I'm afraid?"

"Well, your more recent projects don't capitalize on your skills. It's obvious you're good at comedic acting and romantic dramas. But I think you'd be outstanding in action films and roles of a more serious nature." As the words spill from her pretty lips, my heart races at the compliments.

"You've watched some of my movies, have you?"

"Yes," she says softly. "I have."

I'm flattered. "Did you watch them before or after you figured out who I was?" I tease.

"Ouch." She chuckles and cringes. "I'd seen a couple before, but admit they didn't stick with me. Then I watched a few over the last couple days," she says with a cute sass and tilt of her head.

I blow a puff of air and words I've never consciously accepted pour out of me. "I can't land the roles I really want. Roles where I'm taken seriously as an actor. I audition, but I don't get them. I'm just not good enough." I pause as my own self-critical admission, that's been buried down deep, fills my ears. "I guess I've gotten used to my body getting me paychecks. It seems like the only roles I *can* get have me taking off my shirt because that's mostly what they want me for." I hesitate. "And, shit." I drag a hand through my hair as the realization smacks me in the face. Something sticks in my throat as I force out, "I can't say the same isn't true for my relationships." I ruminate. "I guess, the accolades just — make me feel good. Ugh, talk about needing my ego stroked. Have I seriously turned into *that* guy and didn't even know it?"

I can't believe I said all that. I can't believe, in one conversation with her, she has me cracking open my soul to her. She owns me.

She lifts her chin. "Hey." Her soothing voice is wrapped with tenderness. "Don't be so hard on yourself. Maybe it's time to stop trying to prove yourself using your body and step into your worth of how smart and truly talented you are. And if the women you're with only want you for your body, then they're missing out on a whole lot."

She makes it sound like I'm with *multiple* women. *How much ass does she think I get?* "I'm not with any *women* right now."

"That's…" She pauses and shrugs, cocking her hands out at her wrists. "None of my business."

"I think we need to clear something up. I get that, according to tabloids and because I have money and access, the world thinks I'm getting laid all the time, but I'm a one-woman guy and I've *never* slept with someone I'm not dating."

"Well, that's good to know." She throws her hands up in surrender. "Again, none of my business."

"Okay, enough about me. What about you? What are your fears?"

She doesn't answer right away. Her green eyes look at the flames and she takes a deep breath, blowing it quietly out of her mouth. "Letting life pass me by." Her gaze returns to me. "I know I needed to go through everything I went through in my life in order to get here. I just…I feel like I've lived in disappointment for so long. And, I don't want to find myself another ten years from now in the same uninspired, empty existence. I have so much passion inside me and so many desires I want to fulfill and live. And…" She hesitates. "…I'm scared. I'm coming out here because I know I want a better life. A life filled with joy and happiness and laughter and I have no idea how to begin making it happen."

"But you're doing it." I encourage. "You've made the decision to come out here. That's a huge first step."

"Yeah, but then what?" She shakes her head.

"You'll figure it out, day-by-day." I pause. Things are getting a little heavy. "Hey, you want to try something fun?"

She quizzically tilts her head and raises one eyebrow at me. "Okay," she agrees hesitantly.

"Both shoes have to come off first."

"My shoes?" The skin between her brows puckers.

"Yup, off." I wave my hand toward her feet.

"Oh gosh. What are we doing?" The playfully concerned undercurrent in her tone makes me want to grab her and hold her… and kiss her.

"You'll see. Take the other one off and follow me."

She removes her other shoe and I lead her downstairs to the pool where I pick up my skateboard. "Have you ever?"

Her eyes widen as she steps backwards. "Oh dear. No, I haven't. I have to warn you, my athleticism is pretty much confined to the gym."

"Okay, we'll go slow. It's all about balance and learning how to control your center of gravity." I put the skateboard on the cement. "Give me your hands and just stand on it with your feet facing me. Get used to how it feels under your feet."

She steps onto the skateboard with one foot and it inches forward when she goes to put her other foot on. She squeezes my hands and tugs on me. "Ooooo."

I hold her steady. "It's okay. You've got it. You're on. Don't move yet. Just feel it."

She smiles broadly and bobs her head, looking around.

"Ready?"

"No?" she answers with a questioning inflection and gives me a side-eyed stare.

"I'm going to move you a little before you even start pushing on your own. We're going to start at this end and go to that end." I point to the other end of the pool. "I want you to feel how it feels when you're moving."

"Okay." She looks scared, but is willing and moves her hands to my shoulders.

I put my hands around her waist, my fingers nearly able to touch each other around her lower back, my thumbs on her abs. *Damn, her abs are tight.* A quick spurt of excitement shoots through me. Slowly, I start pulling her. She wiggles and squeezes my shoulders, trying to balance.

"Oh gosh. Oh gosh."

"Come on. Here we go." I continue pulling her to the other end of the pool from where we started, keeping my eyes on her while she looks down at her feet. "Now we'll go back." I slowly pull her back to where we started while she wriggles. "How's it feeling?"

"Hah! Unstable." She laughs as she holds a vicelike grip on my shoulders and steps off the board.

"Now you're going to push, just a little. Start with your left foot forward on the board and you're going to push with your right foot and then put it on the board. Got it?"

"I can't believe I'm doing this. Okay, got it," she says confidently, shaking out her arms like an Olympic swimmer in preparation for a race. Her willingness is so damn sexy.

"I'll be right here." I reassure her.

She takes a deep breath in and blows it out. While she's feigning confidence, her death-grip on my left shoulder tells a different story. Carefully, she puts her left foot on the board. One small push with her right foot and, when she goes to put it on the board, she hits the deck of the board, throwing her balance.

"Woah!" Her arms flail and she is completely enchanting.

The board slides out from under her and I catch her in my arms. *Jesus, I want to kiss her...hard.* "That's probably enough for tonight." I hold her until her feet are solidly on the ground. "How about something a little less challenging? A movie?"

She moves her hand over her heart and chuckles as she catches her breath. "Yes. A movie sounds good. I bet you have quite a selection."

"That I do." I nod. "What are you up for?"

"Any chance you have *The Money Pit*?"

"Aw, I *love* Tom Hanks." She has good taste.

"The most hilarious movie." She smiles her tender smile I'm growing to adore.

"I'll grab the movie. You get the cookies."

"Done." She runs to the bottom of the stairs, stops, and runs back to me. Her sultry green eyes captivate me. "Thank you for dinner." She kisses me on the cheek and runs back to the stairs. I stir in my pants and groan under my breath.

I watch her climb each step. *I can't tell her. Not yet. It'll ruin everything if I tell her now.*

I blow out all the candles and hand her the pile of my clothes she brought back. "Go change and meet me back here."

I find the movie, change into comfortable clothes, and wait for her. "Come on, grab a blanket. We watch movies in style around here." I lead her down to the movie theater room where we recline the black leather two-seater theater-seats of the front row and I start the movie.

She curls up her legs and wraps the blanket around herself. Dimming the lights with the remote, I put the plate of cookies in my lap so she can reach them.

"Mmm, just one more," she says and grabs a cookie off the plate. She opens her mouth and, as the sweetness is about to land on her tongue…I want to be a chocolate chip cookie.

~ 11 ~

Desiree

The room is dimly lit when I open my eyes. I'm nuzzled on Zane's firm chest and bathe in the moment. I think about our night at his parent's house; how welcoming they were and how comfortable I felt with him. He didn't even seem like a huge celebrity, but just a good guy with a nice family. It was unexpected.

I think about the night we had together; how vulnerable he allowed himself to be and how open he was with me. In one night, I learned more about him than I knew about Brad in our five years together. It's the kind of soul-connection I've always desired to have with a man and it terrifies me. He is unexpected.

I'm also starting to wonder if I'm imagining the intense physical chemistry between us.

Okay, it's time for an intervention. Here's the deal; there's your Head, your Heart, and your Body. They're three separate entities. Your Head is the ruler and makes all the decisions. Your Heart will not, I repeat NOT, *be involved in any way. As for your Body; okay, so you've never had mind-blowing sex in your life and now you can't stop fantasizing about mind-blowing sex with the young, gorgeous, famous guy who's popped into your life. It's totally normal to fantasize; there's nothing dangerous about fantasizing. Just...don't...touch. And under* no *circumstances can any one of these bleed into the other. Whew. That's settled.*

"Oh, man." He yawns. "What time is it?"

"I don't know." I get up from his chest, wishing I could stay there longer.

"Let's head upstairs. I may not be able to make us breakfast today. I have a meeting."

"That's okay."

We gather the cookie plate, our glasses, and the blanket and go upstairs to check the time and it's already after eight.

"Hey, I've gotta get ready and go. I have a meeting about a new project this winter. Can I call you later?"

"Yes, of course."

"I'm going to have Bill take you home, okay?"

"Absolutely. That's fine." I nod.

He turns away from me and lifts his shirt off over his head then turns back to me. *Good Lord.* I swallow hard. Heat accelerates from my feet to head; my face is hot. Seeing his broad, chiseled torso in real life is overwhelming. Wide-set shoulders, expansive chest that narrows toward his hips with that sexy v-line, solid pec muscles, eight-pack abs, and perfectly sculpted arms. His body is magnificent and I want so badly to touch him. *Don't stare. Look at his face. Look…at…his…face.*

"Will you go to Sherry's wedding with me?"

I refocus my thoughts *and* my eyes. "The wedding?" I hesitate. "You want me to go with you?"

"Yeah, be my plus one." He puts his hands on his hips, his penetrating smile makes me lightheaded.

"Zane, I don't know." *A family wedding? This is not a good idea.*

"Come on. I can't get in the shower until you say yes, and I *really* need to get in the shower." He wiggles like he's doing the pee-pee-dance.

I wave him away, trying not to gawk at his ravishing chest. "Go, go, get in the shower."

"So, you'll come?" A childlike smile forms on his face as he continues to wiggle.

"Zane Adam Elkton, you are incorrigible. Okay, okay, I'll go with you. Now go." I wave him away again.

"Someone's done her homework. Only my mom uses my

middle name." He flashes me an adorably sinister smile and turns. Halfway around, he turns back and tilts his head, giving me a caught-you-looking smirk. And then he runs off.

That afternoon, Zane texts me.

Chocolate Bear: What are you doing Wednesday?

Me: Nothing at the moment. I don't have any houses to look at that day. Why?

Chocolate Bear: Will you spend the morning with me?

Why does it feel like we're dating? We are not *dating.* Speaking of dating, he's only ever slept with women he's dated? That was an interesting tidbit and not what I expected. I'm not sure I believe him. But he has no reason to lie to me. Why does he keep inviting me to spend time with him? He's Zane Elkton, for goodness sakes. This doesn't make any sense. Why do I want to see him again? I'm trying to sort through the array of feelings coursing through me; angst battling longing.

Chocolate Bear: Where did you go?

Me: I'm here.

Chocolate Bear: So, will you?

Oh gosh. What should I do? Head says, *"Don't go."* But Heart overrules and makes the decision.

Me: What are we doing?

Traitor.

Chocolate Bear: It's a surprise. You'll like it. Wear sneakers. Do you have a sweatshirt? It'll be an early start. I'll pick you up at 5:00 AM.

A surprise? What in the world are we doing?

Me: Okay. Yes, I have a sweatshirt. See you then.

It's the girls' last day here and I spend the day shopping with them while they celebrity-hunt. I'm grateful they're leaving tomorrow. Thankfully, they have an early flight so we make it an early night and go back to the house after dinner.

The next day, once the girls are gone, I get showered and ready for a day of looking at houses with Jerry. We're set up to see three houses today and I'm excited to see what he's lined up.

Before Jerry arrives, I call my friend Lisa and we make plans to get together on Thursday. We met online through our businesses and we've known each other for about four years but only ever saw each other over video calls and talked on the phone. We've been each other's sounding board through difficult business decisions, tough times in relationships, and even family drama. We've built such an amazing friendship and it's going to be so great getting to meet her in real life and hug her. Maybe she can knock some sense into me about Zane.

At eleven o'clock, there's a knock on my door; Jerry's right on time.

I open the door to his bright, smiling face. He stands about my height and is sharply dressed with slicked back hair.

"Hey, another redhead. I'm Jerry," he says enthusiastically, extending his hand.

"We redheads gotta stick together." I smile and shake his hand. "I'm Desiree. It's so nice to meet you."

"Yeah, yeah, it's great meeting you. We have a full day ahead of us. Are you ready?" I love his upbeat energy already.

"Absolutely. Let's go."

He walks me around to the passenger side of his car and opens the door for me to get in. I would expect someone Zane recommended to be a complete gentleman and Jerry hits the mark.

As he drives, I try to pay attention to the roads so I can continue learning my way around.

"Okay, so what I have is a small, cute house with two bedrooms, a fireplace, and preferably a nice view, not necessarily of the beach, but somewhere you can look out and see nature. How am I doing?"

"Yup, other than those few things, I'm honestly not too picky."

"That's the must-have list. How about the would-like-to-have list? Anything on that one?" He looks in his rear-view then side-view mirrors, puts on his blinker, and cautiously passes the car in front of us.

"Oooo, a garage would be nice." I pause. "Although, I'm guessing you guys don't get much snow out here."

He laughs. "No. We don't."

"Right. Still, a garage would be nice. If there's something within, say, twenty minutes of the beach, that would be great. I don't want a big yard, something small and manageable would be good. And if it has space for a hot tub, that would be fantastic. Oh, and clean, it has to be clean and in a safe neighborhood."

"Safe neighborhood, check. That part I got from Zane."

Really?

Within about ten minutes we pull up to the first house and it's darling. We tour the house and head to the next one and finally the third. He's done a great job in listening to what I want and finding homes that match.

On our way back to my Airbnb we talk through each house, what I liked, what I didn't, and prices. They're all a little more expensive than what I want to spend.

"I'm sorry. I hope I'm not wasting your time. I told Zane I was going to be small-time for you."

"Please, there's no need to apologize. I'm happy to help you. Any friend of Zane's is a friend of mine. I owe that guy my life."

"You do? How so?" That's a pretty powerful statement and he has me curious.

"I had some hard times for a while. The market was down

and houses weren't selling. I couldn't pay the bills for my family, let alone pay for my son's college tuition. It was the scariest time of my life. Because we're friends, he knew a little about what was going on. Then one day, he stops by the house and hands me a check for fifty thousand dollars…*fifty thousand dollars.*" He shakes one hand vigorously as he repeats it. "I didn't ask for it, he just…gave it to me. Said it was a gift. He didn't even want the money back. Of course I paid him back over time as the market picked up and I started making bank again. But who does that? That guy's one of kind." He shakes his head. "And the damn tabloids and all that crap they print. They know nothing about him. Saved my ass, that guy. Saved my ass."

Oh my gosh. Here I thought giving waitresses a fifty-dollar tip was a generous random act of kindness. Holy cow.

Jerry pulls up to my house. "Let me do a little more research and I'll give you a call to set up another day together."

"Okay, that sounds perfect. Thanks so much, Jerry."

"You bet! Take care."

"Bye."

I get out his car, lost in my thoughts, and walk to the door with Jerry's story fresh in my mind. He waits until I'm inside before driving away.

Zane sneaks farther into my heart. And I'm seeing him tomorrow for a surprise. A burst of adrenaline flashes through me.

~ 12 ~

Desiree

Promptly at five o'clock Wednesday morning, Zane knocks on my door. I open the door and excitement zips through me at seeing him again. The sky is still dark and there's a chill in the air. He's wearing worn-in jeans, a plain black hooded sweatshirt, and a black baseball hat. *He's adorable.*

"Good morning." The sound of his voice makes my heart beat faster.

"Good morning," I say, my voice gravely from the early morning hour.

"Ready?"

"Yup. Can you tell me where we're going yet?" My curiosity is eating at me.

"No. You'll find out when we get there." A sexy grin dances on his lips.

With the crispness in the air, he's driving a different car, an Audi R8. As he drives, he tells me about his meeting and the movie he'll star in that begins filming in the winter.

"Yeah, it's another one that has plenty of Zane-flesh in it." My mind jumps to the visual of his luscious, bare chest that I've stored in my brain, against Head's wishes. "But you really got my wheels spinning. I spent some time thinking about what we talked about the other night. I'm going to be much more selective about the projects I take on. If I'm going to build the legacy I want to build, I need to go after the roles that will help me do that and not give up." He looks at me. "Thank you. You gave me the swift kick in the ass I needed."

"You're welcome."

"How's the house-hunt going?"

With the early hour, there are only a couple other cars on the road. While I would've taken him to be someone who enjoys driving fast, he travels right at the speed limit.

"Oh, Jerry's great. We saw a few cute places yesterday and he's going to do some more research to see if he can find anything that's a little more in my price range."

"Super-nice guy, huh?"

"Yeah, he is."

"So how were your last few days with *the girls*?" He raises an eyebrow.

"Let's just say I'm glad they're gone."

We both chuckle.

About forty minutes into the drive, he pulls off the road.

"We're here?" I look around us. "This looks like we're on the side of the highway."

"No, we're not there yet. Be patient." There's a mischievous sparkle in his eyes when he smiles. He grabs a backpack from the back seat and pulls out a black and white bandana. "Oh, I brought some waters and snacks in case you get hungry." He folds the bandana into what looks like a headband. "Turn your head for me."

"What's that for?"

"No questions. Just turn around." He winks. I love…*no, I like*… his playful nature.

I comply and turn my head as he wraps the bandana over my eyes. A blindfold, not a headband. I'm a little nervous, a little turned on — *stop it* — and very intrigued. He secures the bandana in a knot. My senses are razor-sharp.

"Can you see anything?"

"No, nothing."

"Good." He takes my hand in his and lifts it to his mouth,

kissing it. I stifle a gasp. His lips are soft on my skin. My nerve endings spark throughout my body. *What's happening?* The uncertainty flusters me.

He places my hand in my lap. "Are you excited?"

"I am," I answer, wondering if I sound convincing. At the moment, I'm a touch more nervous than excited. Well, excited in a way he'll never know about.

I feel his eyes on me and stir in my seat. "Are you looking at me?"

"Yes. Do you trust me?"

Something in his voice eases me and I do. "Yes."

I hear him get back onto the road, the engine hums. For the remainder of the drive, he holds his hand on top of mine. It makes me feel safe. His palms are rough and calloused, evidence of dedication in the gym. The faint scent of his body wash fills my lungs as I inhale.

"We'll be there in a few minutes." He sings along to the song coming through the speakers.

His voice soaks into me as I listen, committing its soothing resonance to memory.

Within ten minutes, I hear the car slow down and fidget in my seat. The sound of gravel crunches beneath the wheels.

"Are we there? Can I look now?" I'm eager to remove the blindfold and see where we are.

"So impatient." His sensual voice drifts into my ears. "No, you can't look yet. Stay right there. I'll come around and get you."

His keys ting as he pulls them out of the ignition. He opens then closes his door. I hear his footsteps crunch on the gravel and then my car door open.

"Here, give me your hand," he says as he takes my hand.

I grip his hand and turn my body, putting my feet on the ground. Then I reach out and he slides his other hand into mine, helping me out of the car. He releases one hand and guards my head as I get out then slips his hand back into mine. The door closes with a thunk.

"I've got you. Just follow my lead," he says, calming me.

He must be walking backwards because he doesn't release my hands. We move from the gravel to something softer, spongy — grass.

"Okay, don't move," he says as we stop.

He releases one hand and moves his body behind me, his chest against my back, his mouth at my ear. My heart rate races.

"Are you ready?" he whispers, sending a shiver down my spine.

"Yes." I nod vigorously.

He unties the bandana and my eyes adjust, focusing on a large, colorful, hot air balloon sitting in an open field. I'm speechless. He's inching deeper into my heart.

Bright colors of the rainbow tile the massive canvas of the balloon. The sun is ascending from behind the mountains in the distance.

"Zane." I breathe as I turn and look at him. "I can't believe you did this."

A boyish grin spreads across his face. "Come on," he says excitedly as he grabs my hand and walks toward the balloon. "Let's catch the sunrise."

I walk alongside him, holding his hand, my heart skittering. *I can't believe this.*

We approach a man standing next to the large woven basket beneath the balloon.

"Hello, Mr. Elkton. It's our pleasure to host you today. I'm Ted and I'll be taking care of you and your guest." He offers his hand and Zane shakes it. "Pete and Mark will help us get untethered and give us some weights so we can stay level while we're up there." He points in their direction and they wave at us.

"Thank you so much for accommodating us, Ted. This is Desiree," he says.

"Pleasure, ma'am." He shakes my hand. "Our business thrives on special requests, sir. It's great to meet both of you." From his statement, I suspect Zane pulled some strings to make this happen. "I just need you both to fill out these waivers and then we should get up in the air. It's going to be a beautiful sunrise today."

We complete the waivers and hand them to Ted who runs them over to one of the guys. Zane steps up the stepstool and climbs into the basket then helps me in. Ted climbs in while Pete and Mark start untethering the lines holding us down. Once we're securely in and Ted gives us some instructions, then the roar of the flame fills our ears. I hold onto the red, vinyl-wrapped top of the basket and Zane tucks himself in behind me, straddling his arms around my body. Unintentionally, but naturally, I lean back into him and close my eyes, taking in everything that's happening. His mouth is at my ear and warmth washes over me.

"I think it's better if you open your eyes."

Another blast of flame shoots above us. I open my eyes and we float up. We rise higher into the sky and I watch neighborhoods grow tiny below us. We glide over rows and rows of grapevines of local vineyards. Trees begin to look like moss and there's green field after sprawling green field.

We continue to climb and he points over to the mountains where the sun is climbing into the sky with us. "Look over there."

"It's magnificent."

The sky illuminates with colors of bright orange to tangerine to dandelion yellow and citrine, with the sun itself a searing, glorious white. Beams of light bounce off the clouds as the sun continues its ascent and the fiery colors slink across the horizon.

We don't say much during our hour in the air. I'm completely mesmerized by the experience and the breathtaking views I'm soaking in as we soar through the air. And Zane is the only person I want to share this experience with. I feel like I'm in a dream that I don't want to end.

Ted stops pumping flames into the balloon and quiet surrounds us as we hang, suspended in the sky. It's so peaceful. Like the birds, I'm free, weightless.

Slowly, we begin our descent.

I turn around to face him. "Thank you for this." Moisture

brews in my eyes. I wrap my arms around his neck and he holds me in his arms, lowering his head into me. Gratitude fills me and I start crying, my body shakes in his arms.

He shrinks back and looks in my tear-filled eyes. "Hey." Sympathy coats his voice. "This was supposed to make you happy."

I laugh as I wipe the tears off my face. "I *am* happy. This has been the most incredible experience of my life."

He shakes his head. "I don't understand. Why are you crying?"

I continue cry-laughing and smile. Then I look around and extend my arms out wide, motioning around us. "No one has *ever* done *anything* like this for me. And my gratitude tends to come out in tears."

"So, you're happy?"

"Yes." I giggle as I sweep my fingers across my face, wiping away more tears. "I'm happy."

He throws his arms around me, holding onto me and lingering for a moment before releasing me. We're silent for the rest of the descent. There's a happiness in my heart that I've never felt before.

Within minutes, we're safely on the ground and climb out of the basket. Thanking Ted, we walk toward the sedan limousine where Bill is waiting to bring us back to Zane's car.

"How was your ride?" Bill asks with bright eyes.

"Spectacular," I answer joyfully as I get in.

Zane pats Bill on the shoulder and follows me in.

"I have no idea how to thank you for this." I place my hand on his leg.

"Your smile is all the thanks I need." His eyes are warm and tender as he puts his hand on top of mine and laces our fingers together. "Hey, I forgot to ask if you ever found a gym you like. I've missed seeing you at Virtue."

"I did. I found a Planet Fitness so I've been going there. Yeah, about that. We weren't supposed to see you that second day at Virtue. We were *trying* to leave you alone, well *I* was. Something tells me your little owner-friend, Johnny, had something to do with that."

He shakes his head and looks out the window as he lies blithely. "I don't know what you're talking about." He returns his face to me with a sly grin spread on his face. "I have meetings the rest of today and tomorrow, but how about I show you around town on Friday?"

Resisting his requests is becoming increasingly difficult the more connected to him I become. And after his heartfelt gesture of the hot air balloon ride and sitting here holding his hand, I can't help wanting to be with him again.

No, thank you, Head answers. "Okay, that would be nice," Heart responds. *Be careful. Don't let him in.* Without my consent, he's fully and completely in my heart.

~ 13 ~

Desiree

After seeing some houses with Jerry the other day and looking at what I have going on today, I'm feeling much more productive than last week. Today I have an appointment to tour the National Holistic Institute's campus and then I'm meeting up with Lisa.

The massage therapy program is eight months long and that's going full-time. Thankfully full-time doesn't mean 9-5 so I'll have time to work on my business. When Brad died, he left me the house and three million dollars in life insurance money. While that's a lot of money, I know the cost of living out here is a lot more expensive than Pennsylvania and I want to build up my business to the point that I don't have to touch that money and can put it away for retirement. Plus, I'm a workhorse and I like to keep busy.

When I check in at the Institute, I'm told I'm the only person taking the tour today so I'll get some personal attention. A woman named Christine meets me and shows me where the classrooms are, the massage practice rooms, and the cafeteria. She also points out some study rooms and the outdoor area that's great for peaceful walks if we need a break. Moving here is starting to feel more real and I'm getting excited to start my life over.

After my tour, I head over to a little café Lisa recommended. Even though we never met, she's become the closest friend I have and I'm thrilled to finally meet her in person. I recognize her right away and wave my hands at her like an excited child on Christmas morning. We move quickly toward each other and immediately hug, swinging our bodies from side to side and laughing.

"Hi. I can't believe it's actually you. This is so great."

"I know. Me either. And you're here. This is amazing." She shares my joy. "Are you hungry?"

"Yes, very."

"This place has great sandwiches and salads. Let's grab a table. We have so much to catch up on."

We decided to meet after the lunch rush so it wouldn't be too crowded or loud. Finding a table in a little corner, we place our orders and immediately launch into catching up.

"So, how's it going so far? You've been here a few weeks now already, right? Tell me all the things." Her bright smile makes me smile.

"Well." I purse my lips together. "It's certainly not gone at all how I thought it would go."

"Oh no." Her pitch drops. "No luck finding a house yet?"

"Oh, no, not just yet, but I've seen a couple cute places I like." I tilt my head and purse my lips together again. "There's just been a few things happening that I didn't expect and *never* could've anticipated." I raise my eyebrows. She has no idea what I'm about to unleash on her and I'm so grateful to have someone outside the ring-of-Zane to talk to. Someone I know I can trust.

"Oooo." She rubs her hands together and eagerness glows in her eyes. "Tell me, tell me."

"I'm going to warn you, you're not ready for this."

"I like the way it sounds already." She smiles.

"Well, I think I'm losing my mind." I become serious.

"Uh-oh. I'm sure you're not, but what's going on?" She must sense the shift in my tone because she shifts hers to match mine.

I sigh. "It started the day after I arrived." I begin. "I met someone."

"Okay, that actually sounds like a good thing, no?"

"You would think so, but this *someone* is *not* just anyone."

"Go on."

"He's someone you would know."

"I would?" She leans forward.

"Oh, you would." I nod. "He's a celebrity. An actor." I pause.

"Really?" The corners of her mouth turn down as her eyes widen.

"I know, not my thing at all." She's well aware that I'm not into the whole wooed-by-celebrities thing.

"No, not at all." She shakes her head and a crease knits between her brows. "So, what happened?"

"We met at a gym, purely accidentally. I didn't know he was who he is, at least not right away. So, *that* was embarrassing. Anyway, he kept wanting to get together and hang out. He took me to his parents' house for dinner and invited me to a party at his house with his friends. And…" I sigh and hold my hands out in surrender. "And then he invited me to have dinner at his house, just the two of us and it was one of the best nights I've *ever* had. Oh, and then," I jet my neck forward, "he took me on a hot air balloon ride." All I could do was stare at her.

"Um, that actually all sounds pretty damn awesome." She scratches her temple and looks at me like I'm crazy.

"I know, right?" I feel ready to bounce out of my seat as I shake my head and wave my hands tightly.

"So, I'm a little confused." She squints. "What's the issue?"

I take a deep breath to calm myself. "There's a few things. First, you know I'm done with the whole dating thing, and we're not even dating. I don't even know *what* we are." I sigh. "I really don't think I ever want to be in a relationship again. I'm so tired of being hurt."

"Okay, I need to stop you right there." She moves her hand across the table and puts it on top of mine. "I get it. I know you've been hurt. And that sucks, that really sucks. But, closing yourself off to the possibility of a relationship with someone who's worth it and the chance at love — you can't close yourself off from that."

I jerk my head back. "Who said anything about love?" I pause. "I don't know. Maybe love just isn't meant for me. I mean, if I haven't found it by now —"

"Nope." She cuts me off. "I don't accept that on your behalf." She waves her hand toward herself. "What else ya got."

"So, second, he's famous."

"*And?*"

"*And* he's stinking famous. I don't want anything to do with that kind of lifestyle. It's not me, Lisa. *Come on.* You know me. And watching him half-naked with other women on massive movie screens. I couldn't handle that. No way."

She nods and looks up. "That *would* be really hard to get used to, dating someone like that. It always seems so stressful when we get the smallest peek into what they have to deal with daily. Yeah, I wouldn't deal well with watching my husband kiss someone else, even if it was his job. I kind of get this one. By the way, do I get to know who it is?" She gives me a giddy smile.

I get my phone and bring up the picture of him and I that Grace sent me. Looking around to make sure no one is near us, I slide my phone to her, put my finger up to my lips, and *shhh* inaudibly.

Her eyes fly open and she leans back. "That's Zane Elkton." She mouths.

I quickly grab my phone as our food arrives. The waiter puts our plates down and we thank him.

"Yes, I know who it is." I smile at her and chuckle at her reaction.

"This *is* unexpected. Keep going." One of the things I've grown to love about her is her genuine interest in our conversations, no matter what kinds of crazy things I throw at her.

"So, there's a third issue, and it's a big one. He's been to rehab for alcohol addiction, which I'm glad he went to rehab, but he's off the sober-wagon." My heart sinks as I tell her.

"Ugh," she groans. "Yup, that's a big one, especially for you. How do you know he's off the wagon?"

"For one, I saw him drinking at least one beer during his party and then he had wine glasses out when I was there for dinner. He took them away after I said I didn't want any. Even if I hadn't seen him drinking, I know the signs. I've lived through it too many times. I won't go there again."

"Oh shit." She blows out an audible exhale.

"Exactly. And now, I'm supposed to go to his cousin's wedding with him and I really think I shouldn't go."

"What are you going to do?"

I grit my teeth together. "I don't know. I need you to talk some sense into me about all this. See why I'm losing my mind?"

"Mmmm."

We take a pause and dig into our salads.

"So, tell me this." She taps her finger on the table. "Take away everything you just told me, just for a minute. Do you like him?"

Now it's my turn to blow out an exhale. "I don't even know how to put into words what I'm feeling about him. I mean, we've only known each other a few weeks and I feel so — connected to him, which seems strange. He's unlike anyone I've ever met before. He's kind and thoughtful and respectful. He makes me laugh." I pause. "When I was at his house for dinner, we talked for hours and I got to see a part of him that the world doesn't get to see. He shared with me his fears and his dreams for the future. It was incredible. And," I put my fork down on my plate and lean toward her. "Do you know what he said to me about my business and starting it up out here?"

"What?" She leans in.

"He said I seem like a woman who can do anything I put my mind to. He doesn't even know me and he believes in me more than Brad *ever* did." I heave a sigh.

Her fork clangs on her plate as she puts it down and stares at me. "Desiree, you really like him."

I shake my head. "But I can't."

"Have you kissed?" She watches my face like she's looking for a sign of guilt.

"No, no." I shake my head again — vigorously — and then

pause. "But I must say, the energy between us is…" I fill my cheeks with air, blow another exhale, and open my eyes wide.

"Oh, really." She taps her fingers togethers as if to say, "Things are getting juicy now."

"Well, he *is* gorgeous. I've never in my life seen a body like his up close."

"I'm sorry, what now?" She shifts her body forward and tilts her ear closer. "You've seen his body?"

Heat fills my face as I turn to the side, recoil my body, and wave my hands.

"No. No, I haven't. Not his whole body, just his chest."

"And how exactly did you come to see his bare chest?"

My face is burning. "I just — well, he…he took his shirt off before he went to get in the shower after he asked me to go to the wedding with him."

"*Desiree.*" She stops chewing, puts her fists on the table, and practically lunges at me, ready to burst.

"What? *What?*" My whole body breaks out in tingles.

"You're hot for him." Her eyes are bulging out of her head at this point.

"Noooo." I pause. "Okay, maybe a little. I mean, what woman in her right mind wouldn't be?" I take a bite of my salad. "My head is so messed up about all this. Part of me does like him and it's been so amazing getting to know him and, at the same time, it's like I want nothing to do with him. Oh, and let's throw in a fourth tidbit, he's *very* young, too young."

"That one's off the table too." She waves at me like she's shooing away a fly. "Age doesn't matter."

"Lisa, please. Talk some sense into me. He's all I think about. I can't even get a good night's sleep anymore because I'm so twisted about this whole situation. What am I going to do? I should *not* go to the wedding, right?"

"Wait. Before we go there, let me summarize." She drums her fingers on the table and touches a finger to her chin. "You met this sweet, amazing guy, who you're already feeling connected to on an emotional level in a way you've never felt before, he's pretty great as far as personalities go, he treats you nicely, *and* you're hot for him."

I sit quietly and listen to her summary, gulping down a bite of my salad. I can't deny anything she's stated.

"Desiree, are you falling for him?"

I squint my eyes as I ponder her question. "No. I can't possibly be." I'm trying to convince myself more so than her.

"No?" She swivels her head slightly and gapes at me, seeming to study me.

"No." I say adamantly, completely lying to both of us. "That's it. I need to stop this from going any farther. I can't go to this wedding with him."

She goes back to eating her salad. "You can't just sweep feelings like this under the rug, you know."

"I can when there are massive issues blockading any chance of things turning out well for me." I take a bite of my salad and know what I need to do. "Thank you for talking this through with me."

"I don't feel like I helped at all."

"You did, really you did. Okay, enough about me and my ridiculous drama. Tell me what's going on with you. How's business? Your family?"

"Okay, but I want updates. You call me if you need to talk." She wiggles her finger at me.

"I will."

We spend the rest of our lunch chatting about our businesses, her family, and how much fun it's going to be to hang out with each other in person from now on.

As I head home, I make a promise to myself that I'll back out of going to the wedding with Zane. The thought is unsettling because I don't like to back out of things, and because I know if I don't go to the wedding, I probably won't see him again after tomorrow.

Damn, tomorrow. Maybe I should cancel tomorrow too.

~ 14 ~

Desiree

I can't do it. I can't bring myself to cancel our plans for tomorrow. I want to see Zane again. I know spending time with him keeps me wanting more of him, but I have to see him one last time, at least to say goodbye.

On Friday, he picks me up at ten and shows me some of his favorite spots, including where he had his first audition. As we drive through downtown L.A., he seems to spot something and quickly pulls the car over.

"Stay here," he says as he gets out of the car.

He tugs down the brim of his baseball hat and walks briskly to a little flower shop that has buckets and buckets of flowers scattering their storefront. He manages to disappear into the shop without being recognized by anyone on the busy sidewalk. I love watching his bow legs and cute butt.

He comes out, carrying a bundle of pink peonies, squats down at my door, and hands them to me through the open window. "For you." He smiles that devilishly crooked smile and my heart melts.

"Thank you. They're beautiful," is all I can mutter, toiling inside about how I'm going to back out of the wedding.

"Hungry?" he asks, getting back into the car.

"Yeah, I am."

"Great. Me too. I know a place we can go and get a good meal and avoid paparazzi."

We drive for about twenty minutes and Zane pulls down a narrow, filthy alley, parking next to a dumpster.

"Where *are* we?" I ask, kind of grossed out, as we get out of the car.

"Welcome to the not-so-glamorous side of being a celebrity," he answers, pulling a large, crumpled cloth from his trunk and draping it over the car. "We know a lot of back entrances."

Taking my hand, he walks across the alley to a black door at the back of a building and opens it. The scent of garlic and freshly made pasta drifts into my nose as we enter the kitchen.

"Mr. Elkton," the guttural voice of a tall, round man dressed in gray suit greets him. "It's so nice to see you. You haven't been here in a long time." His Italian accent is charming.

"Yes, I know, Luigi. I've been busy."

They shake hands and go in for a quick hug and pat on the back.

"Of course, of course." Luigi nods and smiles at him.

"This is my friend, Desiree." Luigi takes my hand in his and kisses the top of it as he bows slightly. "So lovely to meet you." He extends his arm toward the table. "Please, come, sit."

A small round table and two chairs are set up in a tucked-away corner of the kitchen, no doubt reserved for celebrities and VIPs who need a private place to dine. We follow Luigi to the table as his shoes tap on the terra cotta colored tiles. He pulls out my chair and then pushes it in as I sit.

"If there is nothing on the menu you like, just tell me what you want and we will prepare it for you, special." His smile spreads from ear-to-ear and he looks at Zane. "Mr. Elkton, your favorite vino?"

Zane shifts in his chair, almost nervously, and waves his hand. "No. Thank you, Luigi."

Don't dwell on it. So, he has a favorite wine here that he probably has every time he comes. It's none of my business.

"No?" The surprise on his face borders shock. "Okay. What can I bring for you to drink then?"

Zane looks at me. "Waters?"

I smile and nod.

"Two waters, please. One room temperature."

He remembered.

"Coming right up." Luigi puffs his chest as he leaves.

"He means it. I know this place is Italian and their food is amazing, and I also know you like a simple meal. That's why I brought you here. They'll seriously make anything you want, as mild as you want it."

"I appreciate that." And I do. "Don't not have wine on my account," I prod. "If you want some, get some."

"Nah, I'm good." He shifts in his seat again.

I know I shouldn't say anything, but I can't stop myself. I care about him. I've seen too many lives destroyed by alcoholism. I don't know if his friends or his family have said anything to him, but if today is goodbye, I have to say something.

"I know I don't have to tell you this because you've been to rehab and gone through the program, but you know it's a disease, right?"

"Of course I do." He laces his fingers together and rubs his palm with his thumb. "I only have one or two drinks here or there."

Oh, the lies they tell themselves in the grip of the destructive disease.

"So you also know that one or two usually leads to three or four and more?"

"Not for me. I've got it under control. I know when to stop," he says, fidgeting with the silverware as his skin pales.

"That's good." *"I've got it under control." Famous last words.* My heart sinks like a brick. Yup, it still has him in its vicious clutch. "But I think you know better."

"You never drink? At all?" His knife and spoon clang together as he continues fidgeting with them.

"Rarely. I may have one or two for a special occasion, but after that night I told you about back in college, I knew that drinking wasn't part of the kind of lifestyle I want. I'll never again be with someone who drinks regularly." Boom. The words drop like boulders out of my mouth.

His face turns grayish as his Adam's apple moves up and down in his throat.

I look through the menu and see something that suits me. He already knows what he wants. When Luigi returns with our waters, we place our orders.

I need to end this...whatever this is that's happening between us. The emotional connection and powerful physical attraction I have for him are something I can't deal with right now. Even having a friendship with someone who clearly isn't ready to take his addiction seriously doesn't fit into my plans for building a new life. No toxic people. *Tell him.*

"Zane, I'm not sure it's such a good idea for me to go to Sherry's wedding with you."

"Why not?" A puzzled look washes his face as he sits forward.

I didn't fully think through what to say. Make something up.

"Shouldn't you take a beautiful, A-list celebrity to something like that? Besides, I don't have anything to wear to a wedding."

"First off, no. I *am* bringing a beautiful woman with me, period. And second, Grace can take you shopping. I'll pay for your dress."

Did he just say I'm beautiful? Guys as hot as him don't find old women as ordinary as me "beautiful." Why does he say things like that and make this so hard for me?

"No, no, no. I'm not letting you pay for a dress for me."

"I invited you. And you obviously didn't pack for a wedding."

"I really think it's best if you take someone else."

"I can't believe you're backing out on me?" The hurt in his eyes crushes me. "I thought you didn't back out of commitments unless there's an emergency," he says snidely.

Shoot, I can't eat my own words. I gulp.

"Jeez, is there an emergency?" Now, he genuinely looks worried that I have an emergency of some kind.

"No, I just — I thought it might not be my place to go with you to something like that." I sound utterly foolish now.

"Desiree, I invited you. Of course you should be by my side."

Damnit. I cave. "Okay, I'll go with you."

"Yesssss." That charming, boyish grins lights up his face, melting me.

"I'll go with Grace, if she has time, because I have no idea what's even around here, but I'm *not* letting you pay for it."

He arches one eyebrow. "I think you underestimate the kind of power I have." A big, cheesy grin plasters his face.

"I'll figure something out. Is it a black-tie type of wedding?"

"Yup. You'll want to go with a long dress, something fancy. Try not to get shoes that are too high, if you don't mind. I'm obviously not the tallest of guys." I sense a shyness in him, like when he shoves his hands in his pockets.

"Thank goodness you're not. I dated a guy in college who was 6'4". My neck was constantly aching when we kissed. You're a..." before my brain can process the words, they fly out of my mouth, "kissable hei..." Now I hear them. His eyes are pinned on me. "...ght." Whoosh, I think I'm having a hot flash. I want to sink into the ground. *Get a grip on yourself.*

"Is that so?" His cocky grin and slow nod tell me I'm busted.

"Ah, delizioso." Luigi's jolly voice saves me. *Thank goodness.* He puts our plates down in front of us and curls his fingers to his lips, releasing a kissing sound as he pulls away his fingers and spreads them in the air. "Please, enjoy. Let me know if you need anything else."

We thank him and eat our lunch. I avoid *any* talk of kissing or touching or bodies or anything physical. *Physical, lusting, body-thoughts are in the compartment that is not to be spoken of, but kept chained away in your mind,* I remind myself.

After lunch, he takes me home because I have appointments

with Jerry to see two houses. Before Jerry arrives, I text Grace and we set up plans to go dress shopping the next day.

Once again, Jerry does a great job listening to what I want and brings me to some adorable houses I'd love to live in. Once again, it's proving tough to find something in my price range. We shift our strategy to finding me an apartment for a year that's near the National Holistic Institute. This is a more realistic approach and feels a lot less stressful.

During most of my time with Jerry, I'm distracted because I'm mad at myself for not following through with backing out of the wedding. Now tomorrow, I'm going shopping for a dress to wear to the wedding that I shouldn't be going to with a man I shouldn't be falling for.

The longer I wait to say goodbye, the harder it's going to be, and the more it's going to hurt.

~ 15 ~

Desiree

I meet Grace at a swanky boutique shop where I'm afraid to even touch anything.

"Good afternoon, Grace. It's lovely to see you again," says the saleswoman.

"Jennifer, so nice to see you." Grace hugs the woman. "This is my friend, Desiree, I called you about."

Watching them interact, I gather Grace frequents the boutique.

Jennifer is striking; at least 5'9" and looks taller with heels and her platinum blonde hair up in a French twist. Her red dress is snug in all the right places without being revealing and her red lipstick matches it perfectly. Large, sparkly, teardrop-shaped earrings tug on her ears.

"Hello, Desiree. It's a pleasure to meet you. I have a few *gorgeous* dresses for you to try on," she says with a flamboyance that makes me smile. She waves for us to follow her.

"It's nice to meet you as well." *Grace called ahead? And dresses are already selected? Zane's puppeteering is behind this, I know it.* It does feel kind of nice being taken care of in such a high-priority way.

We follow her down a hallway, the walls are painted with wide gold and white vertical stripes. Gold chandeliers dangle from the ceiling. I feel like I'm in a fairytale. Jennifer draws back a white velvet curtain revealing the most luxurious dressing room I've ever seen. Inside, there's a massive, gold, ornate 3-way mirror and a gold mirrored bar-cart with gold-rimmed champagne glasses, Veuve Clicquot champagne in an ice bucket, and Voss water bottles on it. In the corner sits a huge white tufted chair. Five exquisite dresses hang, widely spaced, on a white clothing bar. *Okay, I can see how celebrities like this. Wow!*

"Try them on one-by-one and come out and show us," Jennifer instructs as she pours two glasses of champagne. "Let's have a quick toast first, shall we?" She hands a glass to me and a glass to Grace. "I'd join you, but I'm working." Her high-pitched laugh rings in my ears. "What shall we toast to?"

"New friendships." Grace smiles and holds up her glass.

"To new friendships." I do feel like we're building a friendship and it makes me happy. We clink our glasses and take a sip. "I have to warn you, I'm not a drinker so it doesn't take me much to get tipsy. Plus, it's like truth-serum for me. I may not finish my glass."

"That's okay, I'll finish it for you. Now, let's get you a dress." Her smile spreads widely across her face and there's a twinkle in her eyes.

I go into the dressing room and come out in each one. Jennifer has me stand on a large pedestal in front of three mirrors while they sit on a huge, whited, tufted sofa and evaluate each one. None of them receive approval.

"There's only one left." I remind them as I go back into the dressing room.

"Okay, get in there. Let's see it."

When I open the velvet curtain and step out, Grace removes the champagne glass from her lips. Her eyes widen and her mouth drops open a bit. Jennifer stands up and audibly inhales.

"What? No good?" I ask as I step onto the pedestal and look at myself in the mirror. I don't recognize the person in the reflection.

Grace gasps. "It's sumptuous." She stands up slowly and walks around the pedestal, eyeing me up and down. "It's perfect. You… are…radiant. *This* is the one."

The champagne-colored dress hangs elegantly to the ground.

From above the bustline through the round neck and cap sleeves, it's intricately beaded with delicate pearls and crystals. Jennifer brings over matching champagne-colored shoes, *not too high*, and exquisite crystal drop earrings that dangle delicately just below my ears.

"Grace," I whisper. "It's $4,500. And that's *just* the dress."

"Nice." She nods. "We're under budget."

"Budget? Grace, this is too much. I can't let him do this. It's not right. I'm sure I can find something else."

"Something else?" their voices raise in unison as if I've said the most horrifying thing.

"Too late." Grace winks at Jennifer. "It's already done."

"Grace, I...I don't feel right about this at all." A knot twists in my stomach.

"That's exactly why you should have it. This is how he is, Desiree. He has a big heart and being generous makes him happy. Besides, you're not the type to take advantage so enjoy it and get used to it."

"This is all a little overwhelming," I confess as I go back into the dressing room and change into my clothes. Before I go back out, I sit on the white chair for minute and breathe. *This feels so wrong.*

When I come out, Jennifer has the dress in a long garment-bag and the shoes and earrings in a very expensive-looking shopping bag with ribbon handles.

"Okay, now that this is done, how about we grab a bite to eat? Then we can shop a little more before we go to Sherry's bachelorette party tonight. Oh, you're invited." She smiles.

"I am?" *Why would* I *be invited?*

"Yup, we'll swing by your house and pick you up in the limo around seven. We're going to dinner and then to Oak L.A. to dance the night away." She giggles as she wiggles.

"Oh, Grace. I don't know. That's not really my scene. I'm also much older than all of you."

"Nonsense. I know it's not your scene, but we'd really like you to come and hang out with us. You might have fun. We'll make sure you have fun. And, if you're having a miserable time, we'll have Bill take you home. Will you come with us?" She takes my hands in hers, lifts her eyebrows, and forms a pout with her mouth.

"Oof, you're tough. Okay, I'll come. I haven't been dancing in years. I don't even know what to wear."

"Something cute and sexy." She winks.

"Grace, I don't *have* anything sexy. I'm not the sexy type."

"I'm sure you'll look amazing. Come on. Let's go. Thank you, Jennifer." She waves at Jennifer who waves back.

"Thank you, Jennifer." I wave.

Grace loops her arm through mine and out the door we go.

Clubbing with a bunch of young girls. Oh gosh, this could be like being with Bella and her friends. But, who knows? Maybe it'll be fun.

~ 16 ~

Desiree

"Dancing at a nightclub? What have I gotten myself into?" I sigh as I look through my clothes; nothing seems appropriate to wear to a nightclub — with Zane Elkton's cousins. I don't have time to go shopping so I pick out black skinny jeans; black strappy heels; a wide-strapped, flowy, teal tank top; and my silver choker-necklace with little dangling teardrops.

When Bill arrives to pick me up, I let him know I might leave early. He opens the back door and I get into the limousine with eight other girls, including Zane's three cousins. *Yup, I'm the grandma of the group. I'm so out of place.*

Near the end of dinner, Grace leans over to me and talks into my ear above the chatter in the restaurant. "Come to the bathroom with me."

We get up and I follow her to the bathroom. The chatter fades as the door closes behind us. Grace looks around, we're the only ones in the room.

"Now, I want you to keep an open mind." She reaches into her purse, pulls out a fitted leopard-print top with thin black spaghetti straps and a slightly draped neck, and holds it up to me. "I figured you were an extra-small."

"Grace, I can't wear *that*." My jaw drops as I gawk at the top.

"This is what I call conservatively sexy. Nothing private is hanging out. You're just showing a tiny bit more skin than you're probably used to." She flutters her eyelashes. "Just try it on," she says as she hands it to me and nudges me into a stall.

Begrudgingly, I change my top and exit the stall. I turn in the mirror, trying to decide if I'll wear it or not. The back is open halfway down my back. Definitely more skin is exposed than I'm used to.

She squeals. "You look *so* good and that choker-necklace totally works," she says as she gets eye shadow out of her purse and starts applying just a hint to my eyelids. The final touch is a deep, vixen-red lipstick. When she's done, she turns me to face the mirror and stands behind me as we stare at our reflection.

"You're so pretty, Desiree." She squeezes me gently and a sweet smile draws across her face.

I swing around and hug her. "Thank you, Grace. I feel kind of pretty." And I'm not lying. I've never seen myself as pretty, but right now, I do feel pretty. I neatly fold my teal tank top and put it in my purse.

"Okay, let's go dance!" She shakes her body and sways her arms in the air.

Bill drives us to the club and we pile out of the limousine.

"How will I reach you if I want to leave?" I ask him as he holds the door open.

He reaches into his coat pocket and hands me a business card with his name and phone number on it. I reach up to hug him and scurry to catch up with the girls.

Sherry leads the pack to a back entrance where she mentions Zane's name and we're swiftly let in. As we enter the club, the music pounds in the dimly lit room, lights dance to the thumping beat, and a sea of bodies undulate. The bar is massive, extending almost the full length of the room, and topped with white marble. Tan leather booths that line the walls surrounding the dance floor spill over with scantily-clad women and well-dressed men. Each sleek black coffee table in front of the booths holds bottles upon bottles of champagne. I think I even recognize a few celebrities. *I am* definitely *out of place.*

The girls saunter up to the corner of the crowded bar. Sherry catches the eye of a bartender who seems to know her and they stretch across the bar for a hug. They order drinks and shots while I gaze across the room, taking it in.

"Here." Grace hands me a glass. "I didn't think you'd want a shot so I got you a chocolate martini."

"Grace. Oh my gosh." I take the martini from her. "Okay, but I'm only having one." I may not be a drinker, but I do love a good chocolate martini when I have an occasional drink. I'm not driving and I'm not seeing Zane so I sip on the martini.

Toasts are cheered, drinks are downed, and the dancing begins. During dinner, I got to know a few of Sherry's friends. They're very nice, not at all like Bella and her friends. I have to admit I'm having fun. I finish my martini and let myself enjoy dancing. It's been ages since I've been out like this.

It's not long before Sherry grabs my arm and corrals all of us back to the bar. Another round of shots and drinks. Grace beams her smile at me as she hands me another chocolate martini. I don't feel the effects of the first one so I indulge and take the second.

"Are you sure you don't want to join us for one shot?" Her wicked smile makes me grin from ear-to-ear.

"*One*, Grace, *one*." It actually feels kind of good to let loose a little. Thank goodness I'm not seeing Zane tonight. Heaven only knows what kind of mess I'd get myself into.

I didn't think her smile could get any bigger, but it does. "What's your poison?"

"Jägermeister, please."

"Ooo, girl, nasty." She makes a cute tiger-roaring sound and orders my shot.

The group cheers already happened so Grace and I have our own little toast.

"Thank you for coming, Desiree. Cheers!" She clinks my shot glass.

"Thank you for inviting me. Cheers." I clink back.

We stand in a circle, talking and laughing until we finish our drinks.

Back out to the dance floor we shuffle and find a spot near the edge where we can all fit together. I'm feeling pretty tipsy by this point and allow my body to flow and bump to the pounding music. Out of nowhere, hands wrap tightly around my waist, pulling me into a dark corner. The hands abruptly spin me around.

Zane's lust-filled eyes burn unrelentingly into mine. *Shit! What's he doing here?* Heat races feverishly through my relinquishing body as he pulls me into him. The martinis and Jägermeister drive my action and I sensually grind against him. *Danger! Abort!* I don't think. I let the alcohol and the music drown out decision-making Head and let myself go. Our bodies entangle, hot and aflame with passion.

He slides his leg between my thighs. *Oh God. What's he doing?* His hands are on my hips, twisting me into his pelvis. I feel *everything* behind his jeans that I've only fantasized about. *I want this man so badly right now.* Two damned martinis and one stupid shot are all it takes and I've lost my ability to control myself. *Damnit, girl. But he feels so good.* His gyrating pelvis is ceaseless, making me even more intoxicated.

I can't think straight. I wrap my hands around his neck and dig my nails into his trap muscles. He backs me against a pillar, lifts my leg at the knee, and grinds himself into me in the darkness. My entire body explodes with tingles and I think I might faint. This man knows what he's doing, there's no doubt about that. *What's gotten into him? Why's he teasing me like this? Body: Who cares? Stop analyzing and enjoy his hot sexiness because you'll never be in a situation like this again.*

He releases my leg down. The music pounds our bodies together, seducing us as he seduces me. We're both starting to sweat.

He presses against me, his breath hot against my face as the strobe lights disorient me. *This is so hot.* He has me all worked up, I'm out of my mind. *Why did I have that damned shot?*

We pump against each other with my arms wrapped around his strong neck. His eyes drill into mine, our faces so close. *Oh my God, is he going to kiss me? Please kiss me.* My heart pounds in my chest and my breath heaves out of me.

"Stay here and don't move. I'll be right back," he says and walks away.

I take a few deeps breaths, trying to clear my head. *I know what this is. It's infatuation, that's all. A hot guy is paying a little attention to me and it feels good. That's all this is, infatuation. I've got to sober up and collect myself. I can't be tipsy around him. I'll say something or do something stupid. Tipsy? Shoot, I think I'm bordering drunk. Damnit. Get it together.*

Zane

I don't know how, but this woman manages to be adorable and beautiful and hot as hell all at the same time. *Holy shit, I'm craving her.* But not tonight. Tonight, I need answers.

I duck my head down, hoping not to be noticed, and find Grace.

"Hey," I shout so she can hear me over the music. "What did you do to her? I know that's not her top she's wearing."

"I got it for her," she shouts back. "And I did her eyes up a little. Doesn't she look pretty?"

"She's sexy as hell. I just know she doesn't usually dress like that. You know she doesn't drink, right?"

"I only gave her two martinis. She took them willingly. Oh, and a shot. She's just a little tipsy." A devilish smile spreads across her face.

"Two? And a *shot*? Grace," I scold.

"She's okay."

"Thanks for texting me. I'm going to take her home." I turn to leave.

"Hey," she says and I flip back around. "Take care of her."

"I will."

"Oh, and alcohol is her truth-serum." She winks at me. "Have fun."

Interesting.

I weave through the crowd looking for her and see her dancing by herself right where I left her. I can't take my freaking eyes off her. *Damn, she knows how to move her body.* Her hips pump and wave, gliding up and down and from side to side. *The sweet, sexy image of her moving on top of me overtakes my brain.*

"It *is* Zane Elkton!" a high-pitched squeal erupts next to me, hammering down the rise in my pants.

I'm surrounded by five drunk women who start groping my chest, touching my hair, and asking me to sign their body parts.

"I'm sorry, ladies. Not right now," I say, trying to push through them.

Desiree is watching and slinks back into the darkness.

Finally, I break free from the women and quicken my pace to her. I grab her hand, pulling her behind me, and head toward the back entrance.

"Wait." She releases my hand and hurries over to a woman in a black dress and high heels who came out of the bathroom. Toilet paper is stuck to her shoe. Desiree sneaks behind her and puts her foot on the toilet paper that releases from the woman's shoe and is now stuck on hers. She shakes her foot a couple times and the toilet paper falls to the ground. The woman slinks over to a man in a suit who puts his arm around her. She kisses him on the cheek, oblivious that Desiree just saved her from a little embarrassment. *This woman has a heart of gold.*

She quickly returns to me and slips her hand back into mine. "Okay, go." She smiles. We hurry through the door to the back ally where Bill is waiting for us, holding the limousine door open.

She wraps her arms around Bill. "I told you I'd probably go home early." She smiles at him and climbs in.

I quickly get in behind her and Bill is back in the driver's seat in a flash, taking off.

"You belong to them," she states bluntly.

"Who?"

"Women, your fans, the world. You belong to them." Her frankness smacks me in the face again.

"Only a part of me does." I know this piece of my life makes her uneasy.

"I have no idea how you keep your cool and manage it with such politeness and ease."

"I work hard at it and it's not always easy."

"I'd never want to deal with all that."

This conversation will only lead somewhere I don't want to go so I change the subject. "Looks like you had quite a night."

"I did actually. I wasn't expecting to have fun. I haven't been dancing in years. Back home I rarely see my friends and I'm usually by myself working. Your cousins and their friends are all really great."

"You look nice." *Smokin' freaking hot.*

She looks down at her top. "Oh, this was Grace." She gasps and smacks her chest with her hand. "I didn't say goodbye to her or the other girls."

"It's okay." I put my hand on her thigh. *Damn, every muscle on this woman is tight.* "I found her and told her I was taking you home."

"Oh, thank you for doing that. I don't want them to think I skipped out." She looks at me with her lustrous eyes. "Hey, do you have Pop-Tarts and hot cocoa?" she asks as she takes off her shoes.

"Pop-Tarts and hot cocoa?"

"Yeah. When I was your age, maybe younger, definitely younger, and I'd go out with my friends drinking and dancing, we'd always have Pop-Tarts and hot cocoa when we got home to prevent a hangover." A silly grin forms on her face. "I'm not drunk, but, wooow." Her eyes widen. "I'm definitely a little tipsy. It's not good for me to drink."

"I'll make sure we have some. Any particular flavor?"

"Um, frosted strawberry Pop-Tarts and Godiva hot cocoa if you have it. Mmm."

I chuckle at how unguarded she is.

When Bill drops us off, I send him back out for Pop-Tarts and hot cocoa.

She's tiptoeing across the driveway in her bare feet and I run in front of her, kneeling down and putting my arms out to my sides. "Get on."

"Piggy-back!" She giggles and climbs onto my back, holding her shoes and miniature purse at my chest.

I carry her into the kitchen and put her down, making sure she's steady before I let go.

"I'll be right back. I have to tinkle." She puts her shoes on the ground, her purse on the kitchen island, and runs off down the hallway.

I have to kiss her. I can't not kiss her. I'm dying to taste her sweet lips. Just a kiss though.

When she gets back to the kitchen, she plants herself against the wall and leans her hip against the countertop.

While she was in the bathroom, I poured room temperature water for her and cold water for myself, which I should've dumped on my crotch. "Let's get some water in you." I bring the glass over to her and put my hand on the wall next to her shoulder, trapping her between my arm and the countertop.

She swills a large gulp of water.

I lean in, putting my face close to hers and locking my eyes onto my sexy little vixen's eyes. "Are you attracted to me?" *Because I'm insanely attracted to you and I want to make love to you this instant... but I'm only going to kiss you.*

She squirms. "What?"

"You can only answer either yes or no."

"I — I can't ans —" She breathes, seducing me with her faintly audible words and I clench my teeth.

I quickly place my finger on her lips and shake my head. "Only yes or no. Are you attracted to me?" I fix my eyes on hers.

Another breath as her chest visibly raises and lowers. "Well, yes, but —"

There's a stiffness in my pants.

I lean in closer, cutting her off. "Have you thought about me kissing you?" *I know you have, but I want to hear you say it.*

Silence hangs painfully in the air. She peers over my arm and bites the left side of her succulent lower lip as though trying to plan an escape. With my free hand, I gently curl my index finger under her chin, drawing her face back to mine.

Her lips are slightly open. The shine of unmistakable desire in her eyes answers me. And the stiffness springs to full attention in my jeans. She breathes and swallows.

"Yes," she purrs, her voice barely a whisper. *I have to taste her.*

I lower my forearm to touch the wall, our noses only inches apart. I hear her soft breathing quicken. Desire rages through me as my own breath speeds up.

"If I kissed you," I pause. "Right now, would you be mad at me?" I don't think I can wait any longer to kiss this gorgeous woman who doesn't even know how unforgivingly sexy she is.

Her sultry eyes flit from side to side as she pants ever so slightly. My jeans are now uncomfortably tight.

My phone rings, abruptly breaking the hot tension. *Shit.* Bill's back with Pop-Tarts and Godiva hot cocoa, as requested.

I get the bag from him and relieve him for the evening. He also picked up miniature marshmallows and a small bundle of vintage-pink roses in a vase. The guy is a true gentleman with a big ol' romantic heart.

She's on the sofa, remote in hand, trying to turn on the TV with no success. I microwave a mug of almond milk for her cocoa and set the roses on the island.

"Do you want your Pop-Tarts heated?"

She jumps up from the sofa and joins me in the kitchen. "Ooo, yes, please." Noticing the flowers, she sticks her nose in one of them and inhales. "They're beautiful." She's the cutest, sexiest woman I've ever seen.

"Do you know what you're doing over there?" I ask, putting the Pop-Tarts in the toaster.

"No clue. There are too many remotes. You men love your gadgets." She shakes her head.

"I was surprised to hear you had a few drinks tonight."

"I really shouldn't have. That Grace and her cute smile; she can talk anyone into anything. I told you, I don't like to not be in control of myself. And," she pauses. "I admit to things I shouldn't admit to." She looks me squarely in the eyes, a hint of indiscretion sits in her radiant green eyes. "If I knew I was going to see you, I wouldn't have had anything."

"Why's that?"

"It's hard enough to think straight around you when I'm sober." Her face immediately cringes as though she just heard the words come out of her mouth.

The toaster dings. I turn off the kitchen lights and we bring her Pop-Tarts and hot cocoa to the living room where I set them down on the glass coffee table that spans the length of the black leather sofa. Leaving the lights off, I turn on the fireplace and TV that hangs above the fireplace, lowering the volume.

"Desiree, why do you resist me so much?" I've felt her pull back from me again and again since the day we met and I want to know why. This may be my only chance to get unfiltered answers out of her with her guard down.

"Zane, I'm forty-three years old. I'm not some Hollywood starlet who belongs by your side. Your life is filled with fame and movies and traveling and women and adventure and drugs and drinking and…and…my life is simple and boring and just very, *very* different than yours. I came out here to start a new life." She puts down her Pop-Tart and gazes at the fire. "A new life for *me*. No men. I'm done. I'm just done." The words fall, unbridled, out of her mouth.

"What do you mean, you're done? You keep saying that."

"You asked me about love the other night."

"I did." I confirm, wondering where she's going.

"The thing is, I think I'm — broken somehow."

"Broken?" The view she has of herself pains me.

"Broken. Not meant to have love. Every relationship I've had has failed. I make terrible choices when it comes to men and I lose myself. I'm always too much of this or not enough of that. My boobs are too small, I'm not sexy, my butt is too big, I'm too smart, I'm boring because I don't drink, I'm too healthy, blah, blah, blah. And because I'm such a pleaser, I turn myself into who they want me to be or who I think they want me to be instead of just being myself. I guess, because I know if I'm just me — no one will love me."

Damn. She must've dated a bunch of raving assholes who treated her like shit. She's absolutely incredible and she doesn't even see it.

She clasps both of her hands around the warm mug of sweet, steaming cocoa. "I can't be in a relationship again." Her gaze remains on the fire. "I don't want to. It's not worth it." She puts her mug on the coffee table and takes a deep breath. A sheen veils her eyes. "You put your whole heart into it. You invest yourself, you know? And you trust. And...and you take things at face value. And then, what you were told was a way to cope turns out to be a habit, a preference, an addiction — a way of life.

"Drunk every night and all weekend long. And you put up with it and put up with it because you have a good life." Her words tumble out. "Then you're all alone in this relationship and you're empty and lonely and you're five years in and you love him, but you're so alone. And then," tears well in her eyes. "One night he... he flies out of a parking lot and...and..." The tears flow as she quivers, sucking air in rapidly. "And lands in a field and...and *dies*." Whimpered cries spill out of her. "And you wonder why you're even here. He has *kids*. And I tried." She cries. "I *tried* to stop him. I..." She gasps for air then whispers, "I didn't try hard enough." Her body hunches. She's trembling and sobbing.

A sadness digs deep into my flesh. I wish I could ease her pain. I move close to her and put my arms around her, letting her sob into my chest. My heart aches with intense pain for her.

Once her convulsive crying tempers, her tear-soaked eyes meet mine. Mascara smears down her face. "Oh my gosh. I'm so sorry. I...I don't know where that came from," her voice is shaky. She pushes her body away from mine and wipes her fingers under her eyes.

"It sounds like maybe you needed to release some of that."

"But not here, not *now*, not with *you*," sadness colors her words.

"Desiree, it's okay. I want to know this. I want to know *you*."

"This is so embarrassing. Do you have a washcloth?"

I clench my teeth. In an instant, she's pulled back again, erecting her guard like an iron wall.

"Yeah, there's one in the closet in the bathroom."

She excuses herself and goes to the bathroom. When she comes back, she looks more like herself. She's washed off the eyeshadow and lipstick and cleaned the mascara off her face. Even after crying, this woman is naturally radiant. She sits back down and sips her cocoa.

"Desiree, I'm so sorry for what happened. I don't think you should feel guilty. It sounds like you did everything you could."

"If I did, he wouldn't be dead and his kids would have their father."

"You don't know that. Something would probably have happened eventually. You're owning guilt that's not yours to own."

"Maybe." She pauses. "I told you, nothing good ever comes from drinking."

"Did he drink a lot when you first met? I don't mean to pry, it just seems odd that you'd be with a guy who drinks a lot when you don't." My entire torso hardens as I recall her saying she'll never again date someone who drinks.

"That's the thing, he didn't when we first met. He'd have a few beers from time to time and, because I'm kind of sensitive about the whole drinking thing, I asked him about it. He told me it was how he dealt with his ex-wife, but that he wasn't a big drinker. And I foolishly believed him. When we moved in together, 'from time to time' became more frequent. As time went on, his drinking got progressively worse and became a daily habit. It got to the point that every night after work and all weekend he'd be out in his garage getting drunk.

"We never spent time together. We never went out and did fun things together. I was in the house, working, cleaning, and picking up after him and he was out in the garage drinking. After a while, I got used to the loneliness. The part that hurt the most was that he deceived me. He loved drinking, it was his favorite hobby. Once I finally figured that out, I knew, if he had to choose between me and alcohol, he'd pick alcohol."

Nerves launch inside my chest.

We sit quietly, watching the flames.

"Heh." She heaves a breath. "And after he died, I found out he was having an affair for the last six months. Left her two hundred and fifty thousand dollars too." She shakes her head. "So typical." Her cynical tongue stings me.

"Not all guys cheat, you know," I retort quietly.

"The ones I pick do. Every…single…one." *Damn, she's been hurt, badly.* My stomach churns and a bone-deep loathing of every guy who's ever hurt this incredible woman fills me. She stares silently into the flickering flames and then her eyes meet mine, I see so much pain and vulnerability in them. She turns her body toward me, lifting her leg onto the sofa and curling it under her. "Zane, in a few weeks I'll be gone and we'll both move on with our lives. This has been a blip in time that we'll soon forget. Nothing more can come of…" She gestures her hand between us. "…whatever this is."

"I disagree with you. And, for the record, I don't care how old you are."

"Zane, we're from different worlds. I don't belong in your world." Sorrow etches her eyes.

"Says you and some preconceived fear." I escalate quickly to frustration. She's maddening.

"It's not a fear. I couldn't handle what you have to deal with on a daily basis. People taking your picture everywhere you go, not having any privacy, your every move splashed around on the internet." She pauses. "And, to be brutally honest, I would *not* deal well with you being — intimate with other women." Her eyes evade mine.

I reach over and gently take her chin in my hand, swiveling her face to mine. "That's just work."

"To you." Her soft voice sounds wounded.

God, I don't want to cause this woman any more pain.

"Can you please let this go?"

I now have a much better understanding of what she's been through and why she continues to push me away. But I'm not willing to let her walk out of my life. I'm falling for her…hard. I'm going to be patient. I'll wait until she's ready. I'll wait forever. She's worth it.

"No," I say firmly, and hesitantly change the subject. "Desiree, I have to tell you something. And right now, I'm not sure if you're going to be happy or angry with me."

"What is it?" One eyebrow furrows as she stares at me.

"I bought your house."

She draws back her head as she peers at me through narrowed eyes. "You what?"

"I bought your farmhouse."

"I don't understand. What do mean you bought my farmhouse?"

"I mean I bought it — for you. You said how much you love it and I want you to still have it. It can be an investment. We can turn it into an Airbnb and go there whenever we want."

She stands up, her eyes darting back and forth. "This…this is crazy. You're crazy. You can't just go buying people's houses. I mean, *you* can, but…" She holds the sides of her face with her hands. "…this is *nuts*. Airbnb? I don't know anything about running an

Airbnb. And what do you mean *we* can go there whenever we want? We're not — " She starts pacing and breathes in deeply, blowing it out. "I, I don't even know what to think right now."

I can't tell if she's pissed or pleased, but I'm thinking she's pissed. "I thought it would make you happy. I know how much you love it and this makes your move here a lot easier and you don't have to get rid of things you like."

She stops pacing and stares at me, eyes piercing through me. "I know, but Zane. This doesn't make any sense." She taps her temples with her fingers. "I don't know what to say. It's not that I'm not happy. I just — I'm a little dumbfounded."

"We'll figure it out. It'll be okay, I promise." I may have made a huge mistake on this one.

Letting out a huff, she sits back down. "Do you *always* get what you want?" She squints at me.

"No." That's a lie. "Usually, but not always. Okay, most of the time. Pretty much, yes."

"This discussion isn't over, but I'm *not* up for it right now."

I need to cease the tension. "How about a movie?"

She inhales deeply and breathes. "Yes. Your pick tonight. Can we stay by the fire?"

"Sure."

I choose *Jumanji: Welcome to the Jungle*, hoping the humor in it makes her laugh and eases the emotional night she's had. About an hour in, I pause the movie.

"Snack time," I announce. "More Pop-Tarts? Water?"

"No, thanks. I'm full. I'll have more water though."

I grab two waters from the kitchen.

She has one of the remote controls in her hand and is pressing buttons.

"You don't know what you're doing with that." I sit back down and take the remote from her.

"I can figure it out." She reaches for the remote.

I tease her and hold it across my body, out of her reach.

Stretching her tight, slender body across me, she's laughing and trying to get it from me. In one swift movement, I encircle her waist with my arm and lay her down beneath me on the sofa, my body hovering above her. I pin her arm over her head.

"Zane, please." Her breathy words are pleading.

My skin prickles with desire. "Please, Desiree." Years of falling in love with her in my dreams, weeks of falling in love with her in real life, and days of pent-up lust pulse through me.

Her breathing quickens. I look into her eyes and see so much longing in them. Lowering my body, I capture her mouth with mine; desire, craving, passion all combust the second our lips touch. I sweep my tongue in and out of her moist mouth, deepening my reach with each sweep. My mind goes hazy. I'm hungry for her. She pushes against my chest with her free hand. I'll stop if she wants me to. *Jesus, I don't want to stop.* Then I feel her hand on my back, pulling me toward her, her mouth eager, reaching for mine.

I'm on fire in seconds; my lust unleashed.

Each muted whimper at the probe of my tongue into her mouth fuels my passion. I want to hear every whimper, every gasp, every moan. My body hums with anticipation. I wrap my arm tighter around her waist, drawing her pelvis to mine, gently thrusting against her. She lifts to meet me, sealing our bodies together. Releasing my grip, I move my hand under her top and fold it around the warm, bare skin of her tiny waist. She's panting.

I press my thumb gently into the tender skin just inside her hip bone, she quietly gasps; *a sensitive spot.* My fingers extend halfway across her lower back. She arches, pushing into me again. Then she hooks her hand around the back of my neck, clutching me tightly as I sweep my tongue into her mouth. This is far beyond anything in my dreams. A hushed whimper releases from her and I swallow the sound. "Jesus." I heave a breath. Her whimpers become more audible, driving me wild.

"Hey, you guys up?" Declan's voice jolts our bodies apart.

"Are they here?" Jasmine asks.

We sit up quickly, startled. They don't come around the corner so don't see us.

"Hey, yeah, we're here," I answer, my heart beating wildly as I try to slow my breathing.

"Bro, we're gonna crash in the spare bedroom, okay?" Declan declares.

"Yeah, yup, it's all yours," I call out, looking over at Desiree.

They disappear down the hall.

"What time is it?" she asks, trying to catch her breath.

"Almost two-thirty."

"I think we should get some sleep."

I'm definitely *not* ready to go to sleep, but comply. I need her to know I'll do as she asks, even in the frenzy of passion. "You take my bed and I'll sleep out here."

I bring her to my bedroom, lift her into my arms and kiss her…deeply. She kisses me back with raw desire and I'm lit up again — everywhere. My body is swimming in hunger. Sweet whimpers provoke me and I desperately want to make love to her. *Now isn't the right time.*

I put her back down, find her a pair of sweatpants and a T-shirt, and kiss her lightly on the forehead. "Sweet dreams."

"Good night," she whispers.

Desiree

I lay awake in his bed — Zane Elkton's bed — wearing his clothes — again. My tipsiness has worn off and a cluster of emotions war inside me. Head says, "Don't let him in." But my rebellious Heart is allowing him to sneak in. And my Body, *holy crap*. So many naughty sensations descend upon me, like I've never felt before.

He's kind and thoughtful and attentive. He makes me feel important. He's encouraging and believes in me, something I'm not used to. I've misjudged him time and time again based on my own bad experiences and preconceived notions about celebrities. He's shown me nothing but kindness and treated me like a queen. And my attraction to him is exploding into unbridled craving. I replay his unrelenting kiss over and over in my head, tormenting myself. I know I shouldn't, but I want more of him.

I'm powerless to my intensifying desire for him, everything about him...well, almost everything.

Finally, fatigue forces me to sleep.

Zane

My nightly insomnia and vibrant, passion-induced thoughts of her keep me restless. I lay on the sofa recalling various conversations we've had and moments we've shared, both tender and scorching hot. I'm overcome by how she embodies so much of what I want in a woman. She's intelligent, driven, kind, loving, ambitious, classy, sophisticated, beautiful, passionate, open to adventure, and freaking sexy as hell. I love how she challenges me and inspires me. I have to keep this woman in my life. I have to make her mine.

I swallow tightly. A leaden weight settles deep in my stomach and my chest aches. I have to tell her. I have to tell her about my dreams. I know she doesn't need to know, but it feels like I'm keeping a secret from her and I don't want to keep secrets from her. But I can never tell her that I know *her* secret.

And I have to get back to my AA meetings and my regular calls with Jason, he always got me through tough times. He'll be disappointed to know I've been drinking again. She's right and I do know better. I'm disappointed in myself. *This fucking disease.*

A few hours pass while I wrestle for sleep. I can't stop fantasizing about her and I'm not comfortable on the sofa. *I can do this.* I go to my bedroom and turn on the fireplace so I can see without turning on the lights over the nightstands. Building a wall of pillows between us, I notice that the covers are down at her thighs. My T-shirt has risen above her waistline and the glow of the fire hugs her shape. I trace the silhouette of her body with my eyes.

She must've taken off my sweatpants during the night because I can see the thin black line of her G-string panties curve over her hip. My steel rod pushes against my underwear. God, I want to touch her. *Grandma's underwear. Grandma's fucking underwear! Who am I kidding? Even Grandma's underwear would look sexy on this woman. Ugh.*

I drink in her image, taunting myself with my desire for her.

~ 17 ~

Desiree

Sunshine fills the room, letting me know it's morning. I roll over, half asleep, and burrow in. Something doesn't seem right. I wearily blink my eyelids as I force them slowly open to focus. I'm lying on Zane and have nuzzled into his chest, my leg slung over his.

Last night happened. I wasn't drunk, but I was tipsy. *Why did he kiss me? I've never been kissed like that…ever. And I've never felt that kind of passion. Was it the martinis?* Why *did he kiss me? Oh this is* not *good, but it was sooo damn good.*

The sheets are all on his side, covering only a portion of his leg, his glorious body exposed. The sun warms me and I don't move. Maybe he didn't feel me and he's still sleeping.

I cautiously lift my head and peek up at him to see if he's asleep. His eyes are closed and his breathing is slow and rhythmic. I return my gaze downward, my eyes trace every magnificently sculpted muscle from his chest down to his rippling abs and…*oh, good morning to* you, *down there.* I want to run my tongue down his amazing body and taste his skin. *You're in dangerous territory, Desiree.*

I run my fingers delicately, deliberately across his mouthwatering, creamy skin; luxuriating in every savory stroke, knowing I shouldn't be, but unable to stop. *If I keep this up, he's going to wake up. Cut it out and quietly get out the bed.*

Zane

She rests on my chest. That faint scent of creamsicle drifts into my nose. I love the way she feels on me. I love the way she smells.

I remember the day I took my shirt off in front of her. I admit it was a tease, but I wanted to see her reaction. To see if there was any kind of physical interest on her end. Because I *know* there is on mine. I'm not gonna lie, I enjoyed catching her check me out. The pink that flushed her cheeks makes me think she was embarrassed, like she's never seen a guy as stacked as me. It was so damn cute. It turned me on. Now, she's touching me. After hearing her admit that she's attracted to me and that hot kiss last night, I'm going out of my mind.

I keep my eyes closed and focus on my breathing. Her stroke is subtle, sensual. Desire shoots through my body at her slightest touch. Keeping my breath steady is hard. The slowness of her pace as she touches me intensifies the sensations swarming me. Her secret indulgence is a freaking turn-on. Lust curls inside me like hot flames, torching my blood. I'm consumed by it, no longer able to focus on my breathing. "Mmm…"

Desiree

Oh God. Tactical error. Busted. He felt me touching him. He softly strokes my hair. I close my eyes and let him caress me for a few minutes, not wanting the moment to end. *But it has to.*

I slide my bare leg off his and lift my body off his chest, thirsting for him. Propping up on my elbow, I look down at him, let out a big sigh, and shake my head in disapproval.

"What? I built a pillow-wall," he says, playfully trying to defend himself. "You busted through it."

"This is why I don't drink." I'm exasperated with myself.

"Nothing happened, I promise." His tone becomes serious

and the look in his eyes shifts from playful to earnest. "That's not something I would do."

"What do you mean, nothing happened? You kissed me." *And I want you to kiss me again, right now.*

"Yeah, well there was that." He lifts himself to rest on his elbows and teases me with his provocative smile. "But that was all, I promise."

"Zane, I owe you an apology."

"You do? For what?"

"I know I've been making it hard for you to get to know me and that's largely due to the fact that I've been quietly misjudging you."

"After what you've told me, I guess I can understand why."

"No, that's not fair of me. You've been so good to me and so kind." I pause. "I'm sorry."

"Apology accepted." His smile is my forgiveness. "Are you hungry?" He gets out of bed and — *dear God.* His black boxer briefs fit snugly around *every*thing. The man's body is pure perfection. Every rippling muscle captures my attention. He's got all the right stuff in all the right places. He puts on a T-shirt and pair of gym shorts from his dresser. "I'll make breakfast." He leans down and kisses my forehead.

I lay there a moment, listening to the lulling hum of the fireplace, letting the sun bathe me, and trying to burn the vision of his hot, sexy body in my brain because I know I'll never see it again. I climb out of his bed and put on my jeans, leaving his T-shirt on.

As I approach the kitchen, I hear Declan talking. "So, did you give the 43-year-old her first orgasm?"

I freeze in the doorway to the kitchen. *What did I just hear?!* That's when they see me. Fury burns behind my eyes and I'm seething. Adrenaline swarms hot, pulsing through my veins and everything appears red and blurry through my eyes. My entire body tenses and my fingers curl into my hand, nails digging into my palms. Anger, rage, hurt, betrayal, and mistrust simultaneously smash into me like a tsunami.

Zane jumps up and I run to the bedroom, forgetting that my shoes and purse are in the kitchen. He chases after me, the thud of his footsteps down the hall echoing in my ears.

"Desiree, wait. It's not what you think."

"It's not what I think?! Then what is it Zane? Tell me exactly what it is!" I'm frantically looking for my shoes and purse. "Was Bella whispering sweet mortifying nothings in your ear while she was practically licking your chest?!" I stop and glare directly at him. "Was I some kind of...of...bet?"

"No, *no*! It's not like that."

"What else did she tell you?" I continue stomping around his bedroom, scanning for my shoes and purse.

"Nothing." He pauses briefly. "I mean, she told me about your boyfriend and the crash."

"What?!" Deception bites me, slashing at my heart. "So, this whole time, before I even told you, you *knew*? Is this some kind of sick joke you people play? Was I supposed to be another notch in your belt? Let's see if Zane can bang the 43-year-old whose boyfriend just died?" Words are spewing out of me.

I stop moving and shove my hands through my hair, holding my head. "I can't believe I let this happen. I'm so stupid. I can't believe I let you in." I pause, anguish engulfing me. Hot tears threaten to spill out of my eyes. "The things I told. I *trusted* you." My voice catches in my throat. "I'm such an idiot." I storm out of the bedroom toward the kitchen.

"Desiree." He follows me. "Please wait. Let me explain."

"Explain what?! There's no explaining this, Zane."

"Please, let me take you back to your house and we can talk about this."

I see my shoes and purse and grab them. "I'll get an Uber. Just *please*, leave me alone."

Declan tries to block me. "Desiree, I'm sorry. I didn't know you were still here."

"And if I wasn't, *that* would've made it okay?!" I glare at him.

"You can tell whoever bet that he would, that he *didn't.*"

I storm out of the house. The sun usually soothes me, but with the rage boiling inside me right now, the heat is oppressive, suffocating me, burning under my bare feet that are propelling me agitatedly forward. My brain is going a hundred miles an hour trying to figure out what just happened. A few minutes later, as I'm pounding down the sidewalk and trying to hold back my tears, Bill pulls up beside me. *Of course he sent Bill to get me.*

He rolls down the window. "Desiree, let me take you home," his tenderness coaxes me.

Emotionally drained, I don't say a word and get into the passenger seat, letting tears flow out of me.

Zane

Declan's face drops. "Dude, I'm so sorry." Standing at the kitchen island in his boxers, he puts his hands on the sides of his head and sighs. "Shit. What can I do?"

"You've done enough, dickhead." Anger thickens my voice. "I should've known that somehow, some way, this would come out. Why would you even say that? Whether she was here or not." I throw my arms up in question.

"I…I wasn't thinking." He rubs his fingers over his mouth.

"No, you weren't. You're the *only* person I told and now she thinks I'm running around telling people and making bets. Fuck." My accidental betrayal is exposed and I can't take it back. She was never supposed to know I knew her secret. "This is so bad." I thrust my fingers into my hair. "How am I going to fix this?"

I know I need to give her space and I need time to figure out what I'm going to do. *Can I even fix this? I can't lose her.*

That night, desperate to talk to her and fix things, I text her.

Me: Can I please see you?

She doesn't respond.

I toss and turn all night in bed; the bed where I want to fall asleep next to her every night and wake up with her snuggled on my chest every morning. When I do sleep, visions of her monopolize my dreams.

The next morning, I call Grace. I know she and Desiree have become friends and I hope she can help me figure out what to do. We set plans to meet up that afternoon at her house.

I call Desiree and leave a message. "Hey, it's me. I know you don't want to talk to me right now and I get it. But I really wish you would. I have to explain all this to you, but I…I don't want to do it on your voice mail. Please call me back."

I pull up at Grace's and text Desiree.

Me: I know you're mad at me. I really screwed up. Please give me a chance to explain.

Come on, answer me. As I suspect, she doesn't respond.

I go inside and plop myself on a stool at Grace's white granite-topped kitchen island. She hugs me and sits on the stool next to me. Grabbing a lemon from the brightly-painted porcelain fruit bowl, I toss it around in my hands and tell her everything that happened.

"What should I do? She won't return my calls. She won't answer my text messages. I have to explain things to her. Not that the truth is *good*, but it's better than what she thinks happened. How do I get her to talk to me?" My level of frustration is soaring and I'm desperate. "Grace, I can't lose her."

She grabs the lemon from my tossing hands. "Zane, what is it about her? Don't get me wrong, I adore her. But I want to know from *you*," she says with the lemon in her fist, pointing a finger at me. "What's going on between the two of you?" She tosses the lemon back to me and grabs two water bottles from the fridge, placing one in front of me.

"What is it about her?" I ponder, tossing the lemon between my hands again, then sigh and stop tossing. "Jeez, so many things. Everything. She's the personification of everything I've ever wanted in a woman. And things I didn't even know I wanted. If I could custom-build a woman from her intelligence to her drive to her sense of humor and how playful she is and the things we have in common. She challenges me in ways I've never been challenged… by anyone. She's sweet and kind and she doesn't want me for my fame or my money. And physically, *Jesus*. And we haven't even had sex. She's it. Everything she does, everything she says makes me want her in a deeper way. I want to give my whole heart to her."

"Are you in love with her?" Boom. Grace goes for the jugular.

A blaze of adrenaline shoots through me as she says the word — *love*. I don't answer. I take a deep breath, letting it fill me and drop my forehead to my hands. My chest aches, my heart stings, and my skin buzzes. I lift my head, lean back, and let my head hang back. Sitting forward, I heave a sigh. "Is that what this is? Is this what it feels like?" I ask because the answer eludes me. I've never felt so emotionally and physically connected to a woman, not even Veronica.

Grace cocks her head to the side and her eyes light up as her mouth curls into a smile. "It sure sounds like it."

"I can't be. It's only been a few weeks."

"Sometimes that's all it takes, when it's right."

Am I seriously in love with her? Holy shit. I'm in love with Desiree. "So, what the hell do I do?"

"Honestly?" She touches my hand and looks into my eyes. "I think you need to give her some time. She came here for a reason, to start a new life. You've been a curve-ball — a massive curve ball in her plans. And not that long after her world was turned upside down already. Let her focus on what she needs to do. Give her some space. You'll be with her at the wedding and maybe she'll be ready to listen then."

"The wedding? That's a week away." I don't want to wait that long. "She probably won't even come now."

"I'll make sure she comes," she says, caring and determined.

I leave Grace, feeling completely defeated. My heart is aching and a gloom spreads through me. In the following days, I do as Grace suggests and don't call or text Desiree. Being between projects is sheer torture. I have nothing to focus on but her, the beautiful woman from my dreams who now owns my heart. Days drone on and nights are endless. She occupies my thoughts during the day and possesses my dreams at night.

Now that I've spent time with her, my dreams are more vivid, rooted in my soul. Having tasted her lips and felt her body against mine, my desire for her is ceaseless.

A scotch sure would numb this damn misery. I haven't touched it since I got out of rehab, only beer and wine.

No, I won't go there. But, fuck, if anyone can break me, it'll be Desiree Capstone.

~ 18 ~

Desiree

I drive aimlessly along Pacific Coast Highway, trying to drive Zane from my thoughts. I'm furious with him. And I'm furious with myself for even allowing myself to be so recklessly vulnerable and develop feelings for him. I'm also angry with Bella and her blabbering. As far as I'm concerned, whatever little friendship we had is over.

My phone rings. *Please don't be him again.* I've been tormenting myself, listening to his voice mail over and over, his rueful voice tugging at my heart. Thankfully, it's Grace.

I pull off the road and answer. "Hi. What are you up to today?"

"Actually," she says cheerfully, lightening my mood. "I'm calling to see what *you're* up to. Can you meet up for lunch? I know it's last-minute."

"As it turns out, I'm just driving around. And I'm hungry. Where do you want to meet up?"

"There's a cute little place called Intelligencia. I'll text you the address."

"Sounds good. I'll head over now."

While Grace reminds me of Zane, I'm actually looking forward to seeing her and not being alone with my exhausting thoughts. I park my car and go into the café. She's already there, perusing the menu. We hug and place our orders at the counter, grab our food, and go out to the patio. The floor is tiled and huge potted plants are scattered around. Each quaint two-top and four-top is adorned with a dark green umbrella to keep patrons cool from the heat of the California sun. The brick walls bring a coziness to the space.

I can't help myself. "Did he put you up to this?" I ask, leading us to a table at the outer edge of the patio, hoping for some privacy.

"God, no. He'd have a fit if he knew I was with you." She follows behind me.

I find a tucked away table and we settle in across from each other.

"I take it he told you what happened?"

"A little. The details aren't my business. All I know is that he's devastated and wants to fix whatever happened."

"He can't fix it." I take a bite of my sandwich. "There's no fixing this, Grace. He lied to me."

"He did?" She jerks back her head and arches her eyebrows in disbelief.

"Well." I pause, thinking about my word choice. "He didn't lie, but he deceived me and kept things from me. And I think I was some kind of twisted joke or bet or something."

"Desiree, are you sure?" She tilts her head, putting her sandwich back on her plate. "That doesn't sound like Zane at all."

Confusion swarms me. "Well, no." I pause. "I guess I'm not sure. I'm not sure at all. None of this makes any sense. I don't know what to think. All I know is that he kept wanting to make plans with me and do things together. He's been so sweet, but I don't know why. And then he kissed me and I have no idea what that was about. Then Declan asks him if he gave me an…" I whisper, "… orgasm."

I shake my head. "Bella and her big mouth. She also told him about my boyfriend dying and God only knows what else. Why else would he spend time with me and get to know me and *kiss* me unless it was some kind of prank? I don't know what to make of any of it." My last sentence comes out flustered; my emotions are a mess.

"Desiree." Grace speaks tenderly but firmly. "In all your analyzing, did you ever consider that maybe he likes you and there's been a misunderstanding of some kind?"

I don't answer, but quietly process her words. "Well, no. That would be crazy. He's," I quickly scan around us to make sure no one is close. "Zane Elkton," I whisper his name, "for goodness sakes. Women across the world fantasize about him. He can have any woman he wants. Young women, beautiful women, women with, you know, perfect bodies like his."

"But that's the thing. You don't know him. That boy is a hopeless romantic. He believes in true love. Yeah, he's all buff and masculine and all that, but underneath, he's a softie." Compassion sits in her eyes. "That stuff doesn't matter to him. He only wants *you*." Her sincerity strikes me. "I've never ever seen him like this. Not even when he was with Veronica."

"Veronica?"

"His first love. Well, who knows if it was *love*. They were young and together for four years."

"Right." I remember seeing pictures of them together when I looked up Zane online. I read bits and pieces about their breakup, but you never know the real truth. "What happened?"

"I think she broke his heart. He never told us what really happened. I think it hurt too much. He didn't date anyone for a long time after her."

"Oh." Maybe he's not quite the gigolo I thought he was. I wonder what happened between them. "But, Grace, I'm no one."

She takes a sip of her soda and looks straight at me. "You're someone to *him*."

"I don't know. I mean put yourself in my shoes. Okay, not with your cousin, but you know what I mean. Would you really be okay with your boyfriend living his lifestyle? That's just a whole different world. I would have no idea how to even function in his world. Every move he makes is made public for the world to see. And watching him on massive screens being intimate with other women." I shake my head. "I couldn't handle that."

"But, when you set all that aside, he's really just a good guy with a big heart who wants a normal relationship with *you*. I think you should give him a chance. He might surprise you." She winks at me and picks up her sandwich, taking a huge bite.

"Even if I was willing to see if I could handle the famous part of him and his intimate work with other women, I absolutely will *not* get involved with another alcoholic. I can't do it. I've had too much of that toxic crap in my life and I won't do it again."

"I know it's a tough battle for him and it seems to go hand-in-hand with the celebrity lifestyle. He was really good for a long time after he got out of rehab. I think he slipped a little after a couple of roles he didn't get. He's really hard on himself."

"I'm sure you know that a little slip is just the top of the slide to a massive downfall with that disease," I say and take a bite of my sandwich.

She casts her eyes down and sighs. "Yeah, I know."

"You two seem pretty close. He has so much going for him. I'd hate to see him plummet and let it destroy him. Maybe you can encourage him to get back on track."

"You know what? You're right. And we *are* close. I should've talked to him about it when I first saw him have a drink after he got out of rehab." She pauses thoughtfully. "I can do something now and I will. Thanks for the nudge. You really care about him."

I nod, gripping tightly around my glass of water and take a swig. "I do. More than I should. And that scares me. I'm trying to restart my life and I don't want any distractions. I don't want to let myself get any closer to him."

"I get it." She reaches over and touches my hand. "It makes me sad, but I get it."

We're quiet for a moment. I enjoy the feeling of the gentle breeze against my face, pacifying me.

"You're still coming to the wedding tomorrow, right?" she asks.

I put down my sandwich and squeeze my eyes closed. I had forgotten about the wedding and now feel conflicted about whether or not to go.

"Desiree, please tell me you're still coming."

Shoot, I did make a commitment that I'd go and there is no emergency. "Yes. Yes, of course I'll be there. I think it's best I go by myself. Can you text me the address? I'll let Zane know I don't need him to pick me up."

She wipes her fingers on her napkin, gets her phone out of her purse, and texts me the address.

Brushing my fingers on my napkin, I grab my phone and text Zane.

Me: Hi. I'm with Grace and she gave me the address for the wedding tomorrow. There's no need for you to pick me up. I'll see you there.

Chocolate Bear: Are you sure? I want to pick you up. I want a chance to talk to you.

It's like I can feel the disappointment in his words even though I can't hear his voice and it's crushing me.

Me: I'm sure. It's for the best.

Chocolate Bear: Okay. I'll see you there then. I miss you.

Ugh. My heart sinks. *I miss you too. How am I going to get through this wedding with him?*

~ 19 ~

Desiree

Me: Hi. Do you have time to talk? I could use a friend.

Lisa: Absolutely! Does now work?

Me: Perfect.

Wearing his T-shirt, blankets cocooning me, I call her from my bed. Lisa always has a way of grounding me when I feel like I'm riding a spin top toy.

"Hi. What's going on?"

"Well, you wanted an update and, boy, do I have an update."

"Lay it on me."

I give her the highlights of dress shopping with Grace, the bachelorette party, and *after* the bachelorette party: my breakdown about Brad and the kiss with Zane. I also tell her about the whole orgasm debacle.

"So, obviously I caved. I didn't back out of the wedding and now I'm going with him tomorrow. Well, I'm meeting him there. At least I managed to get myself out of being trapped in a car alone with him. I'm like a big tumbleweed of crazy emotions, totally out of control and all I want is to be *in* control."

"That does happen sometimes."

Grabbing a pillow, I clutch it to my chest. "It's like on one hand, he's the most incredible man I've ever met and we're aligned in a lot of ways that are important to me. Then, there's this cloud of muck with his lifestyle, well really it's the making out with other women for his job part that's the hardest to swallow, and his drinking. And now this whole thing with me not having an orgasm from sex. And I'm so angry right now. He keeps calling me and texting me, wanting to explain. Honestly, I don't think there's anything he could say to explain this." I sigh. "What a mess."

"You weren't kidding when you said you had an update. Phew. You know with my psych background, I want to jump into the emotional stuff. But, I know right now, you want the voice of reason. So, here's what I've got for you, take it or leave, it's up to you."

"Okay." I prop my head on my pillow, ready for her words of wisdom.

"You've made it clear to the unemotional part of yourself that you want nothing to do with him. Then a bunch of wild things happened in the last few days and now you're committed to going to this wedding with him."

"Right."

"I think, and this is just my opinion, you owe it yourself to at least hear what he has to say about the orgasm thing. Up until that, he seemed like a pretty damn good guy. Okay, aside from the drinking. If you're determined to end your friendship, at least give it a chance to end with you not feeling like shit about whatever the misunderstanding is. Then you can walk away knowing what happened and not hating him."

I let her words sink in and blow out a loud exhale, clutching the pillow tighter then releasing my grip on it.

"Maybe you're right. I don't want to end things being angry with him. Okay, I'll give him that chance tomorrow."

"Good. I really think you'll feel better."

"Thank you, Lisa. I'm so grateful for your friendship."

"Anytime at all. We're always here for each other, always."

"Okay, I'm going to let you go and try to get a good night's sleep. I have a feeling tomorrow's going to be tough."

"Give yourself, and him, some grace. Good night."

"I will. Good night."

I know there's something between us, some kind of indomitable force that keeps pushing me toward him. Could I ever get past the part of his job that has him naked with other women? If I could, I still don't think I'd be able to get past his addiction.

With all the thoughts and questions going around in my head, I knew it would take a while to fall asleep. I have no idea what time my brain finally shut down.

Zane

Desiree walks into the church and heads turn. She is stunning. Although she's not one of Hollywood's elite, she certainly looks the part. I can't help but stare at her, appraising her beauty. She's the epitome of graceful glamour. I walk over and stand directly in front of her, taking both of her hands in mine.

Leaning in, I whisper, "You take my breath away."

She glances away, not saying a word.

"Desiree, please let me talk to you and explain things."

She returns her face to mine and releases my hands, "We'll talk. This isn't the time or place though." Her sullen green eyes shift down and back up to mine. "Let's get to our seats."

We walk closely, but don't touch.

During the ceremony, I put my arm around her; around her waist when we stand and around her shoulder when we're seated. She doesn't reject my grasp and I revel in being close to her again. Whether her anger is subsiding or she just doesn't want to appear rude, I don't know and I don't care. I just want to be close to her.

Once the vows are spoken and Sherry and Jim are pronounced husband and wife, the celebration begins. Guests exit their pews and make their way down the aisle to greet and congratulate the newly married couple. I put my hand on the small of her back, guiding her. When we reach the bride and groom, we hug and congratulate them, swiftly keeping the line moving.

Desiree starts walking away and I grab her hand, stepping in front of her.

"You're coming to the reception, right?" Even if I've screwed things up so badly that she never wants to see me again, I have to tell her the truth about everything. I owe her that.

Her eyes sparkle as she looks down at our hands laced together and then back into my eyes. "Yes, I'll be there. I have the address. I'll see you over there." Her angelic voice both soothes and arouses me.

I wish she would've let me pick her up so we could have private time together to talk, but I'm not going to push her. I arrive at the reception before her and wait anxiously.

The cocktail and hors d'oeuvre hour is almost over when I see her. Within seconds, we're being ushered to take our seats in the ballroom for the arrival of the bride and groom and bridal party. We find our table and clap and cheer as each couple is announced. Upon the entrance of Sherry and Jim, we stand and applaud as they make their way to the dance floor for their first dance as husband and wife.

Desiree dutifully watches them dance. I devotedly watch her, with a yearning in my heart.

Each impeccably orchestrated step of the evening is flawless. As cake plates are cleared, the music shifts to club-music and Grace runs over to us, pulling Desiree onto the dance floor. Three songs in, Nat King Cole's voice charms the room. Grandpa walks over to Desiree and holds out his hand. My heart melts.

Desiree

"I believe this is our song." A bright smile plays on Grandpa's lips and I can't resist him.

"I believe it is, Grandpa." I glide into his arms.

The sound of his humming comforts me, the way Zane's voice does when he sings in my ear. He draws back a bit and looks at me with soulful eyes. "I don't know what Zane did and it's none of my business, but I know he regrets it."

I squeeze his hand gently. "It's nothing for you to worry about." I know how much Zane confides in him and I admire their relationship. I'm sure he's spared him the intimate details.

"Did he finally tell you about his dreams?"

"His dreams?" My curiosity is whet. "What dreams?"

"Well, my dear girl," he starts, gingerly turning us as we dance. "It seems there's been a mysterious woman visiting my grandson in his dreams since he was about fifteen years old and the woman who keeps reappearing," he pauses, tilting his head slightly to the side, "is you."

"Me?" My cheeks fill with heat as my mind tries frantically to piece things together. Clarity and confusion fill me simultaneously. Knots wind in my stomach and my throat tightens as I swallow hard. *Zane Elkton has been dreaming about* me *for half his freaking life?* I'm not one to curse much, but *what the fuck*? This must be why he kept wanting to see me. I mean, if I dreamt about someone for that long and then met them, I'd be curious too. *But why didn't he tell me?*

"You," he confirms. "Now, here you are and I believe he's scared. But, it's none of my business." He smiles and continues rotating us.

I swallow the lump in my throat. "Thank you for telling me this, Grandpa. It doesn't change the fact that we're from two *very* different worlds. I don't belong in his world."

"It's not true, you know, all that rubbish in the tabloids and on the internet. My Zane is a good boy. He has a good heart. And he's been waiting — for you." The twinkle in his eyes touches my heart.

My eyes moisten as Zane catches my gaze from across the room. He's swiftly out of his seat and approaching us.

Zane

"Grandpa, may I cut in?" I ask politely, eager to have Desiree in my arms again.

Grandpa holds her hands in his, kisses her on the cheek, and gives me a pat on the back as he hands her to me.

I clutch her hand and wrap my arm around her waist. "I think Grandpa's smitten with you." I pull her close, tight, body to body. "You can't escape me now. You look beautiful," I whisper in her ear and feel a slight shudder through her body.

"I feel like people are watching us." She's stiff in my arms.

"They might be. I haven't brought a woman to a family function since Veronica."

"You haven't?"

"No."

"Oh." She pauses. "But you dated other women since her." I can almost see her curious mind churning.

"No one I was serious enough about to bring with me to something like a family wedding."

"Oh." Her tension seems to ease as she settles into my arms.

We dance in silence. I close my eyes and shut out the world.

"Grandpa told me."

I open my eyes. "Grandpa told you what?" I ask, speculating and a little concerned.

"About your dreams."

I separate our bodies to face her, my blood picking up speed as it courses through my veins.

"What do you mean, my dreams?" My nerves pique. I know there can only be very particular dreams Grandpa knows about and I'm scared she now knows about them before I got the chance to tell her.

"The dreams you've been having about me since you were fifteen." Thunk. My heart drops to my feet. *Oh, shit.*

We stop moving. Adrenaline zaps me and I lower my head. "Oh my God." I raise my head and look in her eyes. "I'm, um, I'm sorry. He —" I shake my head in disbelief. "He wasn't supposed to tell you anything about those."

"It's okay. I'm glad he did. It doesn't change anything, but I'm glad I know."

"Well, you don't very well meet someone and say, 'Oh, by the way, I've been dreaming about you for over half my life.' You know? It's kind of a creepy thing to say."

She chuckles and continues moving, basically taking over the lead of our dancing. "Yeah, well, that's true." Her voice dims again. "Knowing about them makes a few things make more sense. But what I don't understand is why you didn't tell me about them."

"I wanted to. I tried to. But the timing never felt right. And I was afraid if I told you, it would scare you away. There isn't really a good time to tell someone something like that. And," I sigh. "All I wanted to do was find a way to keep you in my life."

The song ends and she stands still in my arms, looking into my eyes. I don't want to release her. I want to kiss her and erase the last few days. Thumping music invades the moment.

"Can we please talk. I need you to know what happened the other day."

"Not here." She walks at a leaden pace out to the veranda and I follow her.

She nestles into a nook away from others on the stately veranda that overlooks lush green grass, extending as far as the eye can see. Crossing her arms, she holds onto them with her hands. With the night air cooling, I know she's cold.

"Here," I say, taking off my tuxedo jacket and handing it to her.

"Thank you." She takes it from me, puts it over her shoulders, and leans against the ornate railing that's draped with flowers, dusting romance through the outdoors. "It's beautiful here."

The sun is setting, its glow casting a radiant fuchsia on the underbelly of the wispy clouds. As the clouds link and stretch across the horizon, the fuchsia subdues to a cotton-candy pink, softening the sky.

Being unsure of her temperament, I stand close to her, but don't touch her. She faces me, waiting patiently for answers.

"Please know I never meant to hurt you or deceive you. I..." I shake my head, "I don't even know how it all got so messed up.

All I know is that I had these dreams about you for most of my life and, out of nowhere, you were here and I just…I didn't have a clue what to do. I was freaked out. Then I *accidentally* overheard your conversation in the gym with Bella that first day we met. One of the microphones from my show was still turned on and I didn't know it until I was back in Johnny's office and we heard you talking.

"Hearing what you said and knowing that *very* private thing *really* made things messed up. There was no bet." I shake my head. "I would never do anything like that, Desiree, I promise you. Declan isn't just my little brother, he's my best friend and I told him because I was trying to figure out what to do. There you were, standing in front of me and not in my dreams. I kind of became obsessed and knew I needed to figure out how to be with you and keep you in my life. And then everything got so out of control and…and…I think I lost you. Did I lose you? Please tell me I didn't lose you." My words are flying out of my mouth.

"Zane," her voice wobbles like she's on the cusp of tears. "We'll always be friends, I hope. I want to stay friends."

That one word…friends…sucks up all the oxygen around us. A heaviness descends on me.

"Friends?" A vice-like grip squeezes my heart.

"Zane…" She inhales deeply as a tear releases, tracing down her cheek.

"I don't want to be just friends with you. I want more. I want you, all of you. I want you in my life. I want to be with you. I want to go through the rest of my life with you by my side." I point to my chest. "*I* want to be the one you take on the world with."

She turns her face toward the setting sun and I see her fighting to compose herself as she wipes away the tear with her delicate fingers.

"You don't even know me." Returning her gaze to me, she's almost whispering. "What if I don't live up to your dreams, your fantasies? What if you can't handle my quirks you don't even know about yet? What happens when you *do* fall in love with your next leading lady and shatter my heart. I couldn't handle that." Another tear escapes.

"But, the reality, *you*, are *so* much more than my dreams. And I'm not *that guy* who gets all caught with his leading ladies. Okay, I dated one once, but I was a kid. I'm extremely professional about my work."

"You can't control who you fall in love with," she says, sadness penetrates her words.

I step in closer, holding her gaze hostage. "I know that." I lift my hand to cradle her face and circle her waist with my arm, drawing her in and kissing her deeply, and she lets me.

We part our lips. "Please, can you forgive me? I'm so sorry for how all this happened."

She gently pushes away from me. "Zane, you didn't just break my trust, you broke my heart." In that moment, I know she's fallen for me.

I know that kind of hurt. It's the kind that feels like your heart just exploded into a million pieces and you'll never be able to put it back together again. It's the kind of pain I suffered when Veronica broke my heart. Heaviness fills every corner of my body, weighing me down.

"But it's not really your fault. I should've known better. I should never have let my guard down. That's on me." She pauses. "And I told you, I'll never be with someone who drinks. This could never work between us." Whomp. Her words punctuate my fear: my drinking, my addiction, is a deal-breaker. "I can't do this. I just can't. I'm sorry, Zane. I have to go." She steps away from me.

"Desiree, wait." I quickly reach for her arm and pull her back. I'm losing her. *Don't say it. Shove the words back down. They'll reveal too much and you might lose her forever.* But my irrational heart blurts out the words. "I know this sounds crazy, but I think I'm falling in love with you."

Tears fill her eyes. "Please don't say that." She backs away from me. "I have to go, Zane. I'm sorry."

Right then, I know I've lost her...and dread floods me with an intensity that matches the love I feel for her.

~ 20 ~

Desiree

Still in my dress with his suit jacket on, I lay on my bed, curl up in the duvet, and let the tears flow. Images of Zane's face saturate my mind as his words play over and over. *He's falling in love with me?* I wrestle inside myself. *That's not possible. He can't be. Okay, check-in.* Head: This is for the best. You have no business being with him. The fame, the love scenes, the drinking, no. He'll forget about all of this in a few weeks and you'll forget about him. *Yes, logical.* Body: Girl, you are so damn hot for this man. *Pipe down!* Heart: You're falling for him. *Ugh. I'm so foolish. Why does this hurt so much?*

I pull the duvet tighter around me and sob until I fall asleep.

In the darkness, I push open my swollen, crusty eyes, toss the duvet aside, and find my phone. 2:12 lights on the screen. I groan. No message from him. *Good. Is it?* Rarely ever going to bed without brushing my teeth and washing my face, I simply don't care. I unzip my dress, climb out of it, and lay it on the chair. Still haunted by him, I put on his T-shirt and crawl under the covers.

Daylight ruthlessly wakes me and I sluggishly get out of bed, thankful it's Sunday and I don't have any house tours scheduled with Jerry. I walk past the bureau and catch my sallow reflection in the mirror. Stopping, I turn to get a better glimpse. I look as haggard as I feel. Tidying my hair, I poke at the puffiness under my eyes and head to the bathroom to wash my weathered face.

I have to get him out of my head and focus on the things I need to get done while I'm still here. Moving my body always helps to clear my head so I drive to the beach to go for a long walk.

It's still early and the parking lot is sparsely-filled. Pulling into a spot, I grab the light sweatshirt I brought in case the breeze by the ocean is too cool for me to be comfortable. Getting out of my car, I wrap the sweatshirt around my waist and head toward the beach, my flipflops clapping my heels as I walk. When I reach the sand, I step out of my flipflops, carrying them in my hand, and let the sand seep between my toes. The tension in my shoulder blades softens.

As I walk toward the water, seagulls sing above me, floating on the salty air. I take a deep inhale as I walk, filling my lungs and feeling calm settle in. Reaching the water, I walk on the wet sand where the waves are crashing and spreading. Being at the water's edge, the wind strikes me and I unwrap my sweatshirt and put it on, wishing I'd thought to wear jeans instead of shorts.

My mind and heart return to Zane. His words echo relentlessly in my head, "I think I'm falling in love with you. I think I'm falling in love with you." Each time I recall the moment, my pulse races and hummingbird wings flit inside my chest. My mind is chaotic and jumbled. Muddled confusion plagues me as the same battle resumes, like a twister, churning inside me.

Ever since we met, I dream about him more often than not, bedeviled by vibrant memories tucked in my subconscious. I think about the time we've spent together, how thoughtful and kind and encouraging he is. I think of being with him, kissing him, listening to his stories, touching him. I'm overwhelmed by my feelings for him and how intense they are in such a short time. I've never felt such a powerful emotional connection or intense physical attraction for a man.

Then there's his lifestyle and his job; the fame, the lack of privacy, the grandiosity, the women…the sex scenes. And, even though he says he's never had sex with anyone he's not dating, maybe there's a temptress down the road who will break him. It's so strange and foreign to me. I really don't think I could ever get used to it. And the much bigger issue: his alcoholism. Whether I *am* falling in love with him or not, I just can't go there again.

There's no one around me on the beach now. I sit in the sand just above where the ocean is pulling the waves back home. The dark blue water rolls in, cresting as it nears the sand. With a soothing crash, they stretch their foamy bodies across the sand, making a hushed fizzy sound as they're dragged back into the ocean. I direct my gaze farther out to where the sun glints on the peaks of the dancing water. To my right, there's a long stretch of massive rocks. As the frothy caps strike them, sea spray springs to life in the air above them.

With the sun cloaking me in its warmth and the salty breeze whirling my hair around my face, I decide to be grateful for the time we had together and move on with my life. *Why did I tell him we can be friends?* I can't be *just friends* with him, that would rip me apart; to be with him and not be able to hold his hand, to touch him, to kiss him, to want him. My chest is hollow.

It's decided. I fulfilled my obligation in going to the wedding with him and we don't have any more plans together. I'll simply fade out of his life. We'll both move on and forget about each other. It's for the best. *Then why doesn't it feel that way? I'll never forget about him. He's deep in my heart.*

I get back from my walk, eat breakfast, and jot down items I need to pick up at Whole Foods. I busy myself with looking for a bank and dry cleaner. Zane defiantly creeps into my thoughts and I drift between daydreaming about kissing him and barricading him out. The struggle is exhausting.

The parking lot at Whole Foods is packed. I was hoping to get in and out quickly, but it doesn't look like that's going to happen.

I only have a week left so I don't need much. I fill a small cart and get in a checkout line. Glancing at the magazines while I wait, I'm hit with panic.

The headline reads, "IS ZANE ELKTON OFF THE MARKET?" In smaller letters underneath the headline, "Zane seen getting into limo with mystery woman." A picture of me and Zane getting into the limousine at the back entrance of Oak L.A. is staring me in the face.

I hear a whisper behind me that sounds in my head like it's echoing through the store's loud speaker. "Is that *her*?"

My heart races. As discreetly as I can, I slide the ponytail holder out of my hair so it covers my face. *What in the world? How did they get that picture? I have to get out of here. How do they do this?*

Thankfully, I'm next in line and get out of there as fast as I can. As soon as I get in my car, a text message chimes on my phone, startling me.

Chocolate Bear: We didn't get to say goodbye.

Annoyed and distraught, I text back, against my better judgement.

Me: Go to your local grocery store and get *Stars Exposed* to see a picture of me and say goodbye to that.

Within seconds, my phone rings. "Chocolate Bear" appears on the screen. *Argh.* I toss my phone in my purse and drive to the house without another stop. Resolved to staying in for the rest of the afternoon, I decide to rent a few movies. Avoiding Zane is proving difficult as two of his movies pop up as viewing options on the menu selection guide.

Before going to bed, I check my phone. Zane texted hours earlier.

Chocolate Bear: I'm so sorry about the picture.

"Well," I say out loud. "That's your life, Zane, out in the open for everyone to see."

The following days are filled with apartment tours with Jerry, opening a bank account, and anything to keep myself occupied and distracted from thinking about him. Once a day, he texts me or leaves a voice mail.

Chocolate Bear: I hope your house-hunting is going well.

Chocolate Bear: I miss talking to you.

Every night, I wear his shirt to bed. I'm helpless against my wandering mind. I recount sweet moments, tender moments, and oh, so steamy moments. My thoughts tantalize me in agony. As much as I try desperately to deny it, I've fallen for him — and I never want to see him again.

My return home is set for Saturday and by Friday, there's not much left to do. I go for a long walk on the beach to wallow in the sunshine and warmth before flying back to the cold, gray skies of Pennsylvania. I'll close on my house, that now belongs to Zane, and will be back in California in a few weeks, building my new life.

Having lived in the Airbnb for over a month my belongings are scattered around the house. I decide to start gathering and packing up some things. Zane's T-shirt lays on my pillow. I sit on the bed and pick it up, immediately picturing him in it, smiling his crooked, dazzling smile that melts me.

I can't keep this reminder of him.

Without thinking, I grab my phone and call him. He picks up on the first ring.

"Hi — hi. How are you?" He stumbles over his words, sounding surprised.

"I'm fine, thanks. How about you?"

"Good, yeah. Uh, how did the house-hunting go? Did you find anything you liked?" I know he's trying to sound casual.

"I did, but they were all a bit more than I want to spend so I'm going to rent an apartment for a year. Hopefully, Jerry and I can solidify things once I'm back in a few weeks."

"So, you haven't left yet?"

"No, not yet. I leave tomorrow. I was just packing and I have your T-shirt. I wouldn't feel right keeping it."

"Can I see you before you go?"

"That's not a good idea. It'll just complicate things." My stomach churns.

"You can give me back my shirt. I think you have my suit jacket too."

Shoot, I didn't think this through. "That's right, I do. How about I send them with Bill?" I attempt to sidestep his request.

"Come on. I didn't even get to say goodbye to you. Let me make you dinner. I'll be on my best behavior. Promise."

I'm silent. Head: Danger! Body: I'm with Head on this one. Don't even think about it. I can't control myself around him. Heart: I'm yearning for him. *Shoot.*

"Desiree, please."

Resisting him is impossible.

"Um, okay." *Danger!* I immediately doubt my decision.

"I'll send Bill to get you in about an hour, okay? I'd come myself, but I'm trying to lay low after the picture in *Stars Exposed*."

"Okay, bye."

"I'll see you soon. Bye."

Regret and anticipation battle inside me as I put on my pastel seafoam-green dress that's dotted with lavender and white hydrangeas. Each thin spaghetti strap is trimmed with a narrow, delicate, flowy, ruffle.

Bill arrives as scheduled, he never misses a beat.

"You look lovely." He says, as I open the door. His jolly grin always makes me smile.

"Thank you, Bill."

Without another word, we get into the sedan-style limousine. I stare blankly out the window as he drives.

"You're quiet tonight," his voice is calm and nonjudgmental.

"I don't know what I'm doing." I confess quietly.

"We're back here again, are we?"

"I'm going to say goodbye."

He looks at me. "Is that what you really want?" he asks, unknowingly zinging me.

I don't answer. A lump swells in my throat as I choke back tears. "I don't know." My words comes out strangled. "Thank you for your kindness and help these last few weeks. You've been wonderful to me."

"It's been my pleasure, Desiree. When you're back in town, you have my number, if you ever need anything, you give me a call."

He pulls into Zane's driveway and opens my door.

I step out of the car, reach up, and put my arms around him. "Thank you, Bill."

Before we part, he looks me in the eyes. "Follow your heart," he says softly. Another unintentional zing.

Zane's waiting at the top of the stairs wearing blue jeans, a white T-shirt, and no shoes. I approach him and he wraps his arms around me in a quick embrace. *I love being in his arms.*

"Oh." He releases me. "Is a hug okay?"

"Yes, it's fine." My nerves are hot.

We go inside and he's prepared another simple, delicious dinner. As we eat, I keep the conversation casual, talking about the homes and apartments I'd seen and things I'd done. He follows my lead.

Not sure I have the right to ask or to know, curiosity gets the better of me and I shift out of casual-mode. "Zane, what happened between you and Veronica?"

His eyes open a little wider, I've clearly caught him off guard. But he doesn't seem upset. He takes in a breath and blows it out slowly.

"I don't talk about her — with anyone." His face resembles a wounded puppy.

"Okay." *I shouldn't have asked.*

He takes a bite of his chicken, chews, and swallows, then gulps a swig of water.

I stop eating the moment he speaks, my attention intently focused on him.

"I thought we were in love. I thought *I* was in love. I thought I was going to marry her. Maybe I was just young and dumb and naïve, I don't know. We had a good thing going for a while. And one night, when I was away filming, she cheated on me. Apparently, it went on for a few months. When I came home after the film was done, she told me, and we ended it right then." He pauses. "She crushed my fucking heart."

My heart stings. Pins and needles cover my skin like thousands of tiny lacerations.

"We did a good job keeping the details private. I had no desire to disrespect her or her reputation. People screw up. And when you screw up in our world, it just gets twisted and blown out of proportion. Really, I just wanted her to be happy."

I'm leveled. In his devastation, he could've decimated her and instead, he chose to honor her.

"Zane, I'm so sorry. I guess being famous and having money doesn't erase pain."

"Heh. No, it sure doesn't." He takes another drink of water.

"You deserve to be happy too."

"Yeah, well." He pauses. "I think I kind of held people at arms' length after that. Hell, maybe I still do."

"Mmm…I've perfected that." I pick up my fork and take bite of chicken.

"Oh, yeah? Another personal rule?"

"No. Just too much disappointment."

"How so?"

"If I think about it, it probably stems from moving around so much. Every time we moved, I had to make new friends. I was a pretty quiet kid and never felt like I fit in so it made making friends kind of hard. When I finally did make a couple friends, I was ripped away from them because we had to move again. So, little by little, I just stopped letting myself get close to people, because I knew that, eventually, one of us would have to leave." I stop and a realization I never consciously had before hits me in the face. "I'm pretty sure I let that bleed over to my relationships with men. Never let them get too close. Hah. Which actually wasn't too difficult because none of them had any depth to them anyway. It's just as well. My mother let a man destroy her. I won't let a man destroy me."

"Brad didn't?"

At first, I'm taken aback by his question. But, as I ponder, I can see why he'd think that based on the little bit he knows about our relationship.

"No. At least not entirely."

"Why didn't you ever leave him if he was an alcoholic and you weren't in love with him?"

Thunk! I physically sit back in my chair at the gravity of his question.

"He was a good man. He took care of me and gave me a really good life. He never hit me or got violent with me. I had a roof over my head, food in my belly, and someone who cared about me. I thought it was the best life I could hope for."

"Mmm." He nods and doesn't press me for more.

We finish eating and easily launch into our comfortable habit of cleaning up together after we eat. It's a habit I'm going to miss.

He excuses himself and I go out to the balcony for one last look at the gorgeous view and sun setting into the ocean in the distance. Sadness twists around my heart.

His warm body is against mine and he grips the metal railing on either side of me. A bolt of electricity shoots through me.

"How about a walk?" His sultriness is incredibly persuasive.

"Okay."

We walk back inside and I take off my shoes at the door as he puts on his.

"Will your feet be okay?"

"Better without them than with them. They're *not* made for taking a walk." I smile.

As we walk, he asks what things I need to do when I get back home and I rattle down the list.

"I meant what I said. You take whatever you want to bring here with you and you can leave the things you really want to keep, but can't bring with you. I know there will still be things you want to get rid of regardless. You do what you want with all of it. It doesn't matter to me."

"Okay. I won't leave you a mess though."

"I know you won't."

"This is very weird that you're going to own my house." I look over at him, his face void of expression.

"I want you to think of it as still being your house. I bought it for you."

"No, it's yours now and I'm okay with that." I look down, making sure to avoid stepping on the seams in the sidewalk that would hurt my feet.

We're quiet for several paces and it's like I can sense him thinking.

"I..." he starts cautiously. "Heard you describe an Untouchable that day when I accidentally overheard you and Bella talking."

My skin burns a little at the reminder of that conversation and the things he learned by unintentionally eavesdropping.

"That's really how you see us, isn't it?" An innocent curiosity rides his tone and my irritation fades.

"It's how it is, Zane," I answer honestly. A breeze tousles my hair.

"I guess, being the one living it, I never saw that perspective." He almost seems sad, maybe hurt.

I wish he'd never heard that conversation.

We're only a few blocks from his house when we feel raindrops.

He looks up at the sky and puts his hands out. "What's this? It rarely rains here."

Ominous charcoal-gray clouds spread across the sky as the wind picks up, whirling around us. Silky ribbons of water pelt down on us ceaselessly then unleash a downpour.

He grabs my hand. "Run!" he shouts.

"Ah!" I run and laugh.

We race back to house and into the kitchen, dripping and laughing.

"That came out of nowhere. It looked like a perfect night for a walk." He's bent over with his hands on his thighs, breathing heavily.

"It did." I'm also trying to catch my breath from the sprint.

Kicking off his shoes with his feet, he peels off his rain-soaked shirt that's clinging to every muscle on his torso and drops it on the floor. I can't take my eyes off his glistening, rippling chest and abs. He steps closer to me, his virile body enticing me, his smoldering eyes entrapping me.

Danger! Retreat!

~ 21 ~

Desiree

He wraps his strong, gentle arms around me, pulling me into him, and I let him.

Head has a sock in its mouth. Heart is smiling. Body is in charge and under his spell.

He moves closer, locking his lips onto mine, slowly parting them with his tongue. A hot current goes through me as I meet his tongue with mine and they dance. His kiss has the same effect on me as the first, sending my head spinning, making my blood boil, and forcing my body to surrender. His mouth leaves mine and wanders inch-by-inch down my neck, dropping hot, feathery kisses. My breath quickens and I close my eyes, dizzy with anticipation.

He lets out a deep, guttural moan, telling me he's savoring me.

He skims his soft lips across my flesh, delicately kissing my neck, the sensitive hollow above my collar bone, and out to my shoulder. Tiny gasps escape me when he hits a sensitive spot and lingers there, teasing me.

Picking me up, he carries me to his bedroom and places me gently back down. He grabs a remote and presses a few buttons. The fireplace glows and seductive music saturates the air. The storm passed quickly and the setting sun permeates the room, bathing him in its glow. Taking my hand, he puts it on the warm skin of his chest. "Touch me," his voice is soft and low.

I recoil my hand and he grabs it, placing it on his chest again and holding it there. "Touch me." He kisses me and looks deep into my eyes. "I'm not untouchable. Not to *you*, Desiree."

I can't contain my desire for him any longer. I explore his bare chest with both of my hands, lightly running my fingertips slowly over his tight muscles, down his massive arms, and around to his strong back.

"Mmhh." His moan lets me know he's enjoying my indulgence.

As I look into his deep blue eyes, they beckon me to continue.

Hot blood heats my body as I soak in every inch of his chest and arms. I lean in, gently kissing his chest, gliding my tongue slowly over his hard nipples.

"Mmhh." His sound is louder. He closes his eyes and the veins in his neck tense as he tilts back his head and tightens his grip on my hips.

Opening his gorgeous eyes, he looks down at me. A blaze of intense heat rushes through my body as I tilt my face up to his, succumbing to my desire. He slides his swirling tongue into my mouth and I feel myself losing control, letting out a hushed moan. His lips release mine and he holds my face in his hands, looking deep into my eyes. He kisses me again. I hear my whimpers and can't stop them as my mounting passion for him possesses me.

He releases me again and strips off his wet jeans, using his feet to kick them off at the bottom. Before I can admire him, he pulls me into his body, meeting the skin on my neck with his lips, traveling across to my shoulder again. With one finger, he slides the wet strap of my dress off my shoulder and tickles my skin with his tongue. I gasp.

"Desiree." His voice is like melting caramel. "I need to know you're okay with this. I'll stop if you want me to." His exhale is intense.

My breathing is quiet and erratic. "No. I don't want you to stop."

He keeps his mouth at my shoulder, tantalizing me, and unzips my dress. With his other hand, he slips the strap off my shoulder and peels the rest of my wet dress down to the floor.

Lifting me into his arms, he carries me to the bed and gently lays me down. Slowly, he takes off his underwear, his eyes never leaving mine, and I drink him in, all of him. As if waiting for my approval, he sits next to me on the bed and tugs lightly at my panties. I lift my hips and he slides them down my legs. I quiver with anticipation.

He opens the drawer of his nightstand, grabs a condom, rips open the packet, and rolls it on. Climbing into the bed, he slides his body between my legs then holds himself above me. *My God, this man is magnificent.* My heart pounds like a base drum in my head.

He looks at me with his mesmerizing eyes. "You're beautiful, Desiree." His voice is quiet and smoky, like the music seducing us. Lowering his body, he sweeps his confident tongue into my mouth, going deeper and deeper. He lifts himself above me again and gazes into my eyes.

"Do you trust me?"

"Yes." My heart pounds harder.

Slowly, he takes my hands and holds them by my sides.

"I want to touch you," I say through stilted breaths.

"And I want you to touch me. But right now, *I* want to touch *you*," he says as he journeys slowly down my body with his hot mouth from my neck to my stomach.

He finds my breast, circling my nipple with his tongue. I grab at the sheet beneath me. He sucks gently and I moan. Continuing down the center of my body, he seduces me with his lips. Whispering kisses as he travels, he stops at my navel ring and flicks at it with his tongue then makes circles around it. *Dear Lord, he knows how to tease.* I've never been with a man so confident and it's driving me absolutely wild.

In his exploration, I know he's searching…searching for spots that elicit my body's reaction. He lingers at the sensitive, tender skin just above and inside my hip; the spot he found the night he first kissed me. My body involuntarily responds, flinching at each nibble of his teeth and squirming at each sweep of his lips across my heating flesh. Lust invades me.

He has complete control. His touch provokes me. *God, I*

want him. He releases my hands from his grip and I grab his butt, panting, trying to pull him into me, but he resists. I can't halt my begging whimpers.

He takes both of my hands and holds them in one hand above my head. With his other hand, he softly touches my cheek.

"Patience," he whispers into my ear, his breath hot against my cheek.

I want his lips on mine and he knows it. He kisses me, long, slow, and deep. I love how he kisses me. I'm lost in him. He skims my skin with his hand, starting at my arms he's holding above my head, gliding down to my breasts. Cupping one in his hand, he takes it into his mouth and tugs gently on my nipple with his teeth. My back arches in response and I twist my hands in his grip.

I groan.

He leaves little electric shocks as he kisses my skin. Seeming to relish in his teasing and my response to it, he slides his hand between my legs and dips his finger in, lighting me on fire. Lingering and rubbing, he sends me into a frenzy. My pulse races, my breathing is rapid.

"Zane, please..." I beg.

One more passionate kiss and, finally, he releases my hands and lets me have him.

"Oh fuck, Desiree," he says with a groan as he slides into me.

A loud, pleasurable moan escapes me.

He moves above me, rhythmically changing the speed of his thrusts, rocking his hips and scooping into me. I've never been with such a sensual, confident man. My passion intensifies with each carnal plunge.

I wrap my hands around his neck and lift to meet him. His entire torso moves like a wave as he curls his hips, sending him deep inside me. As though he can feel my body tensing, preparing, he slows his movement, prolonging the pleasure. Skillfully, he knows just when to quicken his thrusts, pumping faster and faster.

"Jesus," he grunts on an exhale. "You feel too good."

Then he stops moving. His eyes are closed. I know he's focusing to hold back. But I don't want him to hold back. I squeeze my walls around him, his eyes fly open and his body stiffens. His passion-infused growl encourages me. I squeeze again. Another animalistic growl. He drills his eyes into mine, his arms rippling tight with tension.

"Desiree." His loud exhale is shaky, like he's trying to control himself with all his might. "I won't last if you keep doing that."

I want to please him as much as he's pleasing me. I squeeze and clamp tighter around him.

"Oh fuck me." He moans and pounds into me faster and faster again. His gratifying groans grow louder.

"Zane..." *Oh God.* I release my hands from around his neck and lay back. My heartbeat races. My breathing accelerates. My body is on fire and clenching. "Zane...Zane, *Zane*, oh God." *Oh... my... God.* I've lost all control and he brings me to a place no man ever has. Ecstasy vibrates through me as my body surrenders to him with visceral moans. Every nerve ending on my body is aflame.

He lifts my hips and pulls me mercilessly into him faster and harder. I feel him throbbing inside me and he moans loudly again and again as his body tenses and shudders over and over. "Holy shit," he grunts.

Collapsing next to me, he curls his sweaty body around mine and wraps his arms around me. I feel his breath, blowing hot and hard against my bare skin.

He interlaces his fingers with mine. "I love you, Desiree," his breathy words prick my heart.

My heartbeat still pounding in my head, tears blur my vision and I close my eyes; grateful he can't see my face.

I love you too, Zane, Heart wants to respond.

We lay spooning, breathing, while the seductive music whirs around us and the glowing fire lights the room.

As my heart rate begins to normalize, he releases me.

"Stay right here," he says, getting out of the bed. He opens his dresser, grabs a pair of underwear, tosses me a T-shirt, and leaves the room.

Body: That was the most intense sexual experience I've ever had. So *that's* what mind-blowing sex is like. Nice. *Shhh!* Heart: I don't want to hurt him, *but I'm about to.* Head: Hey, I've got nothing, there's still a sock in my mouth.

I put on his shirt and pull the covers up. *I've just let this get very complicated. How am I going to tell him?* My chest tightens and acidic pangs jet around my stomach.

A few minutes later, he comes back with a mug of marshmallow-topped hot cocoa in each hand and that crooked, boyish grin on his face. "Mmm..."

He hands me a mug and gets back into bed.

"Thank you." My grip tight around the mug, I take a sip. "Um, I have a question for you."

"Ask me anything you want."

"When did you get the condoms? Did you plan on this happening tonight?"

He nearly spits out his mouthful of hot cocoa. With the most earnest expression, he answers me. "I got a box the afternoon we met. I haven't been with anyone in a long time and didn't have any. When I saw you in real life, I hoped to God I'd be lucky enough to have you in my life and, at some point, make love to you. And, no, I definitely did *not* plan on this happening tonight. I promise you that."

I gaze at him, studying his face.

"Desiree, I admit I kept things from you that I shouldn't have and I own that, completely. But, I'm not a liar. I've done some stupid shit in my life, but I don't lie and I don't cheat." His tone is steadfast.

"I believe you." And I do, wholeheartedly. My heart twists in disappointment of myself at how unfairly I've misjudged him over and over.

I sip my cocoa, delaying the conversation I know I have to start.

"Will you stay with me tonight?" he asks with a hopeful grin.

Why did he have to ask me that? Yes, I want to say. *Ugh, here we go.* I put my mug on the nightstand and try to swallow the massive lump in my throat. "Zane, I'm leaving tomorrow." I start hesitantly. "I'm going back to my life and you're going back to your life. And that's the way it has to be."

He stares at me incredulously. "What do mean, that's the way it has to be? You're coming back here, right?"

"I am, but." I choke back tears and swallow. The air in the room suddenly feels heavy. "We can't be together." The pain in my heart is oppressive.

"Why? I don't understand." He furrows his brows. The hurt in his eyes and confusion painting his face is tearing at me.

"You *do* know why. We've been over this. Your lifestyle and occasional job requirements aren't something I can handle and your addiction isn't something I want in my life...no matter what my feelings are for you." I lay it all out there and watch him wilt from my words.

"Do you love me?" Surprise grips me as his question pierces my heart.

For a moment, I hold my breath, his question reverberating off the walls in my head. Tears threaten to spill over my lashes like a waterfall and it takes me a second to find my voice. "I can't..." *I have to get out of here. I have to get out here!* Feeling like I'm about to hyperventilate, I push the covers off and quickly get out of the bed. Going to his dresser and opening drawers, I grab a pair of his sweatpants and put them on.

He jumps out of the bed and holds my shoulders in his hands, looking me dead in the eyes. "Desiree, do you love me?" His eyes plead with me.

I can't pry my gaze away from his dominating bind on me. I'm about to burst into tears. "Please don't make me answer that," I pleadingly whisper, choking down the lump in my throat.

"Just give me a chance. Please."

"A chance for *what*?"

"A chance to earn your trust back. A chance to earn your love." He pauses.

"I don't even know what love *is*," I blurt out. Saying the words makes the truth of them hurt even more. I don't know what being in love even feels like, but I think it feels something like what I'm feeling for him.

"Then let me show you," he says softly. "Desiree, I want to be with you. You've been haunting my dreams, haunting me, for so long. And now you're here, in flesh and blood, standing right in front of me. All I want to do is hold you in my arms and kiss you and be with you and…love you."

"Zane, that's a dream. It's a fantasy, not reality. None of this is real." I'm a tangled ball of mixed emotions and confusion; desperately wanting to be with him and terrified of being with him.

He cups my face in his hands, weakening me at the knees.

"But it *is* real." His soft, deep voice sends a quiver through me. "You're here, we're here, together." He lowers his head and kisses me…deeply.

I whimper at the intensity of his kiss, wishing our last kiss wasn't like this. "I don't know what to say."

"Say you'll stay." The yearning in his voice slashes at my heart. He touches his forehead to mine. "Stay," he whispers.

I push him away, clasping my hand over my mouth and folding my arm around my stomach. *This is killing me.* Tears flow rapidly. "I can't do this." I run to the kitchen, grab my purse and shoes, and run out the door.

"Don't leave like this!" I hear him call out as I leave.

~ 22 ~

Zane

She broke me.

When she ran out the door, she took my heart with her. Although she refused to answer my question, I know by her reaction that she loves me. I felt it already, but that moment sealed it. And now she's gone — again.

My lifestyle and job are a blessing and a curse. My addiction is a soul-sucking demon I battle every day. Both have driven away the one woman I've ever truly loved. When I look into her eyes, I see my future. Now, my only chance at something real is gone. A once-in-a-lifetime love ripped away. Devastation swallows me.

I lay on my bed and punch at it, roaring in frustration and anger. I want her in my life. I want her to let me love her. I can make almost anything happen. Anything except this.

One thing about demons, they don't ever fully go away. While I know it won't solve anything or give me the answers I want, I need to numb myself. I get out of bed, grab my phone, and go to the kitchen; deep in warring thoughts.

This isn't the way. It won't bring her back. It will help me forget about her, at least for right now. Who am I kidding? I'll never forget about her, not now, not ever. She wants nothing to do with me. *I can't live without her.*

I open the freezer and put my hand on the forbidden block of ice, dislodging it from the built-up frost. Forbidden because it encases a key, a key I never wanted to use. I slam the block on the counter, grab a meat tenderizer, and whack at it, but only small shards spring off. Rage forces my movement and I smash harder and harder until chunks break off. No longer feeling like I'm in my body, I smash until I can see a piece of the key. Hastily, I grab the block and hold it under hot water. As the ice around the key melts away, my stomach twists. Watching my hand tremble, I turn the key over in my hand — over and over. I curl my fingers around it in my palm and strike the counter with my fist, the sound of a thunderclap echoes through the room. "Arrrr!" Rational thought evades me and I'm thrust into the grip of my addiction.

Self-deception rules my thoughts and consequences of my actions vacate me. My movements are calculated. Slowly, I insert the key into the keyhole of the bottom cabinet, the metal scraping down the tunnel of the keyhole. As I turn it, the click clangs like the strike of a bell in my ears. My stomach twists tighter. As I open the cabinet door and look inside, adrenaline surges through my body, fast and furious. I reach in and take out one whiskey glass and the bottle of scotch that was meant to be my reminder of the crutch I never wanted to covet again.

Quickly filling one-quarter of the glass with the amber liquid, I toss it in my mouth, throw back my head, and swallow. My throat stings the instant the liquid splashes down. "Aaaaarrrr," I growl.

I pour again — deliberately — defiantly — and toss it back.

Putting the glass back down, I grip the counter with my arms widespread, rage building inside me. I hang my heavy head, listless, through my shoulders.

Another pour. My stomach twists even tighter. This time, my hand shakes. Lucifer seduces me. I throw the evil elixir down my throat, feeling painful pleasure as it burns on the way down.

Consumed by my devil and enveloped by rejection, I grab my phone and text her.

> **Me:** I know you don't want to see me or hear from me so this will be the last time I text you. You will always be in

my heart, Desiree. No matter where you are and no matter where I am. A piece of me may belong to the world, but my heart belonged to you long before we met and it always will. I'll love you forever. ~Zane.

With the glass still in my hand, I wipe the residual moisture off my top lip, spin around, and hurl the glass into the wall, shattering it. Overcome with heartache, I slide down the cabinet until I'm sitting on the floor and let tears come out of me.

I've lost her.

~ 23 ~

Desiree

As I enter the house, a text message chimes on my phone. *It's probably Zane. Don't look at it.*

I can't not look at it.

> **Chocolate Bear:** I know you don't want to see me or hear from me so this will be the last time I text you. You will always be in my heart, Desiree. No matter where you are and no matter where I am. A piece of me may belong to the world, but my heart belonged to you long before we met and it always will. I'll love you forever. ~Zane.

My heart rips open and I crumple onto my bed, wailing in tears.

Head: I tried to stop you. Body: This is way deeper than me. Heart: I know Head over there wants to exile him out, but it's too late. You've fallen madly, hopelessly, deeply in love with him.

He's the man I've always longed for, but didn't believe existed. And I can't deny that he's shown me a love I've never known, a love I don't want to let go of, only, I have to.

Not having slept well from a turbulent night of combative thoughts and feelings and then traveling all day, I arrive back in Pennsylvania, emotionally and physically exhausted. I've got a busy couple weeks ahead of me so I unpack and get in bed, remembering how good it felt to be in Zane's bed with him, snuggled into his chest.

He dominates my thoughts as usual. I can't erase the pained image of his face from my mind. *I have to let him go.*

For the next couple weeks, I go through my house, separating things to pack, things to donate, and things to leave for Zane. I schedule the movers and close on my house. Since no one is moving in, there isn't a need for me to get out quickly, but I have to close this chapter of my life. With the closing going so quickly, I arrange for an Airbnb to stay in when I get to L.A. and a storage unit for my things until I can move into the apartment Jerry found me.

I'm ready for a fresh start.

Zane

"Zzzaaannneee." The low, distorted, slow-motion sound of my name echoes through my hazy head. "Zzaannee." Someone is shaking me.

It takes all my energy to lift my heavy, throbbing head. My face is numb. I have to consciously exert myself to move, every motion morphing painfully slowly into the next. I'm lying face-down on my black leather sofa with one arm and one leg hanging off.

"Zane." Grace's soft voice finally registers in my thudding head. My body feels like it weights five hundred pounds.

As I strain and push myself up to sit, the room spins. My mouth hangs open, my throat is parched, and my eyes are dry and burning. "Yeah?" I manage to form a word as I blink my eyes, trying to stop the room from tilting.

"Zane, are you okay?" she asks, her voice still warped in my ears.

I have to physically think about closing my mouth. The heaviness of my head causes it to flop back and I fight to keep it upright. Forcing my eyes to open wide, I blink more, trying hard to focus.

"Yeah, I'm good." I lie.

"No, you're not. You're hungover...again. And you look like shit." She touches my lip. I'm starting to feel my face again. "Do you even know you cut your lip?"

I touch my lip, a sting shoots through my face. "Shit."

"You weren't at your mom's house for dinner last night."

"Yeah...yeah, I know."

"Where were you? You know she was disappointed you didn't come and hurt that you didn't even bother to call and let her know." She hovers above me with her hands on her hips and elbows out to the side.

"Yeah, I know. I should've called. I was here."

"You were here? By yourself. Getting loaded."

"Hey, I didn't go out and then drive." I hurl my words at her.

She sits down next to me and takes my hand in hers, looking directly into my burning eyes. "Zane, I'm worried about you. Your drinking's gotten worse and I'm watching you spiral out of control. I love you. I can't sit here, doing nothing, and watch you crash and burn. I know you were crushed when Desiree left. And I know you love her. But you know that *this*...this won't bring her back." Her voice trails off as she stares at me.

"I know it won't, Grace," I say through gritted teeth, my tone heavy.

"Then what are you doing to yourself?"

"Fuck, Grace. I don't know. I'm numbing myself." Annoyance threads through me.

She squeezes my hand in her clasped hands. "It's time to stop numbing yourself and move on. To start living your life again." Her calm, loving words mollify my irrational and misplaced frustration.

I rest my head back, starting to feel my body again. "I know. I'm sorry," I say, removing the harshness from my behind my words. "I can't believe I let myself get sucked back in like this."

"Zane, it's a disease. A disease you need to learn how handle with the right tools so it can't drag you back in when life challenges you. Don't be so hard on yourself. You're only human."

"I'll get it under control, I promise." I deceive myself.

"This isn't something you take on by yourself. You know that." She pauses. "You know what you need to do." She encourages, inviting me to fill in the blank.

"I know. I need to get my ass back into rehab and take it seriously this time."

"And not to get Desiree back, Zane, 'cause that'll land you right back here."

"I know, I need to do it for me." My head is clearing and I sit up.

"That's the only way you can get your life back...get *yourself* back." I swear Grace's heart is bigger than anyone I know, almost anyone.

"I know." I withdraw my hand from hers and lean forward, resting my elbows on my thighs and dropping my head in my hands. I can't hold back my tears.

She tenderly rubs my hunched back, soothing me.

My tears eventually stop. I rub the heels of my hands into my eyes and get to my feet, holding out my hands to her. She grasps my hands and stands up.

"Thank you, Grace." I hug her tightly and release her. "How'd you get to be so amazing?" I smile.

"Oh, well, you know." She winks. "It's in the genes."

After she leaves, I go to the bathroom and check out my lip. It's split and coated with dried blood, but doesn't need stitches. The blood is smeared down my chin. *Damn, I* do *look like shit.*

Though I know Grace is right, I'm in the darkest place I've ever been. Lucifer's talons are buried deep in my flesh and the quicksand beneath my feet continues swallowing me.

~ 24 ~

Desiree

Tomorrow I hit the road to L.A. and start my new life. Surrounded by bubble wrap and boxes, I'm packing up the last few things when my phone rings.

"Hi," Grace's usually-perky voice is dull.

"Hi. How are you doing?" I ask politely, not really in the mood to talk.

"I'm okay. I just wanted to check in on you and see how *you're* doing."

"Things are coming along. I have most things tied up on this end and at least have a place to stay and store my things for a while over on your end."

"That's good. How are you *doing* though?" I know what she means.

I put down the half bubble-wrapped ceramic pitcher I'm wrapping. "Honestly, Grace, I'm empty. I don't want to think about him and I can't stop thinking about him. It's unnerving. I just need to put everything behind me so I can move on. But one thing I'm glad about is that I got your friendship out of all this."

"I'm glad we're friends too." She pauses. "Are you sure that's what you want, Desiree?"

A sigh flies out of my mouth and I lie back onto the old wooden floor. "I don't know what I want." I pause. "I know I shouldn't ask but, how is he?"

"He's not good," she says, her tone downbeat. "He's not at all good. I'm really worried about him."

I sit back up abruptly, the floorboards creak beneath me. "No, that's enough. I don't want to know any more. I shouldn't have asked. It's not fair to put you in the middle. I'm sorry."

"It's okay."

"Listen, I've got to finish up this packing. I'm heading out early tomorrow. How about I give you a call in a few days once I'm settled in and we'll set up a lunch together?" I want to get off the phone and not have any more Zane-fuel feeding my thoughts.

"Okay, that sounds good. You travel safely and we'll see each other soon."

"Thank you, Grace. I will."

"You bet. Bye."

The drive is long and I've spread it out over four days. Four days of windshield time. Four days of being alone with my thoughts — thoughts of Zane. *What did Grace mean "He's not good?" Why is she worried about him? I hope he's okay.*

I get to the Airbnb late in the evening on Friday. Tired from my drive, I order dinner and find a movie to watch. About halfway through the movie, my phone rings.

"Hi. You're on my list to call tomorrow."

"Desiree." Grace's voice is panic-stricken. "I'm so sorry to call you. Bill's on vacation and I can't get a hold of Declan or Eric. I need your help." Her speech is rapid.

"What's going on?" Panic now jolts me.

"I'm on my way to pick up Zane. His friend Steve called me and he's really messed up. I'm going to bring him back to his house, but I don't want to leave him alone. And I can't stay with him. We're flying out at four o'clock in the morning and I have to get back home. I'm so sorry to ask this, but can you please stay with him?"

Without hesitation, I answer. "Yes, of course. I'll meet you there."

"Thank you, Desiree. I'm so sorry."

"It's okay. I'll see you there."

Grace's car is in the driveway when I pull in. Not knowing what to expect and my nerves hot and piqued, I run inside.

When she hugs me, I feel the tension in her body. "I haven't seen him this bad in a long time." She paces in small circles. "I told him he needed to go back to rehab. I'm sorry to do this to you." Stopping briefly, she looks at me and goes back to pacing. "I know I'm putting you in a situation you don't want to be in. And I know him." She shakes her head. "If I take him to rehab right now, he'll freak out. I know he'd want to go by his own will, not by my forcing him. I didn't know who else to call. I still can't find Declan or Eric." She stops again and stands in front of me. "I know I can trust you."

I take Grace's hands in mine. "Yes, you can trust me. It's okay. I'm here."

"I really have to go." She points her head toward the open glass doors. "He's down by the pool."

"Okay, I'll make some coffee. You go. I'll take care of him."

"Thank you, Desiree." She squeezes my hands, hugs me again, and leaves.

Though I know he drinks Four Sigmatic, this situation calls for hardcore coffee. I find the coffee, pour water into the coffee maker, and hit the brew button.

Pssshhhhh. A splash comes from the pool.

He's swimming?

I walk out to the balcony and drop my eyes to the pool. He's fully clothed, face down, and the water surrounding his head is turning blood-red.

"Zane!" I scream.

Adrenaline-fueled, I run to get my phone and dial 911 as I run down the flights of stairs to the pool.

"911, what's your emergency?" asks the woman on the other end of the phone.

My heart is pounding and words torpedo out of my mouth. "I'm at Zane Elkton's house. He fell in his pool and it looks like he's bleeding. I need help!"

"Okay, ma'am. I need you to stay calm. We have the address and I'm sending help to you now. I'll stay on the phone with you. What's the situation?"

"I don't know, I don't know. I was upstairs." I reach the pool, put my phone on speaker, and toss it on the ground. "He's face-down in the pool. I'm going in." I dive into the pool, swim over to him, and roll over his listless body. "Zane!" I shout, looping my arm across his body and kicking my legs as fast as I can to get him to the edge of the pool.

"Ma'am, is he breathing?"

"I don't know yet. I don't think so. I need to get him out of the pool. He's bleeding." Panic shoots through me.

I climb out of the pool, curl my arms under his underarms, and, with all my strength, I pull and heave. His dead-weight of muscle-mass fights against me. I pull again until his upper body is out of the water.

Quickly, I tilt his head to the side to let any water out of his mouth. Blood pools under his head. I put my ear next to his nose and close my eyes. There's no sound and I can't feel his breath on my cheek. I open my eyes, his chest isn't rising. "He's not breathing!" I shout. I'm covered in blood from a gash at the back of his head.

"Does he have a pulse?"

"Oh God, I don't know." I'm shaking. I push against his carotid artery with my blood-covered fingers and close my eyes again, waiting. "No, no! I don't feel anything!"

"Okay, I need you to perform CPR. Do you know how to do that?"

"Yes."

I clasp my hands on top of each other on his chest and apply thirty compressions. "One and two and three..." I whisper to keep track. Then I tilt back his head, my hand on his blood-soaked hair, and blow two breaths into his mouth. I continue the cycle over and over and over. Blaring sirens grow louder and louder as I persevere. The adrenaline pulsing through my body is being overtaken by exhaustion from my repeated compressions. Just as the paramedics dash down the stairs, vomit spews from his mouth and he begins coughing.

"Ma'am we're here," a paramedic shouts to me. I feel his arms around my languid body, pulling me off Zane. "Are you hurt?"

My head is spinning in the chaos. "No, no, I'm not. He's been drinking. I don't know how much."

"Are you sure? You're bleeding."

I look at my bloody hands. "No, no. It's his blood. He has a cut on the back of his head."

"Did he take any drugs?"

"Oh God. I don't...I don't know. I just got here. I don't think so, but — " I shake my head. "I don't know." Adrenaline rages through me again.

Within seconds, the paramedics have Zane on a gurney and are carrying him up the stairs. The paramedic with me wraps a stiff, rough blanket around me and loops my arm around his neck, supporting my trembling body with his arm around my waist. He walks me up the stairs and helps me into the ambulance.

The siren echoes in my head as I sit, shivering, staring at Zane's still body and pale face. A wet chunk of his dark hair curls on his forehead that's wrapped in a bandage. His sunken eyes are closed and he's intubated. The same type of rough blanket that's draped over my shoulders covers his body. I trace the IV tube up to the bag where I see the cardiac monitor and watch the waves move with each beep...beep...beep...beep.

When we arrive at the hospital, everything moves quickly. Zane's unloaded and whisked away while the paramedics hand me off to nurses. One of the nurses probes me with questions, takes my information, and brings me to a private room. Once alone in the room, I let my weak, heavy body slink into a chair and cry.

No. This, I can not *do.* My decision to end our friendship was the right thing to do. I won't be in another toxic relationship with another alcoholic. I don't care that I love him. I can't do it. *Why did I fall in love with him?*

Once I stop crying, I go to the bathroom and my reflection startles me. His blood covers my clothes and is smeared across my face and arms. Mascara and eyeliner are smudged around my eyes and my hair is still wet and disheveled. Moving wearily, I remove my clothes, take a wash cloth, and run it under warm water, watching it turn red as it hits the dried blood on my hands. I squeeze out the water and move the cloth across my face, around my eyes, and down my neck; wiping away his blood. Methodically, I repeat the ritual until his blood is gone. I take the scrubs and booties the nurse gave me and put them on then lay on the bed that waits for him.

Time drags on for what seems like hours. Exhaustion overcomes me.

"Desiree," a soft female voice says my name and I feel a warm hand on my arm.

I blink my eyes sluggishly until they focus on an unfamiliar but pleasant face. The sterile hospital scent invades my nostrils.

"Your friend is here. We need to transfer him to the bed," the woman in scrubs says gently as she holds out her hand to help me up.

He's wheeled into the room. Though my head is groggy and my arms are heavy, the sight of all the tubes coming out of him whips me alert.

"Is he going to be okay?" I ask as I get off the bed.

"He's got a nice gash on the back of his head, but he's going to be okay. He's lucky you were there and performed CPR on him or he may not be here right now."

I watch as he's transferred from the gurney to the bed, his body limp and lifeless.

"You can stay with him if you'd like. He'll probably be asleep for a while. The doctor will be in to check on him in about an hour."

"Yes, I'd like to stay for a bit. Do you have a blanket?" With the adrenaline of the night no longer raging through me, I'm ice-cold.

"I'll find one for you." She smiles sweetly and leaves.

Once everyone is gone, I stand at his bedside, looking down at him. His skin is ashen-gray under the incandescent lighting of the hospital room and his strong body now looks so frail. I watch his chest rise and fall as he breathes rhythmically.

Around 3:00 AM, the doctor comes in, extubates him, and takes some notes.

"How's he doing?"

"A lot better than when he arrived. Downgrading him to an oxygen mask is a positive sign. He'll be here a couple days so we can monitor him," he says and leaves the room.

I drag a chair close to his bed, curl my legs under my body, and rest my head on my folded arms next to him.

Zane

Everything is a blur; a haze drapes over the room. I look around, trying to figure out where I am. *Damn.* My body is heavy and I hear something beeping. An oxygen mask covers my nose and mouth and I'm wearing a thin hospital gown. *The hospital? What am I doing at the hospital?* Although disoriented, I see a figure resting by my side. *Mom? Dad? Grandpa?*

I strain to focus my eyes and struggle for strength. Despite my lethargy, I manage to raise my arm enough to put my hand on the head of the figure sleeping by my side. The figure stirs. I sluggishly, clumsily pet its hair, still not knowing who it is. As the figure moves, my hand slides onto the bed. She lifts her face and turns toward me. I blink a few times to focus. It's Desiree. *She's here.*

Lethargically, I move my hand up to my face and tug the oxygen mask down with my finger. "You're here." Barely audible, my words are slow and shaky.

"I'm here," her tender, celestial voice confirms, comforting me. She unwraps from her blanket, gets up from her chair, and stands beside me.

For a moment, nothing else exists and time stands still.

She reaches down and softly runs her fingers through my hair then caresses my face. I feel her hand holding mine and I weakly squeeze it.

"Do it again," she whispers. "So I know I'm not dreaming."

I squeeze again, barely.

"What...happened?" My speech still faint and scratchy and my throat hurts.

"Well, I can only tell you what I know. Grace called me to come stay with you because you were drunk and she couldn't reach Declan or Eric and she couldn't stay with you. When I got to your house, you were down at the pool. I started making coffee and heard a splash. And when I went to check on you, you were face-down in the middle of the pool with blood coming out of you. I don't know exactly what happened. You must've slipped and hit your head somehow because you had a big gash on the back of your head."

"Ow," I say faintly as I feel the throbbing at the back of my head.

"I called Declan and he should be here soon." Sadness hovers in her eyes as she clasps both of her hands around mine. "Zane." Her gaze drops to our hands and then back into my eyes. "I can't do this again." The skin between her eyes crinkles and she struggles to get the words out. "I can't let myself fall in love with another self-destructive alcoholic." Tears swell in her eyes. "I'm sorry. I'm so sorry." It hurts me to see the pain in her eyes. Pain I caused.

She lifts my hand to her heart and chokes out, "Please take care of yourself." With tears streaming down her face, she puts my hand on the bed, leans over, and kisses my forehead. The heart monitor beeps more rapidly.

Declan walks in the room just as she turns and brushes past him, running out.

"Desiree," I try to call out, but the burning pain in my throat strangles my voice.

"Dude, what the hell happened?" Declan asks.

A man wearing a white lab coat and carrying a clipboard walks in.

"You're a very lucky man, Mr. Elkton. If you're friend hadn't pulled you out of your pool and performed CPR on you, you wouldn't be here right now."

Desiree saved my life? It took a few seconds for me to process. *Desiree saved my life.*

And this time, I'm pretty sure she's gone forever.

Desiree

I'm not thinking clearly and my emotions are in shambles. I'm in the lobby of the hospital with nothing but the hospital scrubs and booties and my phone. Bill's on vacation so I schedule an Uber to bring me back to Zane's house.

When I walk in, I stand silently, breathing in the stale air that dries my throat. Hesitantly, I go out to the balcony. The area where I gave CPR to Zane is still spattered with his blood and I dry heave. Not wanting him to come back home to that, I go down and get the hose out. Snippets of the night before flash through my mind as I wash away his blood. When I'm satisfied with my effort, I go back upstairs.

It's the last time I'll ever be in his home. Not quite ready to let him go, I walk into his bedroom where we made love together, taunted by the memory. As I go to walk out, I see my dress in the mirror of his open closet door. The top Grace gave me and my dress hang in his closet. It looks like he had them cleaned. Grazing the silky fabric of my dress arouses the memory of his gentle touch on my skin when he slid the straps off my shoulders. I close my eyes and take a deep breath. *Get out of here.*

I exhale, open my eyes, and go back to the kitchen. Again, my mind wanders — to dancing in his arms on the balcony under the stars, deep conversations by the fire, and making cookies together.

It's time to let him go.

~ 25 ~

Zane

I know two things. One: I will *never* again allow my addiction to take over my life and Two: Desiree loves me.

The doctor keeps me in the hospital for two days. The day I'm released, I check into rehab, ready to change my life — for good.

Focusing on my recovery is the most important thing. I even back out of my winter project so I can commit myself fully to the program. I know my addiction will always be a never-ending struggle and I'm determined to do everything in my power to get sober and learn the tools to *stay* sober.

Last time, I went through the motions. This time, I'm taking it seriously. Though I'm doing it for myself, I'd be lying if I didn't admit there's a piece of my heart that's also doing it in hopes of somehow being part of Desiree's life again someday. To be the kind of man she deserves. And maybe earn back her heart.

I'm scared to death to face my demons.

Desiree scratched off the scab of my deepest, darkest fear. A fear that became a self-fulfilling prophecy. Every failed relationship and every role I didn't get, I never felt like I was enough. I beat myself up with lies that I needed to be better and work harder. I pushed myself harder, over-critical of every move I made. In a twisted way of thinking I was protecting myself, I connected my body with my self-worth. I did it. Me. Working out and sculpting my body was the one thing I felt like I could control. I began to see myself the way I thought others saw me; a body and nothing more.

My face and my body attracted women. Even though I knew they weren't *the one*, it didn't matter in my distorted head. My body got me shallow roles, roles that paid my bills and gave me a lavish lifestyle, so I took them. Exploiting that identity became how I defined my success. And I perpetuated it, no one else. I gave up on myself and years of resentment festered inside me, gnawing at my soul.

Somehow, Desiree knew. Like she could see all my bullshit, she ripped off that scab and loved me enough to stick my fear in front of my face. I wasn't ready to deal with it at the time. But I'm ready now.

During the three months in rehab, I dedicate myself to my recovery, attending every meeting and therapy session. The sessions are grueling and emotionally exhausting, making me dissect the ugliness I'd created inside myself. This shit is hard.

All the while, Desiree stays in my heart.

Desiree

The apartment Jerry found me is close to the institute and a reasonable drive to the beach. I keep myself busy with school, building my business, and getting together with Lisa and Grace every now and then. I'm even starting to make some new friends and L.A. is beginning to feel like home.

Zane is never far from my thoughts. The good memories have stayed with me. The time we spent together was unlike anything I've experienced with a man. Emotionally, he's supportive and willing to be vulnerable. Mentally, he's intelligent and not afraid to have deep conversations. Physically, he's intense and passionate. From the day we met, I was drawn to him, in a way I can't explain. Some kind of magnetic, ethereal attraction that I don't even know how to describe. All I know is, it was powerful.

Whether or not I'm meant to have love, I have no idea. But what I now know is what it feels like to be in love with someone who loves me and it was the most beautiful, magical thing I've ever felt. For that, I'll be forever grateful for him.

I miss him. I miss him so much my heart hurts.

Completely escaping him is hard to do in a city like L.A.

Running my weekend errands, I stop into Whole Foods. A vaguely familiar voice calls my name. "Desiree?"

When I look up, I see the bright, smiling face of Sabrina and smile back. "Sabrina, how are you?"

She embraces me in a hug. "I'm doing okay, I suppose. How are *you*? You're here for good now, right?" She pulls her cart next to mine.

"Yes, I am. I've been here a couple months now. Things are going really well. I have an apartment and school started. Between school and working on my business, I've been keeping busy."

"That's good to hear. I was hoping we'd see you." An expectant smile spreads across her face.

Ugh, this is uncomfortable. "Yeah, um, Zane and I had a bit of a falling out."

"Yes, he told me. You know him, no details. But I was disappointed to hear you weren't seeing each other." She pauses. A mistiness veils her eyes. "And now he's back in rehab." She shakes her head. "We always encouraged him and supported him. Now I wonder if we made a mistake. I hope that world didn't destroy my sweet boy."

After Grace got back from her trip and I told her everything that happened, we've kept our conversations strictly about each other and our lives. We never talk about Zane. While I know rehab isn't somewhere anyone wants to be, I'm pleased to know he's getting help.

I take her hand in mine. "Oh, Sabrina. If he's in rehab, it's the best place for him to be to do what he needs to do for himself. He has so much strength and unyielding determination in his heart." I tilt my head and smile. "I think he got that from you." Pausing, I squeeze her hand. "He'll find his way back."

When she smiles at me, a tear falls from her eye and she wipes it away. "Thank you, Desiree." She squeezes my hand back. "Well, I shouldn't keep you from your shopping. I'm glad I ran into you."

"Me too. It's so nice to see you."

"I do hope you'll come around. Maybe to a family dinner with Grace? Zane will be away a bit longer so it wouldn't be uncomfortable for you."

"Okay, that would be nice," I say. And I mean it. I remember how much I enjoyed his family.

"Wonderful. I'll have Grace let you know when the next one is. Probably in a week or two."

"I'll be there." I hug her and we go about our shopping.

As promised, Grace lets me know about the next family dinner and, although I feel a little awkward going to dinner at Zane's parent's house without him, Grace and I have become good friends so I feel comfortable going. When I walk through the door, I'm welcomed with open arms, just as I expected I'd be. Everyone was there, including Sherry and Jim this time. Everyone except Zane.

Being in his childhood home, surrounded by his family, *not* thinking about him is impossible.

After dinner, Grace and I sign up for dish-duty. The rest of the family pitches in by bringing all the dishes from the dining table into the kitchen. Grace fills one sink with warm water, squeezes in some dish soap, and puts in a few of the pots from the stove.

"How's that anatomy class? I know it's been a beast." She rinses off a dinner plate in the adjacent sink and puts it into the dishwasher.

"Oof, that it is. But it's going well. There are so many organs and muscles and tissues and nerves, it's a lot to remember. But, I'm getting there. Well, you know, I've been studying like a mad-woman. The final is in a few weeks and I'm planning to get an A."

"Of course you are," she says with confidence, continuing to rinse dishes and load them. "And you will. Should we plan a celebration lunch?" An expectant smile beams on her face.

"Let's wait until I pass, first," I say, grabbing the dish drying towel from the oven handle.

"Deal." She pauses. "I went to visit Zane on Tuesday." Her soft voice holds delicate hesitation.

"Yeah?"

"I know we haven't talked about him since that night. And I fully respect you not wanting to."

"You know I appreciate that." While it's true, not talking about him doesn't mean I don't think about him — every day.

"I know." She nods with a warm smile. "I did think you'd want to know that he's actually doing really well."

"Yeah? That's good." It brings me relief to know he's doing well.

"Yeah. He's been very committed and really taking it seriously. He's one of the most determined people I know."

"That really is so great to hear."

"And you know what he told me?"

"What's that?"

"He told me he's not going to take any more roles that have him getting naked and having fake-sex with women." She puts the last plate in the dishwasher and looks at me.

"Seriously?" My neck juts forwards in an involuntary response.

"Yup," she says, then reaches into the sudsy water, pulls out a pot, and rubs it with the dishcloth. "He said there are plenty of distinguished actors who play remarkable characters who never get naked and he wants to transform his image."

To say I'm surprised is an understatement, but I'm also incredibly proud of him for making such a courageous decision for himself.

"Well, good for him. That's really admirable considering he got a lot of work because of his physique."

"It is. I'm really proud of him. I only visit once a month and I saw such a difference in him this last time."

"I'm so happy for him. It sounds like he really is doing great."

"He is." She rinses the pot and hands it to me to dry. "Do you think there would ever be a possibility you could..." She shrugs and offers a hint of a smile. "...give him a second chance?"

I put the pot on the counter and look at her hopeful face. I sigh. "I don't know. I guess I...hadn't considered it."

She stops washing the dishes and turns her face to me. "I know you love him. I know you never stopped loving him."

"Not loving him was never the issue." My heart still aches to be with him.

"I know what the issues were," she says, her voice gentle and compassionate. "And it seems like, maybe they don't exist anymore. Or at least there's improvement." She presses her lips together in a sweet smile.

I shake my head and can't help but smile at her. "Maybe."

Her smile broadens.

"Come on, let's get these dishes done."

As he does most nights, Zane creeps into my thoughts. I think about the conversation I had with Grace. If he's serious about no longer taking roles where he's intimate with other women, that nullifies that reservation. Then the biggest thing that's left is his alcohol addiction. According to Grace, he's taking his recovery quite seriously.

My heart flitters with curiosity, a spark of hope. Maybe we could work. Maybe we have a chance. Maybe I'm finally ready to take a leap of faith.

Maybe...

~ 26 ~

Desiree

Little by little, my business has been growing and I'm thrilled to have picked up two new clients over the last few weeks. While I'm networking my butt off and it's paying off, something in my gut tells me Zane has been playing secret marionette, having his friends hire me. I have no proof, but the very thought of him being a guardian angel from afar comforts me.

I'm also staying on top of my schoolwork at the institute and love what I'm learning. Managing both has been challenging and tiring.

Having finished a brutal test at school earlier this afternoon, I decide to treat myself to a walk on the beach. I love the warm sun on my face, the gentle breeze, and the salty smell of the air as the waves lap onto the sand. I'm so happy I moved out here. As I'm bathing in this bliss, my phone rings.

"Hey, Grace."

"Hi. How'd the anatomy test go? I know you were studying your ass off."

"Ugh, it was tough, really tough. But, I think I did really well on it."

"That's great. Of course you did."

"I'm just glad it's over. Onto the next one." I laugh.

"How'd you like to blow off a little steam and come over for a barbeque? It's time for that celebration, right? I know, it's last-minute, you know me." She chuckles. "I'm having a few people over around five-ish. Nothing big. What do you say? Wanna come?"

"Yeah. That sounds fun. What can I bring?"

"Are you okay with chip-duty?"

"Absolutely, I'll get a few different kinds."

"Perfect. See you in a little while."

"Okay, bye."

I bid farewell to the sun and the ocean and head to the grocery store to fulfill my chip-duty obligation.

I'm the first to arrive at Grace's and help her put food onto plates and into bowls. People slowly start arriving and we're a small group of about fifteen or so. Everyone is friendly and chatting in small clusters, all pitching in to bring food outside and cook. When it's time to eat, we spread ourselves across four folding tables and random chairs.

Zane

I walk into Grace's back yard and stop when I see her. Grace didn't tell me Desiree would be here. Even though she's not facing my direction and I can't see her whole face, just seeing her in person again is enough to send adrenaline pulsing through me. *Damn, she's as beautiful as ever. Who's the guy she's sitting with? I know most of Grace's friends.* Jealousy seethes through me like a raging fire. My heart jackhammers in my chest. No one is good enough for her.

The guy gets up and I head toward her, dousing my temper.

"Hi, Desiree."

She turns around and her stunning green eyes greet me. "Zane." My heart beats faster from the way she says my name. "Hi. I didn't know you'd be here." I watch her eyes search for and find Grace, who smiles mischievously at us.

"Yeah." I chuckle. "I didn't know you'd be here either."

"That Grace." Her lips lift into a sexy grin that she doesn't even know is sexy.

"So, you're here with someone?" My voice sounds dry as I croak out the question.

"Hey." The guy is next to me, handing her a bottle of water. "You're Zane." He holds out his hand to shake mine. "I'm Sam. My wife and I just moved in next door." He motions to the house next door. "How're you doing?"

I grab his hand and shake it. "Good. Good man, thanks. How about you?"

"Yeah, we're great. So happy we moved here. Hey, I'm gonna find my wife and grab a burger. Catch you guys later."

"Thank you for the water," Desiree says, gracious as always.

"Sure thing," he says as he walks away.

"You were saying?" Her eyes twinkle in the sunlight.

"Oh, I just." I point in the direction of Sam. "I thought you were, maybe…"

"Oh no. Gosh, no." She sniggers, pointing at Sam. "I'm not here with anyone." A spark of hope rises in me.

"Oh." *Why do I always feel like a 12-year-old around her?* "Do you want to take a walk?"

"Yeah, I'd like that." Her smile melts me every time.

Grace has a few acres of landscaped property and I lead us to the swings she had put in for our niece and nephew that she hopes will be for her own kids someday too.

"It's good to see you. How've you been?" I ask.

Our pace is slow and I want to take her hand in mine.

"Good. Really good actually. My business is picking up and I'm doing well in school."

"I knew it. I told you I knew you could do anything you set your mind to."

She hangs her head humbly then raises it. "Thank you. I'm pretty happy about how things are going."

"That's great. That's really great." I'm like a nervous kid on a first date.

"And I know you had some of your friends hire me." Her knowing smile tells me the jig is up.

"How'd you know? Who told you?"

"Don't worry, your friends are loyal. No one told me. I knew there was no way some of them just happened to find me. I figured it was you and you just confirmed it." She winks with a big grin.

"So, I ratted myself out is what you're telling me."

The sun shining through the trees casts a glow on her.

She chuckles. "You sure did."

"Well, I thought I might try to change your mind about not being able to rely on people."

"Yeah?"

"Yeah. You can rely on me, Desiree. I'll never let you down again." I tread carefully, not making any assumptions about what our relationship might be like after everything that's happened.

"That's a pretty big commitment." She raises an eyebrow at me.

"It is. And I'm sticking by it."

"Well, that's good. How are you doing?"

"Um, good." I hesitate and my throat constricts a little as I look down at my feet. "I was in rehab for a while."

"I know."

"Heh, of course you know." I lift my head, smiling.

"I ran into your mom a while ago and she told me."

"Yeah? I hear you were at the house for a family dinner too." Knowing how much my family loves her strengthens my desire for wanting her in my life.

She giggles. "I was. Your family's pretty amazing."

"That they are."

We get to the swings and each sit on one. She feels so close and yet so far out of my reach.

"How'd it go this time around?" The tenderness in her voice eases the tension I'm feeling about answering her.

"Desiree, I screwed up, big time. And I've learned a lot in the last few months. I've learned about the kind of person I want to be and the kind of person I don't want to be. Some of that came from rehab and — some of it came from you."

Here we go. I sigh. "I know that night, I would've died if you hadn't saved me. I need you to know you didn't just bring me back to life. You saved my life — in a much bigger way. And I don't know how to thank you or apologize."

"Zane." She reaches over and touches my shoulder. "That's not necessary. You would've done the same for me."

I smile and nod, then pause.

"You kind of ripped my heart out when you left me in the hospital that morning." She looks down at the scuffed-up dirt under her like she's holding in all her sadness from spilling out. "Hey," I say as gently as I can and she looks at me. "It was the best thing that could've happened to me. You leaving me made me realize I was fooling myself for a long time. I thought I was managing my addiction. I wasn't. It was controlling me the whole time and I was too hard-headed to admit it." I pause. "I'll tell you what, rehab was a lot harder this time. And I know it's because I was serious about it."

"I'm glad you took it seriously and got the help you needed."

"Facing my fears and my internal bullshit is the hardest thing I've ever had to do in my life. I know it's made me a stronger person."

We sway silently, barely moving.

"Want a push?" I ask.

"Okay." Her pretty mouth smiles.

I get up from my swing and bend over in front of her, grabbing her swing where the chain meets the base and lift her toward me. The breeze blows her creamsicle scent into my nose and my heart thumps in my chest. I step back, release my grip, and watch her swing, her hair blowing with the motion.

As the swing slows, I stuff my hands in my pockets, the denim rubbing against my fingers. She watches my movement and smiles like she knows something I don't.

"I'd, uh, I'd like to try that friends thing you talked about if you're okay with that."

She rises from her swing and steps toward me, a quick burst of heat whooshes through my veins.

"I'd really like that."

"Maybe, we can get together for dinner sometime?"

She turns and starts walking then looks back at me. "What are you doing tomorrow night?"

"Going to dinner with an old friend?" The smile on my face isn't as big as the smile in my heart. I want to hold her hand, but I can't presume that, because she's willing to be friends, she wants anything more.

We enjoy the rest of our evening and help Grace clean up afterwards; I wash the dishes and she dries them. Before she leaves, we agree on time a for dinner.

"Is it okay if I pick you up?"

"Sure. I'll text you my new address."

She goes over and hugs Grace, they whisper something to each other. Then she comes back to me, touches her hand on my shoulder, and presses her sweet, warm lips into my cheek. The thumping in my chest reappears.

"Good night. I'll see tomorrow." She is the most bewitching creature I've ever seen and I'm incredibly grateful to have her back in my life.

"Good night." *Don't fuck this up.*

Desiree

The moment he shoved his hands in his pockets, it hit me like floodgates opening. Head, Body, and Heart melded together and I was filled with an exhilarating sense of harmony. He has fought for me every step of the way. He shakes my soul.

Seeing Zane again and spending time together reignited all of my feelings for him. Listening to him talk about what he learned about himself and the things that trigger his addiction remind me how much I love his willingness to be vulnerable with me. He seems likes he's in a good place, grounded, and I'm so happy for him.

His kind and encouraging words about my business and school warmed my heart. The steadfast belief he has in me hits deep, drawing me so close to him again.

The instant I saw him, my body lit up and I thought I was going to fall over. My skin tingled the whole night. I love his boyish shyness when he's about to ask me to spend time with him and shoves his hands in his pockets. The man has perfected being stiflingly hot and charmingly adorable simultaneously.

The next night, he picks me up for dinner and we pay a visit to sweet Luigi. Zane tells me more about his time in rehab, the things he discovered about himself, and some of the realizations he had. He's on his best behavior and as charming as ever. When he brings me home and walks me to my door, he doesn't even try to kiss me.

I yearn to feel his lips on mine again.

We see each other every couple of days over the next three weeks and what started out months ago as infatuation has turned into a powerful attachment, a deep soul connection. It's the kind of connection I've always longed for, but didn't believe existed — until him. And now we're rebuilding our friendship, rooting him deeper into my heart.

The more time we spend together, the more I know I don't want to be just friends with him. I feel us getting close again and my heart wants more. Maybe I am meant to have love and maybe it's with Zane. Time and time again, he's proven to be all the things I want in a partner.

One Saturday morning, he tells me he has some good news

and wants to celebrate with me and spend the day together. I share that I have some good news as well.

He picks me up and we head to Beverly Hills. Fulfilling another Life List item of mine, we start by window shopping on Rodeo Drive and then he takes me to a lake.

"This is mine and Grandpa's favorite place to fish," he says, grabbing a picnic basket and blanket out of his trunk.

"It's so peaceful. Can I help you?" I hold out my hands.

"Sure." He hands me the blanket.

"Packed us a lunch, huh?"

"Yup, we're celebrating."

"I'm bursting with anticipation. I can't wait much longer for you to tell me." I don't know what his news is, but he's been like an excited kid all day.

"Always so impatient." He winks at me and my mind immediately hurdles to my excitement of the anticipation of when he took me on the hot air balloon ride and my volcanic passion when he made me wait to have him when we he made love to me. My cheeks warm at the thoughts.

I lay out the blanket and sit while he opens the basket and takes out salads and bottles of water.

"So?"

"So." He sighs with a bright smile beaming across his face. "I didn't tell you when I auditioned because I was too nervous."

"You auditioned?" I'm getting more excited for him. "For what?"

"It's called *The Sorcery of Science* and Ron Howard's directing it. I auditioned for the lead role."

Goose bumps pop on my arms as he tells me. "That's amazing! What's it about? Who are you?"

He laughs at my zealousness. "I'm a brilliant doctor," he says in an announcer's voice. "Who discovers a cure for Pancreatoblastoma, a rare childhood cancer, but only after my own daughter has already passed away from it. All while struggling through a personal journey of grief and self-discovery." He gleams.

"Wow. It sounds wonderfully challenging." My heart swells for him.

"And," he says in a sing-song voice. "I keep my shirt on the whole time."

"You *keep*? You mean you heard back? Did you get it?" My excitement is erupting.

"I got the call this morning." His smile is as big as I've ever seen. "I got it."

Instinct propels me up and he jumps up with me. I throw my arms around his neck and he envelopes me in his strong embrace. My body immediately floods with warmth. *God, I've missed his touch.*

We both linger, longer than friends should. I step back a bit and his eyes lock onto mine. I don't think there'll ever be a day his intense eyes don't turn me into a puddle.

"Zane, this is amazing. I'm so happy for you. You're going to blow their minds."

"That's the plan. I'm gonna work my ass off."

We lower back down to the blanket and I grab my salad he made.

"Hey, you had good news too, you said." He motions his hand for me to share.

"Gosh, mine is anticlimactic after that."

"Well, let's hear it."

"I just got my biggest client yet," I squeal.

"Yeah? What's the job?"

"Not only do they want me for their main home here in L.A., but they also want me to help them with their homes in Naples, Florida and *Switzerland*. Can you believe it?"

"Yes, I one hundred percent can." The conviction in his response makes me tingle with pride. "I think all this calls for a bigger celebration. How about dinner tonight?"

"Yes. Absolutely."

While I'm looking forward to having dinner with him, I know I can't be just friends. I have no idea if he still loves me or if he only thought he loved me amid the haze of his addiction. I love him, but I don't know if I should tell him. I'm ready to fight for him, but the last thing I want to do is interfere with the progress he's made in his recovery by throwing an emotion-filled wrench out there.

I'll see how the night goes. More than anything, I don't want to lose his friendship.

~ 27 ~

Zane

She's back, and I'm scared as hell I'll screw it up. Being sober, my feelings for her are exponentially more intense, but I'm not sure if I should tell her how I feel, it might blow up in my face. I want to be so much more than her friend. I want to be the exception to every relationship she's ever had and every guy she's ever known. Telling her would be a huge risk.

Tonight, be her friend.

I ring the doorbell and, when she opens the door, she steals the breath out of my lungs. "Hi." That sultry voice of hers makes every hair on my body stand up.

"Hi, you ready?"

"Yes, and hungry."

"Good. Me too."

"Where are we going?" she asks as I open her door to let her in the car.

"Grace recommended a place and I thought we'd try it."

"Okay."

I turn on friend-mode and ignore the pressure amplifying in my pants. *Not now, buddy. We're rebuilding this relationship.*

There's no back entrance to the restaurant and no private table in the kitchen, but I was able to get us a somewhat hidden table in a corner. We check in at the hostess stand and, as the hostess leads us to our table, Desiree slides her hand into mine. That's all it takes; her holding my hand. She has all of me.

The hostess brings us through an opening in the corner of the restaurant. Three walls surround us and a curved, cushioned booth is our seat behind a round table draped in a white linen tablecloth. Desiree scooches past the pillows on the cushion and I follow her, sitting beside her. We look through our menus and give the waiter our orders. Absently, I fiddle with my napkin.

"I like it here. It's quaint." Candlelight glows on her fair skin.

"It sounded that way when Grace told me about it. She said the food's excellent." I pause. "Hey, do you have your Life List on you?"

"Always." She pulls her wallet out of her purse, takes out the delicate piece of paper, and hands it to me.

"And a pen?"

She hands me the pen from her wallet, her eyes bright and curious.

I gently unfold her list and see three more items have been crossed off: "Hot air balloon ride," "Window shopping on Rodeo Drive," and "Dance under the stars with someone I love." I put the pen tip next to, "Dance under the stars with someone I love" and look into her beautiful green eyes. Her lips move into a demure smile. *Man, I'm in love with this woman.* I look back down at the list, strike through the bullet, "Save someone's life," and hand it back to her. She stares into my eyes.

"Thank you. You've been my greatest gift in life. And I'm so grateful we can be friends." If I tell her now, I risk losing her friendship. If I don't tell her, I risk staying in friend-mode and possibly losing the woman I love.

"Desiree, I have to tell you something. And I'm scared to tell you. But I'm more scared not to tell you." Her eyes fix on mine and she sits quietly, listening. "I love how you challenge me and inspire me to be a better man. I love your drive and determination and how smart you are. I love that you can snap your toes. I love that you smell like a creamsicle. I love your kind heart. And I love how you feel laying on my chest in the morning when I wake up."

She smiles, but I can't decipher how she's receiving what I'm saying.

"I know I told you I loved you once and I know I freaked you out, but I meant what I said the night we made love. I want you, all of you. I want to be the one by your side, taking on the world together and building a future together. I want to love you in a way you've never been loved before. And, you're not broken. You've just been let down by everyone in your life who should've been cherishing you the way I do."

Tears coat her eyes. *Fuck! I blew it. She's going to get up and walk out.*

She reaches over and takes my hand, holding it in hers. "Zane, I love you. I didn't want to and I was scared to and I pushed you away — a lot. I can see how you've grown and I know how serious you are now about dealing with your addiction and keeping it at bay. And I want to support you in your recovery." She smiles. "You've shown me a love I didn't believe existed and I want more of it, with you." Tears roll down her beautiful face and the love in my heart explodes.

I slide my arm around her back and cup her face in my hand, lowering my lips to hers. The woman from my dreams is real. I'm holding her in my arms and she loves me. Love doesn't get any better than this.

~ Epilogue ~

Zane

Desiree rests on my chest, one leg slung over mine, breathing slow, steady breaths. The job in Switzerland has kept her from me for three weeks and I only have her for a few days before she goes back.

Making love to her last night was as powerful, passionate, and as hot as the first time. Something tells me it will feel like that every time. It's been six months since we've been officially dating and sometimes I pinch myself, wondering if this is all still a dream.

She lets out the most adorable squeak-yawn and tightens her body with a long stretch, then snuggles back in. "Hi," she says in a groggy mumble as she looks up at me with her soft green eyes and smiles.

"Hi." With my arm around her body I squeeze her into me.

"It's so good to be home," she says, lifting up from my chest and dropping a kiss on my lips.

"It's good to have you home."

"Speaking of home, I should go to my apartment today. I need to switch out my clothes and I probably have cobwebs taking over the place." She chuckles, pushes the sheet down below my knees, and shifts her body, sitting on top of me.

I'm immediately hard.

"Oh." She raises her eyebrows and wiggles a little, pressing down into me. "Did you not get enough of me last night?" she asks, shooting me a devious smile and leaning forward to hover above me. Placing her hands on either side of me, her silken red hair sweeps across her shoulders and down toward my face.

Damn, she knows how to turn me on. Gripping her hips, I hold her in place and pump up against her. "I don't think I'll ever get enough of you."

Leaning down, she gives me a taste of her sweet lips and sits back up.

"Do we have anything planned for today?"

"If you sit there much longer, I know one thing we're doing." I pulse up into her.

She leans forward above me again, her perky breasts peeking out the top of her tank top, and my flesh heats.

"How about we eat breakfast and head over to my apartment for a bit? Do you have anything else going on?"

Firmly placing my hand on her lower back, I press her body down into mine. "We can do that. Then we can go to that little diner you like, the one near the cupcake shop."

"Sugar Flour's."

"That's the one. We'll get takeout and come back home." Moving my hand to the middle of her back, I press again until her breasts rest on my chest.

Her breathing quickens. "Okay." A small breath releases as I feel her skin heating against me. "That sounds good."

Locking her eyes on mine, she lifts her body and slides down between my legs, never releasing her gaze. The moment she takes me into her mouth, I close my eyes and tilt back my head, heaving a groan. She has no idea how worked up she gets me.

After we make love, I whip up some breakfast and we head over to her apartment.

As she opens the door, a muggy heat wraps around us like a damp blanket. The sun filtering into the living room illuminates the thin coating of dust that's settled like a veil over the room. Before she went to Switzerland, she'd been staying at my house a couple nights a week and didn't have much time to clean. I know seeing the dust is driving her nuts.

"Ugh." She sighs, looking around her apartment as I carry her suitcase into her bedroom. "This place is so dirty," she says, waving at the dust particles floating in the air, and follows me to her bedroom.

I put her suitcase down and sit on the edge of her bed. As I do, a light puff of dust rises and she rolls her eyes in disgust.

"It doesn't really make sense to spend time now cleaning it when you're going to be gone again in a few days."

"I know, but I still have to live here." She grimaces and continues waving her hand around at the dust.

"You're only here for a few days. Just stay with me."

She stands in front of me and I spread my legs, inviting her to stand between them.

"You're sure you don't mind?" she asks, looking down at me.

"No, I like having you there. You make it feel like home." I pause. "When you're back for good after you're done with your project, I'll help you clean here. Okay?"

"You spoil me, you know." She feathers her fingers through my hair. "I don't know if I'll ever get used to how good you are to me." Leaning her head down, she meets my lips with hers and kisses me then stands straight.

"That's not my problem." I tease her with a tilt of my head and shrug. "Okay," I say as I stand. "What can I do to help while you swap out your clothes? I need to turn the air on if we're going to be here much longer."

"Jeez, yeah, I had set it to seventy-six while I was gone to save money. No need to cool an empty apartment. You're probably sweating."

I nod and wipe my forehead with my forearm.

"Yeah, go ahead. Um, can you run the water in the sinks and shower and flush the toilet for me since they haven't had water flowing through them in a while? I don't want the water to get all stagnant and gross."

"You've got it." I leave her bedroom and go about my tasks.

About twenty minutes later she comes out to the living room, wheeling her suitcase behind her.

"I wasn't thinking. I should've planned to stay here today and wash all my laundry."

"What fun would that be?" I smile and she meets me with a playful, scolding glare. "You can do it all when you get back. Have a laundry-palooza."

She lunges at me and starts tickling me. "A laundry-palooza, huh?"

"Okay, okay. I surrender." I cease her tickling by grabbing her in my arms and kissing her. "Trash bags under the sink?" Sweat droplets bead on my forehead. The air conditioner here is lacking in power.

"Yes," she answers, giving me a quizzical eye.

"All right then. Let's put all the clothes you just dumped in your bedroom into trash bags and bring them back to my house. You can wash them there."

"Okay, I like that idea. I'll grab the clothes. You reset the air conditioning and put in our order at the diner so we can pick it up when we get there."

"Done."

We meet back in the living room, I grab her suitcase, and we drive to the diner. It's a little off the beaten path so it's usually not crowded. The few times I've gone with her, the majority of people respect my privacy.

I find a parking spot and grab my baseball hat from the back seat, putting it on. A little incognito helps. We're able to scoot in and out quickly and, before we head back to the car, I ask, "Do you want a cupcake?" knowing full well she'll say yes.

Her eyes light up. "Yes, but only if you have one with me."

"Okay. Come on."

As she opens the door to Sugar Flour's, a little brass bell at the top of the door dings. The sweet scent of sugar wafts in the air, filling my nostrils. An older couple sits canoodling in vintage soda shop chairs, the kind with the wired heart back and worn red leather cushion. With its nostalgic décor and sweet treats, it's no wonder Desiree's old soul loves this place.

"Desiree, how are you?" asks the woman behind the counter who also happens to be the owner. It makes complete sense that Desiree would befriend the owner. I don't know a single person who doesn't love my kind-hearted girlfriend.

"Hi, Fiona. I'm great thanks. How about you?"

"Well, I'm covered in flour and sugar and loving life." She laughs, wiping her hands on her apron. "What can I get for you today?"

"Let me see." Desiree surveys the cupcakes. "Ooo, this lemon one looks yummy."

"Lemon?" I ask.

"Not Death by Chocolate?" Fiona asks as Desiree continues peering into the glass case.

Desiree sighs. "It *is* my favorite." She pauses then stands upright. "But nope, I'm feeling like lemon today."

"And for you?" Fiona looks at me and smiles.

"Well, I think Death by Chocolate has my name on it." I turn to Desiree. "I know you. You're gonna want the chocolate one by the time you're done with lunch."

"I'm *not* eating two cupcakes." Desiree waggles her finger at me.

Fiona boxes up our cupcakes and we drive back to my house. Desiree brings in our food while I grab her suitcase and go back out for the trash bags full of her dirty clothes. She starts her laundry immediately and I put our lunches on plates, bringing them out to the terrace.

As we eat, she tells me about Switzerland, her decorating project, and some of the sights she took in when she wasn't working, which wasn't often. Once we're done eating, it's time for cupcakes. We bring our plates to the kitchen and she unboxes the cupcakes while I grab a clean plate and napkins. Heading back out to the terrace, I set the plate on the coffee table. As she reaches for the chocolate cupcake, I shove my hands in the pockets of my jeans and she withdraws her reach. Sitting back, she tucks her legs under her and folds her hands in her lap. She looks at me in anticipation, like she knows I have something to tell her.

"So, I've been thinking." I pause. I'm a mix of nerves and excitement. "Your clothes are going to be here when you get back from Switzerland."

Her eyebrows knit together. "Or I could bring them back while I'm still here. I don't want them to be in your way."

"No." I hang my head, shuffling my feet. "They're not in my way. That's the thing, I want your clothes here. I…" I pause. "…I want *you* here. Permanently."

Her beautiful eyes widen as she leans forward. "You do?"

"Yes. I want you to move in here with me. Make this *our* home. I don't know if you're ready for that, but I am. And, if you want to, I'll pay the rest of your lease or you can find someone to sublet. What do you think?"

"Wow. I wasn't expecting that."

Sometimes I still can't decipher her reactions and don't know if her, wow, is a wow-yes or a wow-are-you-out-of-your-mind. She doesn't give me an answer, but her eyes shift around like she's considering what I said.

Unfolding her legs, she stands up and wraps her arms around me. "Okay, yes." She whispers in my ear.

"Yes?"

"Yes." She squeezes her body around me and let's go, settling back down on the rattan chair. "I think this calls for a cupcake celebration."

"Absolutely," I say, sitting down next to her.

"Can I have a bite of your chocolate one? You can have a bite of my lemon." She smiles at me expectantly and holds the lemon cupcake toward me.

"Yes, but I want the first bite. I've been looking forward to that cupcake."

We unwrap half of each of our cupcakes and take a small bite. She grins from cheek to cheek.

"And now for a bite of chocolate so both flavors are in my mouth at once." I hand over my Death by Chocolate cupcake and she excitedly takes a big bite. "Ow. There's something in it. Ew. Something hard."

She quickly grips the hard thing between her teeth and drops it into her hand as I shift off the rattan chair and onto one knee in front her. Looking into her hand, she sees the diamond ring. A gasp flies out of her mouth as her other hand thunks on her chest.

"Well, since you're going to live here with me, I thought I'd take a chance and make it official."

She shakes her head and puts her hand over her mouth, tears grow in her eyes.

"Desiree, I think I loved you before I even dreamed about you. I think I wasn't ready for you until the day you stepped into my life. I couldn't ask for a more perfect person for me. I want to spend the rest of my life with you by my side. Will you marry me?"

Her tears now flow down her cheeks. She doesn't say a word. Clutching the ring in her hand, she crosses her hands across her chest and nods at me. Then she leans forward, putting her hands on my face and touching her forehead to mine.

"Mmhmm." Is all she can seem to get out.

We close our eyes, still in the moment. A breeze washes over us.

Eager to put the ring on her finger, I take her hands from my face and she opens her eyes.

"Come on, let's rinse this off." I stand up, taking her free hand in mine, and lead her to the kitchen to rinse off the ring.

I rinse it clean and take her left hand in mine, sliding the ring onto her delicate finger. "Do you like it?"

She takes a deep inhale, staring at it. Her green eyes sparkle like the diamonds in the ring as she looks at me. "It's just beautiful. I love it."

"See that stone there?" I point to a small stone next to the main diamond.

"Yeah."

"That's from Grandma's ring. When I told Grandpa I was going to propose to you, he gave me her ring and insisted I give it to you."

Her right hand once again flies to her chest and tears swell in her eyes.

"It's kind of small so I had a friend of mine design the ring using her stone." I move her hand around, letting the light twinkle the ring's radiance and return my eyes to hers.

She holds my gaze. "I love you."

"I love you, Desiree." I lower my head and kiss her with all the love in my heart.

As I release her lips, she steps back and tilts her head. "Wait a minute. How did you…when…I was with you every minute since we left the cupcake shop. How did you get the ring in there?"

I shake my head at her. "Always underestimating me." I give her a cheesy grin. "Fiona and I about fell over when you asked for the lemon one."

"How do you know Fiona?" She sounds genuinely surprised.

"I did my research." I nod. "I dropped off the ring the day before you came home and she helped me out."

"Rotten, Zane Adam Elkton, rotten." She throws her arms around me and I wrap mine around her.

Over the next couple of days while she's home, we figure out what to do with her furniture as well as some of mine. I decide to pay out her lease, making it easier on her. While she's back in Switzerland, I arrange for her things to be brought to my house. When she returns home, she pours herself into making my house our home and I'm happier than I ever thought I could be.

Not only is the woman from my dreams real, she's about to become my wife and together we'll build our future, side by side. Life doesn't get any better than this.

Thanks so much for reading Untouchable Zane.
I hope you loved it! If you did, and have a moment,
I'd love for to you write a short review on Amazon and
GoodReads; it helps new readers find my books.
I appreciate you!

**AND PLEASE COME JOIN ME ON
MY SOCIAL MEDIA ACCOUNTS:**

On Pinterest, you can accompany me on the visual creation of each of my novels as they progress. Follow me here:
www.pinterest.com/debbiecromackauthor/

Join me on Instagram (@debbie_cromack_author) and hop into my Instagram stories for some behind-the-scenes and inside-my-life fun!

On Facebook, you can find me at
/DebbieCromackRomanceAuthor

Head over to my website, debbiecromack.com, and join my email list to stay up-to-date on my new releases.

Finally, join me on Twitter, @Debbie_Cromack,
for shorter snippets of fun.

Made in USA - Kendallville, IN
1204748_9780578654201
12.03.2020 0857